About the author

Hedley Harrison graduated from London University and joined a major oil company, progressing to senior management and seeing service in the UK, Nigeria, Australia and the North Sea. He has published five other novels with The Book Guild: *Coup* in 2011, *Disunited States* in 2013, *China Wife* in 2015, *Sorak's Redemption* in 2016 and *Sorak Returns* in 2018.

SORAK'S LEGACY

HEDLEY HARRISON

The Book Guild Ltd

First published in Great Britain in 2019 by
The Book Guild Ltd
9 Priory Business Park
Wistow Road, Kibworth
Leicestershire, LE8 0RX
Freephone: 0800 999 2982
www.bookguild.co.uk
Email: info@bookguild.co.uk
Twitter: @bookguild

Typeset in Sabon MT

Printed and bound in Great Britain by CPI Group (UK) Ltd, Croydon, CR0 4YY

ISBN 978 1912881 345

British Library Cataloguing in Publication Data.
A catalogue record for this book is available from the British Library.

What's out there so often isn't different from ourselves.

CITY MAP

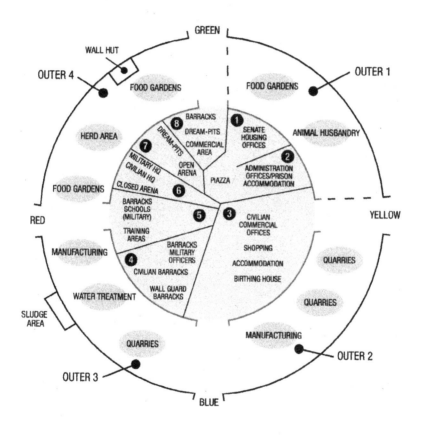

SECTOR ❶ – ❽

1

The shuffling herd of beasts was unsettled. The area between the city walls was usually a sanctuary for them. Since the rebellion, now more than twenty cycles of the distant star ago, they'd had no one to look after them and for several generations had only had minimal contact with the city's inhabitants. There were other herds that provided milk and meat for the people; this one had reverted to the wild. The beasts milled around, uncertain of what it was that had suddenly appeared in their midst. The alpha male kicked out at one of the group of figures that was carefully working their way in to the herd. With new calves, the old male was very protective. The unexpected blow had devastating results. With a hissing groan the figure collapsed and lay still. The beasts crowded around the alpha male sheltering the calves, some instinct telling them to expect retribution. None came.

Frightened by what had happened, the remaining members of the group gathered up their fallen comrade and hastily retraced their steps until they came to one of the ramps leading to the walkway along the top of the outer city wall. They were clearly familiar with the route that they were taking. The light of the first pass of the second moon was just beginning to brighten the horizon as they lowered the body down to the small party who had been guarding their entry and exit point.

As the moonlight suffused the plain surrounding the city, the group of figures set off on their journey to the Edge and the protection of the forest. There wasn't much night left to cover their retreat and, encumbered by the body of their comrade, their progress was slow.

Whatever it was that they'd come to do in the city, went unachieved.

* * *

Sorak hadn't wanted to reinstitute multiple guard patrols in and around the city. Her former experience told her that they weren't all necessary. Although some were, and they were encouraged as a reassurance to the citizens, but patrolling just to give the soldiers something to do, she knew, was demoralising and bred discontent. Abandoning the patrols, particularly outside the city walls, created yet more unemployed ex-soldiers, but these were mostly old and happy to retire.

Sorak had been chairwoman of the Senate for three cycles of the distant star following her and Nasa's return to the city with their son Lenar. Having been thrust into the role of leading the Senate, it had been, and continued to be, a very stressful time. The seventeen cycles of the distant star that she and Nasa had spent in their valley had initially been idyllic, but their very success in making a life for themselves, serviced by the large herd of beasts they'd domesticated to supply their needs, had eventually led to their lifestyle becoming untenable. Increasing numbers of the fierce predators that roamed the planet, confronted with such easy prey, made such inroads into their herd that they decided to leave and find another safe haven. Their journey to do so had been fraught by the post-rebellion chaos in the city as successive male administrations failed to gain acceptance. The aim of finding a new safe haven was increasingly deferred.

The illicit love between Sorak and her slave 1562, that had led to their original escape from the city, had grown into a loving and fulfilling relationship. The female-led society in the city had long since disappeared but they'd had no knowledge of this until they came to return. The turmoil after the demise of the female leadership lasted many cycles, and Sorak and Nasa, as she'd named her ex-slave 1562, since they'd been induced to return to the city, played their part in eventually producing stability in a largely equal society. But of course, in such a complex situation things were never totally straightforward, and the settlement was still very fragile.

Sorak and Nasa had been folk heroes for their initial escape to be together, but after many cycles of unrest and bloodshed, when the men tried to impose themselves on the women, their example had finally been accepted as a model for the future. Women and men were now officially equal but the past was never quite forgotten. Gaining acceptance of gender equality was a major undertaking and was never going to please everybody.

Lenar, now a man of twenty cycles, had gone off to make a life for himself with Desak, the young woman that his parents had rescued on their journey back to the city. In fact, it was the need to find a safe place for Desak to live that had both determined their return to the city, along with Sorak's recognition that she had a role to play in generating a new society.

As in the far-off days of women's rule, the Senate ran the city, but increasingly in name only as Sorak allowed the devolution of more and more of the daily administration to a mixed group of women and men, who, unlike the Senate, had the skills and vision that were necessary. The senators, split equally by gender, were largely older citizens, more conscious of the past than the rising younger generation who'd known nothing of the world that Sorak suspected that some of the senators, especially the women, still hankered after.

"They have no idea! The past they yearn for never existed."

Sorak, as she had done for so many cycles now, shared her frustrations with Nasa, a process that usually assuaged them. It had always been Nasa's sensible approach to the world around him, even as a slave, that had attracted Sorak to him in the first place.

"Maybe next time the people will elect some younger senators."

Nasa, who had no official role in the administration but was regarded by those who knew him as a thoughtful and wise counsellor, would have been the first to admit that those who offered themselves for election as senators weren't the cream of society; it had always been one of the weaknesses of the system that self-promotion often took precedence over capability. But Nasa was optimistic that, with time, they could change things.

But it was a new day. Sorak, who needed very little sleep, was preparing for a reporting session by the overnight patrol leaders. She might have reduced the patrols, abandoning those in the area outside of the city as the most pointless, but the internal ones were still maintained. The patrol leaders' reports often contained information of interest to Sorak, and provided her with an insight into the temper of ordinary people. There was no longer a curfew, so night-time activity, especially around the times of the passages of the second moon, was always informative. The crimes of a free and equal society – burglary, malicious damage, for example – had appeared. In the ordered structure administered in the past by the women's Senate, crime by this sort of definition didn't exist; the discipline had been too harsh. These new manifestations were a worry to Sorak, but largely because she could see no logic in the behaviours, not yet having recognised that there wasn't any.

Sorak, in her far-off days in the past as a military officer, had been allowed, for a short period, to browse in the Senate library; the old administrators were always on the lookout for new talent, and she was thought to be a possible candidate for induction into the administrative categories. But she'd developed into a free thinker, and free thinkers were anathema to the women's Senate.

"The old books talked about crime and crimes," she'd said to Nasa during one of their rambling conversations. "When the Senate no longer owns everything, there are bound to be those who take from others rather than work to acquire things."

It was more a question than a statement. Sorak had still to get her mind around the implications of what she was saying.

Of course, Nasa, who'd only belatedly learned to read, had never had access to the library as a slave and, since the library was burnt down in the rebellion that provoked all the changes to city society, he and everybody else would never be able to draw on the knowledge that Sorak was referring to.

* * *

There were six patrol leaders. Sorak had tried to avoid the rankings of the past but the four men and two women all had the insignia of tenants of former times.

Sorak remembered the debriefings of her own patrolling days, when something of interest to report was a rarity. It wasn't like that now.

"There was some sort of meeting going on in the dream-pit in Sector Seven," Radnor, the oldest of the men, reported. "They had guards posted and as we approached they started singing. But I'm sure that they weren't there to sing to the second moon."

Sorak appreciated the humour but it wasn't the first report of mysterious meetings in that part of the city. The information was noted, along with the previous reports of such unexplained activities.

There was nothing else of interest until they got to Leack's report. Leack was one of the youngest patrol leaders, a good soldier with good prospects. Sorak respected her judgement so she took what she had to say seriously. And what she had to say was intriguing.

"We had to chase a herd right back to opposite Outer Four. They were undoubtedly agitated about something. And when we got them back to their normal grazing area they just milled around and wouldn't settle. It wasn't one of the managed herds and we had to get the herd guardians out of bed. They weren't happy since this herd is virtually wild."

Sorak waited; she knew Leack had more to say, but the young officer wanted to be sure that what she'd said had been understood. Clearly something, more likely someone, had been in the area between the walls and disturbed the beasts; that much was obvious.

"We spent some time looking around on the ground but the beasts had churned it all up. Any footprints would have been trampled over. But one of the troopers found what he said was blood. I think he was right. We checked; none of the beasts were injured."

Alone after the debriefing, Sorak pondered what Leack had said. The area between the city walls was the most difficult to patrol. It was vast, largely open and, apart for the water treatment area, contained virtually no buildings. And both the inner and outer walls were accessible from this area. Along with patrolling the plain outside the city, Sorak had also stopped the patrolling along the top of the outer wall. It didn't, however, occur to her that a night patrol along the top of the outer wall might have seen something; the wall was far too long for that to be a sensible proposition.

With so much else to occupy her, the wandering herd of beasts went from her mind.

2

The city, over the last twenty or so cycles of the distant star, had changed utterly. The female-dominated world from which Sorak and Nasa had escaped was largely a distant memory. Those women, like Sorak, who could remember those far-off days were in their middle years and, with a few exceptions, had come to accept the more equal society that it had taken so long to establish. However, Sorak was aware that some older women with a hankering for the past still probably existed.

The population of the city had declined in the seventeen cycles that it had taken to work through the various male-dominated regimes. This was partly due to the killing that went on during the warfare between the genders, but also because managed breeding of the former times had ceased to exist. Women and men paired off by inclination now and were expected to be responsible for their children rather than them being brought up by the city administration. This latter was a big change and the birthrate had yet to recover to former levels. Many people, both women and men, found the socialising now necessary difficult because, for example, the demarcations between the military and civilians still persisted.

Apart from Nasa, Sorak relied on two other people for advice and support. Pastak was a fellow former military officer whose vision of the future had first prompted Sorak to consider not just a return to the city, but to stay and work for reform. Both women had no illusions about what they'd been part of creating, or about the tensions that still existed amongst some of the women and men. And Pastak, unlike Sorak, eventually retired to Sector Four to live in the old barracks with many of her former colleagues. Not prone to introspection, Sorak only occasionally envied her friend's slower pace of life.

"I guess until all us oldies die off, things will still be occasionally difficult."

Pastak and Sorak, as a part of their ongoing friendship, often walked around the city. Their reception was sometimes hostile amongst the less intelligent of the citizens, especially men. The presence of a couple of male soldiers always lurking in the background usually ensured that the hostility didn't develop beyond sullen stares or turned backs.

Pastak's remark made Sorak laugh. Nasa would have been delighted had he heard her; she so rarely laughed these days.

Sorak's second adviser was more controversial. An elderly black man who never showed himself in public, and who still refused to accept any name beyond his old slave number, 147, had been leader of the last male administration. It was his acceptance of the need for women and men to work together that had catalysed the final change. Having worked at the centre of the original women's administration he was a mine of historical information but also had a facility to think innovatively, which Sorak admired.

When Sorak talked to 147 about the way that the herd of beasts had been disturbed, he was pensive. The idea that something secret was going on made perfect sense to him. He knew that, even in the days of full slavery, occasionally a maverick with more than the normal intelligence had emerged amongst the men; he always cited Nasa, but he was also aware of slave rumours of mysterious beings from beyond the Edge.

It was within Sorak's memory that slaves occasionally escaped from the city. She'd been involved in the pursuit of one such, but the explanation was always given as arising from the misdemeanours of some senior black woman. In those far-off days, Sorak had no choice but to believe such explanations.

Pastak, who'd accompanied Sorak to the talk with 147 and had noted his cautious response, put the reaction down to the man's age.

"How old is 147?" she asked Sorak as they made their way back to the rebuilt Senate buildings.

"At least seventy cycles," was Sorak's response.

For a man, that was old amongst the city's inhabitants.

But Pastak, like Sorak, had such regard for 147 that the thought that something they knew nothing whatsoever about was going on in the city during the night was a thought that wouldn't go away.

In the early days after the original rebellion, and during the days of one of the most vicious of male rulers, all the black- and brown-skinned senators and administrators were massacred in the forest on the edge of the plain. From that time on it was forbidden to visit the Edge at that point, and for all the cycles of the distant star since the whole area had remained effectively unknown to the people of the city, along with the forest, the mountain and whatever that stood behind it.

During their long hours in the chill of evening in the valley home, when their work was done, Sorak and Nasa often talked about the city. Sorak's feelings were more complicated than Nasa's and, as she recognised much later, she'd retained a yearning to see the city again long before the decision to return was made.

But it was Nasa, always clear thinking, who articulated the dilemma that had grown in Sorak's mind.

"If the earliest mothers, people, of the city had come from beyond the distant star, how did they come? Was it in something like the machine that we found wedged in the rocks? How many people came in it?"

The spacecraft that they'd found crushed into a cleft in the top of the mountain had, as far as they could identify, contained no more than seven people, women and men.

"It must have been much bigger," the ever-practical Sorak said. "The books that I saw in the Senate library would have taken up more space than was in the machine that we found."

"There could have been more than one machine," Nasa said.

Sorak acknowledged this, but since her train of thought was more about where the machine was that the founders of the city had come in, she didn't respond to Nasa. Was there another wreck somewhere? Did people travelling in the machine destroy it, or use the material to construct the city? Sorak could think of no obvious answers beyond recalling no materials in the city similar to those that they'd found in the machine in the cleft.

Of course, they came to no conclusions. But they both acknowledged the depth of their ignorance.

Now, many cycles later, and back in the city, the question of where the founders came from and what happened to their machine still sat at the back of Sorak's mind. Much to the bemusement of her colleagues, but understood by Nasa, she instituted a search around what was left of the Senate buildings and the old residences of the female senators. If any of the books from the destroyed library had survived, it would have been because a senator or administrator had withdrawn them to peruse in their private quarters. At least this was what Sorak presumed.

Nothing was found in the form of old books, but in one of the more remote of the senators' houses, largely untouched because of its location right under the inner city wall, a bundle of papers was retrieved. Damaged at some point, only parts of them were legible. Sorak called in one of the aging former administrative slaves whom she knew had worked with old papers in the distant past.

"Two things are apparent from what we could read. The founders of the city knew that there was a plain that would be ideal for a settlement. But if there's any evidence of the machine that brought the founders, it must be somewhere close to the plain and the city. The second thing is less clear, but there appears to be no mention of men in the papers."

How the founders of the city appeared to know about the plain before they arrived, Sorak couldn't imagine.

That the machine, if it still existed, should be somewhere beyond the Edge was a conclusion that no one seemed ready yet to draw.

What also wasn't clear was how soon after the machine arrived on the planet the papers had been written. They were clearly very old and had been damaged even further during the search that located them.

"Fantasy," Pastak said when Sorak talked to her about what they'd learned.

Sorak wasn't so sure.

They also discussed what Sorak had noticed – that the younger women seemed less concerned by the unknown than people like her, and even made guesses about what had happened all those cycles ago that she found disturbing. This was another gulf developing, between the older women brought up in a world of rigidity and their daughters who'd had no restraints placed on them.

That all of this modernity troubled Sorak, Nasa acknowledged. But as Nasa recognised, speculation about how they'd got to the planet and how the city had been built was pointless. It was the future that mattered, and people like their son Lenar, and Lenar's partner Desak, would inevitably be the future.

Nonetheless, the question of what had happened to the wreckage of the machine that had brought the founders to the planet festered in both Sorak's and Nasa's minds notwithstanding.

Something else that was festering in Sorak's mind was the feeling she'd got from her conversation with 147 that he thought something was going on in the city, particularly during the circuits of the second moon, but what? And why would the agitation of a herd of beasts be so important? At least she knew the partial answer to that: something had clearly disturbed the herd, but again what? It was almost as if one of the fierce predators from the hinterland had got into the city. But of course there was no evidence of that.

* * *

In her private quarters in the rebuilt Senate building Sorak felt tired. She'd lived for almost fifty cycles of the distant star and through most of that time had either worked hard or been under stress. The hidden valley, or another like it, never felt more attractive. Lenar and Desak had moved to another part of the city to make their life together. Lenar had become an officer in the city's army; Desak was working in the administrative offices. At least, she was for the moment.

"Why did we come back? Why did we stay? We could have just left Desak and gone."

It was a question that always arose in her moments of stress.

Of course, she knew that if they'd left the city after delivering Desak they would have to have left Lenar behind.

Such a pensive Sorak was someone that Nasa might not have recognised. As she forced herself out of her depressing thoughts, she was conscious that she hadn't felt so uncertain since her unhappy days as a young officer.

"Sorakmam!"

She was instantly alert. She hated being called Sorakmam and had tried hard to get the courtesy suppressed, but the grinning young woman addressing her knew this and they both laughed at the effective way she'd got Sorak's attention.

"There's someone to see you, Sorak. A man, an old man. He says his name is Chackar but you'd know him as Mesrick's slave."

The young woman, Sorak's personal assistant, sounded curious. Perhaps not surprisingly she'd clearly never heard of Mesrick; all those cycles on, only the older women would have known who she was.

Sorak struggled to recall a face. Chackar's slave number didn't leap into her consciousness.

"Mesrick was a soldier in the old days who favoured the slaves and was instrumental in starting the rebellion that swept away the old female-dominated society. She was killed before she could see the horrors that followed her actions. Many of the ex-slaves weren't worthy of her or of the freedom that they'd achieved."

Marwek, named for her mother in the new order of things, clearly didn't know what to say. Folklore said Sorak and Nasa were instrumental in starting the rebellion by their revolt against the restrictive colour-dominated society, but Sorak had always tried to give the credit to others.

She was quiet for awhile.

"Chackar, Sorak?"

"Bring him in."

Sorak's recollection of Chackar was limited. The days when she knew Mesrick were before the rebellion when men were all slaves, and even Sorak was insensitive to any man other than Nasa/1562. Apart from which, it was twenty cycles of the distant star since she'd seen him.

"Chackar, you are welcome."

Mesrick's former slave was clearly infirm. He limped painfully into her room, round-shouldered and with a shrivelled body. Sorak thought that he must be at least ten cycles older

13

than her but he looked very much older than that. He settled uncomfortably.

From what her assistant, Marwek, had told her, Chackar had something to impart to her; Sorak couldn't imagine what.

"Sorakmam, I hope you are well?"

It wasn't a greeting she would have expected; it was a greeting from the far-off former days.

"Chackar, you have something to tell me?"

A mixture of curiosity and impatience motivated her. There were other people to see, things to do. Marwek hovered.

"Sorakmam, they came in the dark times, between the moons."

"Who came in the dark times, Chackar?"

"We don't know who they are, Sorakmam, but Mesrick said that there were people living beyond the Edge."

This is nonsense; he's lost his mind!

Except… 147 had talked about strange goings-on by the light of the second moon. Was Chackar talking about the same thing? But it was the reference to Mesrick that fixed her attention. Mesrick wasn't given to fantasies.

"Mesrick said that there were people living beyond the Edge. How can that be?"

It was more than twenty cycles since Mesrick had been killed. Sorak supposed that the old man's memory was confused. In those days people were terrified of going beyond the Edge. Those who'd done so weren't supposed to have returned. But Sorak knew that much of this mythology had been generated by the old women's Senate to keep people from escaping from the city.

"Mesrick said there were strange things beyond the Edge that faced Outer One."

Sorak's patience was almost exhausted. This was the area where the senators and administrators had been killed. There were all manner of wild stories about this part of the Edge.

But Chackar's next statement had her full attention again. "Mesrick went there," Chackar said. "She saw a strange machine, like nothing in the city, pieces of it scattered in the forest."

Sorak was silent; she didn't know what to say. The idea that Mesrick had left the city and travelled beyond the Edge was inconceivable to her. She knew Mesrick was an unusual woman, but she could see no way how this could have been possible.

But Chackar was fumbling in his tunic pocket. He handed Sorak what she recognised as a piece of metal no bigger than her hand. It had strange letters imprinted in it. She knew that it was metal, and metal different from anything available in the city. She'd seen the like from the other machine lodged in the cleft of the mountaintop when she and Nasa were heading for their hidden valley.

Sorak couldn't help but be curious.

3

No one in the city, woman or man, knew anything about the beginnings of their society. And since the old Senate library had been burnt down during the fighting following the rebellion, no one was ever likely to know. This was not to say that there weren't rumours, exaggerated explanations or just plain fantasy.

The long-range space probe that had finally penetrated the planet's atmosphere had been travelling for two generations. With a crew carefully designed to reproduce itself, a built-in training and education system, and the ability to produce synthetic food, the flight had gone entirely to plan. The planet was one of six orbiting a star distant in a galaxy far from the space probe's origins, and as the craft went into orbit, checking and testing, everything seemed to be as they'd expected it to be. But the most difficult part of the long journey was about to unfold – landing.

The plain that they'd chosen as the perfect landing place was easily identified. There were several such plains on the planet's surface but the chosen one was the largest, seemingly the most level, and also had access to surrounding forest and all the materials that that would supply. The order was given to land. But as they lowered themselves to the surface using the rocket engines, things started to go wrong. One of the rocket engines failed. The probe continued to descend but it also began to tip sideways. And as the rocket power was reduced, the whole vehicle tipped over and was propelled into the forested area adjacent to the plain.

The probe skidded along the ground, destroying itself as it went, until it finally lost all momentum and rolled into a deep gully.

Sorak had been allowed to browse in the Senate library in the days before her awakening self-awareness, and long before the male slaves eventually rebelled. That she, a junior military officer, should have been allowed such freedom was most unusual, but reflected a recognition that she had an exceptional mind for her category. Unfortunately, it was an untutored mind and an ill-disciplined one, something that was not acceptable.

Her browsing had always been very carefully controlled, but as she was seen as a protégée of the only white general in the city she was allowed to see many things that were not normally available to soldiers. But as her real character emerged her browsing rights were terminated.

The early history of the city was one of the things that she found closed to her. In later life, when women and men became equal, she realised that, with the bodies that she and Nasa had discovered on their escape from the city, in the machine in the cleft of the mountain, men hadn't always been slaves. In fact, in that machine, as they were able to explore it, it was apparent that a man had been in command.

Eventually the tolerance of the senator responsible for the library ran out and Sorak was barred from further browsing, but by then she knew that the inhabitants of the city had descended from people who'd come from beyond the distant star, and she had an inkling that the gender relationship might not have been as ordered as it was in her time.

Needless to say, all the glimpses that Sorak had had of the far-off past and the origins of the city did nothing to quieten her growing dissatisfaction and her growing infatuation and then love for her slave 1562.

But as Sorak pondered what the old man, Chackar, had told her, and about what she assumed was Mesrick's location of the machine that had brought the people to the planet, she was excited and confused at the same time.

"Maybe we should send an expedition to find what Mesrick found," she said to herself.

But do we really want to know? What good will it do us to know?

Sorak was all too aware that these were precisely the questions that Nasa, and even her friend Pastak, would ask.

But again, with more pressing calls on her time, her speculation and fantasising were pushed to the back of her mind.

* * *

Although it rained very rarely on the planet, cyclers – violent and torrential rainstorms – did occur, were predictable, and almost invariably happened at night.

The herd was disturbed again, and it wasn't just the lashing rain. Conscious of the disaster that had accompanied their last trip to the city, the figures moved more cautiously. The alpha male was still behaving aggressively but the poor beast had a problem that he couldn't deal with but which the figures were able to exploit. Two of the beasts had recently given birth, in one case very recently, but the dominant male couldn't protect both mothers and calves.

Two of the figures darted into the group, surrounding the older of the two calves, and while one of them grasped the calf and swung it over his shoulder the other fended off the mother with a sharpened pole. Careful to avoid attracting the attention of the alpha male, and with the rest of the party keeping the milling herd at bay, they escaped quickly around the area between the city walls. Followed by the baleful bellowing of the stricken mother, they climbed up onto the city outer wall. The figure carrying the calf held the small beast's mouth closed to prevent its cries from attracting the attention of the alpha male.

At the wall the calf's feet were bound, and its mouth, and it was lowered to the waiting party below.

* * *

With the cycler keeping everybody indoors it wasn't until the distant star arose again that the administration officer responsible for the herds asked for a check of these particular beasts. Something was wrong.

The herd was very agitated, more agitated than they'd ever seen it. The alpha male was at its most dangerous, but it was the continuing anguished bellowing of the calf's mother that attracted the herdsmen's attention.

"She's given birth," the head man said. That much was obvious to him, since he'd checked previously. "But where's the calf?"

The calf was nowhere to be found. From experience, they knew that if the calf had been stillborn, or had died, the mother would have stayed with it for some time.

"The calf must have been taken," the herdsman said. It seemed the only explanation.

"How can it have been taken?"

None of the three had an answer. And following the cycler, the ground was a sea of churned-up mud. Nothing could be learned from the surrounding area.

The loss of the calf was reported; it was an unusual event that attracted more than the normal interest. On one of his occasional visits to the Senate offices Nasa heard the staff talking about it. It made no more sense to him than it did to them. But with nothing pressing to do he set off to find the area where the vanished calf should have by now been contently taking its mother's milk.

But like the herdsmen, Nasa could find nothing that might solve the mystery. The herd had settled and the bereaved mother stood away from the group, a picture of utter misery, Nasa thought. But even she would soon forget, and the alpha male would see to it that the calf was eventually replaced.

"Not sure what I thought I might find," Nasa said to himself as he carefully skirted the herd.

But unbeknown to him he wandered off along the route the figures who'd stolen the calf had taken to get to the city wall. Again, for no reason apparent to him at the time, he climbed the ramp to the top of the outer city wall and walked the parapet. The plain stretched out in front of him, a suggestion of the Edge hazily visible in the distance.

Sorak having shared with him Chackar's tale of Mesrick's trip into the forest, he tried to visualise the forest and the undulations that he presumed were behind it. From his own considerable experience he recognised that there must be mountains out there, just as there were on the other side of the city beyond the Edge. On his and Sorak's original escape from the city they'd encountered mountains on more than one occasion, "mountains" being what Sorak had learned from the Senate library as the name for the high formations.

Nasa studied the plain. The surface was rutted, and there were small streams of water flowing nowhere in particular, left over from the cycler.

Footmarks? There are no night patrols outside the city anymore; how could there be fresh footmarks.

"Are they footmarks?" Nasa wasn't sure. But there had certainly been something going on on top of the outer wall at the point where he'd chosen to look out over the plain. It was unconsciously the marks in the dust on the parapet that had drawn him to the point in question.

And he was sure that something, not the cycler, had left an impression on the boggy surface of the plain.

He moved to the edge of the wall and leaned over the parapet. He could still make no sense of what he thought he was seeing. Then, as he pulled himself upright and prepared to walk away, he glanced down the side of the wall. He knelt and peered down at the ground below.

"Why would the ground be churned up so close to the wall?"

He had no idea. But like Sorak, things that he didn't understand niggled at him. He knew that he was going to have to go down and walk along the wall outside until he could check the ground.

The green gate was nearby. It didn't take Nasa long to find the spot.

"The ground has certainly been churned up," he told himself.

But all he'd done was confirm the mystery. He still had no idea who'd been there or why.

"A calf vanishes. Is that all?!" said Pastak.

Pastak was uncharacteristically angry. She lived in Sector Four in the refurbished military barracks, and although retired from duty she was respected by both women and men and was often a first point of call when something unforeseen happened.

It wasn't all.

"A man has been killed. His throat cut. His body left where it was bound to be found."

Nothing like this had happened since Sorak and her companions had settled the city down three cycles ago. It was the sort of killing that had happened all too often in the days of the men's rule.

"He seemed to be wearing a uniform... or at least bits of one. With insignia. But no one knows what they are."

Pastak's puzzlement worried Sorak. Pastak was rarely uncertain about anything, but this was something new and therefore something worrying.

4

The calf was female, but they knew what they were doing. A nursing mother in what was left of their herd had lost her calf to one of the ferocious creatures that had broken into their compound. It had been a male calf. The calf that they'd taken was female; such an animal was much more valuable.

The small number of beasts that they had left had been brought into a compound in the centre of the encampment. Surrounded by dwellings, and the dogs that they'd managed to tame, it was the only safe place left.

"We must say nothing of this until we know more."

Sorak had heard with dismay Nasa's description of what he'd found. An unexplained dead body within the city was one thing; an unexplained entry into the city by night was something completely different.

"And how, Sorak, are we going to find that out?"

Nasa knew that she had no idea. Neither had he beyond the vague feeling that the answer didn't lie within the city.

The idea that was forming in both Sorak's and Nasa's minds – that there were people somewhere beyond the Edge – was too dramatic a thought for either of them to want to share with the other. But the calf had disappeared and there was clear evidence to suggest that it had almost certainly been lowered down the city wall. Someone must have done that. At least that was the conclusion that seemed obvious to Nasa. But who exactly? And why would someone would want to steal a calf? This second question was something that Nasa had been mulling over in his mind.

What was forming in Sorak's mind, however, was far less clear. What if the people who were rumoured to have gone beyond the Edge hadn't died, but just hadn't returned. She and Nasa had survived well enough beyond the Edge. But how long had they been out there, how long had they lived out there, wherever 'there' was? It was this question, coupled with her half-remembered memories of what the old brown woman at the Senate library all those cycles ago had told her, that was causing Sorak concern. The fact that she alone had knowledge of such things was no comfort to her.

She knew she had to discuss the problems associated with the stolen calf with Nasa; he was bound to have thoughts on what had happened based on what he'd seen.

The conclusion that the two of them were agreed upon, once they'd talked, was that if they wanted answers to all their rising anxieties, someone would have to go out across the plain, across the Edge and search for signs of... It was the signs of 'what' that were the problem.

They both agreed that there had to be an intelligence behind the stealing of the calf. If there were people, there had to be habitations. Were these people friendly? From their experience in their hidden valley, Nasa at least recognised the vulnerability of any herds that might have been formed. It was the increasing loss of calves, after all, that had been one of the key factors behind their own flight. The savage animals of the planet seemed able to take over control of their lives despite their best endeavours. These were thoughts that Nasa wasn't keen to share with Sorak, although he was aware that such thoughts might well have already occurred to her. As he now thought about it, stealing a calf made complete sense to him, if there was a managed herd out there somewhere. Increasingly, he was sure that there had to be.

* * *

The meeting of the Senate was more noisy and more fractured than Sorak could remember. It was a clear sign of uncertainty. The senators were largely older women and men who were inclined to worry about anything that might disrupt the peaceful world they'd established. The more perceptive amongst the citizens might have credited Sorak with the stability rather than the Senate, but the Senate's sense of its own worth had matured to almost the same state as the original women's Senate. As this became increasingly clear to Sorak, so also did the feeling that most, if not all, the female senators still had some hankering after the past.

The agitation was centred on the body that had been discovered and the uniform the dead man had been wearing, or at least what had been presumed to be a uniform. Since only the city's troops wore uniforms the whole thing was outside the general experience.

Sorak, as she watched the senators talk themselves out, recalled 147's comment that something was happening in the dark hours between the moons. He had no idea what it might be but in his own thoughts he was mindful of past history and the formation of groups of citizens to resist the violence and depredations of his predecessors in running the city. For 147, a secret society, a band of ex-soldiers, of unemployed young women, more especially of unemployed young men, were all entirely possible. But he wasn't yet ready to share these thoughts.

Once the senators had gone around the problem of the dead man several times, they turned their attention to Sorak. They didn't know what to make of the killing, or what to do about it. That was what she was for. The most vociferous of the male senators went straight to the point.

"So, what, Sorakmam, are you going to do about this brutal killing?"

Nasa would have noted the anxiety behind the bravado, but Sorak was too concentrated on responding to the question, which the senator had every right to ask.

"I've asked the guard commander to review the night patrols in sectors like Sector Seven where very few people actually live. Social activity has been noted around an old dream-pit in that sector, but apart from being late into the night there seemed nothing unusual about this that we should worry about."

People gathering in the dark period between the moons and being involved in unknown activities during the passages of the second moon, to some people's minds, would have been unusual, but Sorak didn't want to arouse the senators' interest unduly, or at least not until the guard commander had had time to investigate. All of this was another manifestation of the changes and freedoms that Sorak had introduced and which were now developing a momentum of their own.

147 was clearly concerned, and Pastak, when Sorak sought out her thoughts, was certainly of the opinion that he knew more than he was saying. But both her and Sorak's experience with the old man was that he never speculated and wouldn't offer anything more until he was certain of his facts. It was a characteristic that Nasa admired but which frustrated Sorak.

The old black man and former member of the triumvirate who'd run the city before Sorak's return, had retired from view, but he'd not retired from taking an interest in the events that had followed as Sorak had evolved the administration of the city into a less intrusive oversight of the individual citizens' affairs.

So, 147, despite going into secluded retirement, retained contact with the networks that he'd built up when he was in charge of the city, and which hadn't quite faded away once the joint administration came into being. Mostly old ex-slaves who'd worked in the original women's administration, they were very much the former elite amongst the ex-slaves and had been powerful within the administration. Now no longer powerful but nonetheless realistic, they were amongst the first to realise that the future of the city after the rebellion was totally dependent on an accommodation between the women and men. It was Sorak's ability to bring about this accommodation that had saved the city; these old men were quite happy to fade into the background once stability had been achieved, but they were not inactive. So, 147 still had his finger on the pulse of the city, and he still had an organisation of sorts if he ever wanted to assert himself. Sensibly, he didn't, but he still remained potent in the eyes of people like Sorak.

Unbeknown to Sorak, Chackar, who'd come to see her about her old colleague, Mesrick's, foray into the area beyond the Edge, was one amongst these old men, and his visit to see her was a deliberate attempt to forge a new relationship between these old administrators and the younger generation who were now administering the city and who the likes of 147 knew Sorak was fostering. For them it was about security as well as stability and a future in their old age.

The old men might not have known what was going on amongst the burgeoning independent and self-sufficient mixed, and young, population of the new city, but when ripples of excitement ran through the old civilian sectors of the city they were at least aware of them.

And as the violent death in Sector Seven being investigated, huge ripples were running around during a cycle previous to the killing that was now taking their attention, and which illustrated just how much things had changed.

"A white couple have given birth to a black girl!"

Having no knowledge of the genetics of their species, such an event instantly provoked all manner of superstitions. And with the nature of breeding practised before the rebellion, there was no way of knowing whether a black grandfather existed in the family.

After a few anxious days when it seemed likely that the child and parents would be killed, the view began to spread that this was a sign for the future, for how things would be in the city.

Sorak had no knowledge of the event at the time but she would have been encouraged by the way that it was accepted, especially amongst the less intelligent of the ex-slaves.

Equally, Sorak had no knowledge of the conversations that were going on – not about the future but about the past. The emergence of the idea that it might be possible to turn the clock back and restore the women's former administration was beginning to take shape in some of the older women's minds; in its way, another sign of the success of Sorak in freeing people to think their own thoughts and manage their own lives. It was exhilarating stuff but, as Sorak would eventually find out, it had negative aspects.

5

The man found dead in Sector Seven was called Menar, an ex-slave, older than Sorak and Nasa, who had originally worked in one of the commercial areas of the city. An administrator in one of the manufacturing units, he was known to 147 and had been to the other members of the old triumvirate. The thing that attracted most attention surrounding his death was the tunic he'd been wearing.

Nasa recognised it as being similar to the tunics that the Senate prison guards used to wear in the old days. This was even more puzzling, as those guards had usually been drawn from the lowest levels of female society. That's not to say they weren't worthy people, as their son Lenar had discovered cycles earlier when the city was still in turmoil.

"Why would an ex-administration official want to wear such a low-grade garment?"

It wasn't a question anybody had an answer to at the time that the body was discovered.

Menar had been strangled. This, as Nasa knew, was a method of killing also from the old days, when slaves had no access to weapons. In the current times, however, it no longer meant that Menar had been killed by another man.

"But what does the emblem mean?"

It was Pastak who put into words what everyone who'd seen the body was thinking.

The emblem consisted of a black arm and a white arm intertwined. It was obviously intended to be symbolic. Clearly, whoever was behind the emblem was a person of intelligence.

Sector Seven was largely non-residential. There had once been several small commercial units there but what they manufactured had long since been forgotten. There had also been three dream-pits in the days of female rule; again, no one seemed to recall who'd used them, other than the older women like Sorak, or those even older. One of the dream-pits Sorak remembered very well. Used by junior military officers and civilian managers, the mangeneers, it held bittersweet memories for her. The most prominent feature of Sector Seven was the open arena, formerly used to discipline the lower orders of city society. On the other side of the open arena, now derelict, were the two dream-pits once used by the ordinary female soldiers and the civilian female workers. The dream-pits were essentially the only approved places of relaxation for the women of the city, but like everything else they'd been carefully managed, to avoid any irresponsible behaviour. Brawling, nonetheless, as Sorak recalled, was regarded as an acceptable way of working off energy, provided no one got seriously hurt.

The dream-pits in Sector Eight – there had once been two – had been for the senior officers and senior civilians. People like Sorak in her military days would never have had access to them.

Sorak, Pastak and the guard commander Lenrick were refreshing each other's memories of the outer reaches of the city. It was in these areas that 147 had implied that something, undefined, was going on.

Lenrick had come straight to the meeting with Sorak from a gathering of her guard patrol leaders. All patrols were mixed, and the leaders were drawn from both genders and rotated so that a balance was always maintained. This worked very well and, as Lenrick had noted, the women and the men had surprisingly different perspectives on what the patrols needed to be looking for in the aftermath of the killing.

With the freedoms that developed as the old systems had been dismantled, a number of things that were absent in former times emerged. As individuals acquired property in their own right, and the city's ownership of all but essential infrastructure assets lapsed, stealing, robbery, and then robbery with violence, became an increasing preoccupation for the patrols. To the older women this was anathema, but the more enlightened people like Nasa recognised that many characteristics of the inhabitants of the city had been repressed by the harsh rule of the old Senate. It was inevitable in the new more free society that these would emerge.

"Most nights," Lenrick had once said, "houses are broken in to. People are beginning to strengthen their homes."

In the past, locking doors was unheard of; in fact, locks were largely unknown, and citizens were having to use great ingenuity to manufacture the means of preventing their doors from being easily forced.

"During the last circuit of the distant star there were eight reports of houses being attacked and defended. Seven people were injured, and these were only the people protecting their homes."

"You're not suggesting Menar was killed trying to break in to someone's apartment?"

Pastak didn't think Lenrick was, but she needed to be clear. As an ex-soldier Pastak, more than Sorak and Lenrick, was finding the breakdown of the old rigid society the most difficult to cope with. But being a highly intelligent woman, she knew she had to come to terms with the way things were now developing.

None of the three women had heard of the concept of democracy, yet it was exactly that that Sorak had sought to introduce. Used to the uniformity of the past, both Sorak and Pastak were taking time to comprehend that allowing women and men to make their own decisions in life was going to destroy not only uniformity but also universal conformity. And they were slowly discovering the price of this evolution.

"The most unexpected thing that the patrols came across was evidence of the senior officers' dream-pit in Sector Eight having been used recently, and it may have been used regularly. But whoever's been using it has been very careful to try to remove any signs of this. At least as far as they'd been able to see in the moonlight."

"The most obvious thing, Lenrick," Sorak said, "was as a meeting place. There are no longer any bans or controls on private meetings, so if people were gathering there, unless there was evidence that they were planning to do something to threaten the city, there's nothing we can do."

"But," said Pastak, "was there a link to the death of Menar?"

It was the only thing that she was interested in.

From their expressions, neither Sorak nor Lenrick had made any such connection.

However, they didn't manage to pursue the discussion. One of Lenrick's young patrol leaders rushed into the room. Excited, he was in no way overawed by the three women he was interrupting.

"We've found another body!"

He was addressing Lenrick but it was Sorak who responded with the obvious question.

"Where?"

"In the entertainments hall of the old Sector Eight buildings," the soldier said rather primly.

"Dream-pit," said Sorak.

The young man relaxed. Born after the rebellion he was well used to the relaxed manner that Sorak was trying to adopt. He'd delivered his message, but he knew that it would raise many questions. He waited for Lenrick to ask them.

"So, when was this body discovered? There are no patrols in Sector Eight during the day."

The young man actually grinned.

"Pindar – he's always the slowest in the patrol – saw something when we were checking the hall earlier in the night. He was last out of the building and something had lodged in his mind that didn't make sense to him, so he said he was going to go back when we were off duty. We all decided to go with him."

Lenrick was clearly not best pleased by this piece of independent action but the man, having started, was determined to complete his story.

"According to Pindar, it was about doors. Unusually the dream-pit had several rooms with doors. One door leading from the hall was closed. All the rest were open or had been removed. The place had been extensively damaged. The closed door was locked. Pindar kicked it open. That's where the body was. A brown-skinned girl child, just born according to Raneck. She'd been strangled."

Raneck, a female member of the patrol who'd joined the daytime expedition back to the dream-pit, was a mother, and had recognised the child as a few hours' old. A length of cord had been pulled tightly around its neck.

"The others stayed; as patrol leader, I came to report."

Sorak resisted the temptation to go with Lenrick to the Sector Eight dream-pit. Pastak had other plans, so Lenrick and the patrol leader made their way quickly to the site of the latest killing.

Raneck had stayed with the body whilst the other four patrol members made a careful search of the rest of the dream-pit. They had no idea what they were looking for but the first thing they noticed was that the main contact area had obviously been cleaned up. There was no dust or debris, and the few remaining sofas had been arranged in a grouping that was totally different from how it would have been if the dream-pit had been active. It was in use, but not seemingly for pleasure.

The wayward Pindar, upset by what he'd found, hadn't joined the search but had wandered off into the back regions of the dream-pit, to the private rooms, the ones with doors, and the service areas. The whole place was beyond his youthful experience but his curiosity was soon aroused again. This time it wasn't a locked door.

Lenrick had arrived by the time Pindar had returned to the main area of the dream-pit. He was clearly excited again about something.

"There is more to see, Lenrickmam," he said to the guard commander.

He led the way. Lenrick signalled the patrol leader to gather the patrol together as more people from the administration office began to arrive. The normal processes set up by Sorak for dealing with a killing began to take over.

Lenrick, from past memories, recognised the back regions of the dream-pit as she followed Pindar into one of the private rooms.

The light in the room was poor so Lenrick wasn't at first sure what she'd been brought to see. But as Pindar forced open the shutters the room became fully lit. The dream-pit had supposedly been out of use for at least three cycles of the distant star. The room should have been dusty, dirty, but like the main contact area it had been cleaned up and the revealed bed had a cover over it that was very obviously not old.

Lenrick ripped back the cover. Whatever might be under it, from its profile it clearly wasn't yet another body.

"Mother's heart," she muttered.

Under the cover was a set of clothes, personal items belonging to the person living in the room, and a military sword.

"Lenrickmam?"

But Lenrick was poking at the clothes with her own sword. The upper garment that she picked up on the tip of her weapon was that of a woman, which defined who'd been sleeping there without giving any clue as to who she might be.

"Lenrickmam!"

Pindar was seeking a response from the guard commander. He was drawing her attention to the emblem stitched to this woman's upper garment: a black arm and a white arm intertwined. Lenrick, but not Pindar, knew where she'd seen this emblem before.

6

There had been many things that had gone on in and around the city that, notwithstanding the former female Senate's tight hold on the population, they didn't know about.

In the cycles way back before the rebellion, when Sorak and Nasa/1562 were forming their relationship, Mesrick, another military officer who didn't fit the requirements of her category, had finally been relegated to command one of the platoons of the quarry guard. She'd originally worked in the offices of the general in charge of Sector Six but had never been happy with her role in the military setup of the city. Unlike Sorak, whom she admired because of her independence of thought and willingness to follow her own inclinations rather than the norms of the city, Mesrick was considered much more dangerous because of her insistence in regarding men slaves as people equivalent to women, something that totally undermined the Senate's philosophy.

The slaves who worked in the quarries were at the bottom of the pecking order, the least intelligent, brutalised, and capable of extreme violence. The soldiers who guarded them were equally the dregs of the military. Soldiers, and even the odd officer like Mesrick, who didn't respond to the mindless discipline required of them, were as difficult to manage as the slaves. Except that Mesrick was instinctively recognised, by soldiers and slaves alike, as being someone different, someone that they could respect. In an area where respect was in short supply this made Mesrick even more dangerous to the city authorities.

By force of character Mesrick had put an end to the brutal treatment of the quarry slaves by the guards, and she began to improve their lot by giving them better food and teaching those who were willing skills that might allow them to rise above their pitiable status. It was a slow process.

Not all of the guards and officers at the quarries agreed with Mesrick's approach and several of them foretold the sort of troubles that eventually emerged as the rebellion later took hold. Given power, the former quarry slaves didn't know how to use it, and it took several attempts by different groups of ex-slaves to run the city before ex-administrative slaves like 147 took over. It had been a violent and deadly period.

Despite the harshness of their life and environment, some of the quarry slaves were very old. They'd been in touch with the previous generation, and they liked to keep their companions entertained at night with their ghoulish tales from the past, tales of how the city came into being, tales of the arrival of the founders from way beyond the distant star. How much of it was true no one had any idea, but there was little else to lighten the lives of the slaves.

Mesrick and the guards often listened in on these stories, and she began to wonder just where and how they'd originated. There were threads through them and patterns that were retold over and over again. The quarry slaves telling the tales clearly lacked the intellectual capability to have made them up themselves. Mesrick's interest grew and grew.

Surely, then, there must be some basis for them.

To the practical mind of someone like Mesrick, this had to be the case.

Knowing that Sorak had visited the Senate library, Mesrick supposed her friend might have more knowledge than any other person in the military, but isolated in the quarries she had no way of contacting her.

1122 was the oldest slave in the quarries. He seemed to know more of the old tales than anyone else. But he was near the end of his life, almost blind, without teeth, and had increasingly fewer periods of lucidity. Yet Mesrick became convinced that his stories must have a foundation in fact, even if she couldn't visualise what that foundation might be.

I must talk to him.

* * *

The quarries were sited between the city walls, in this case in Outer Two. 1122 lived in a foul-smelling hovel built up against the outer wall. Mesrick found it difficult, because of the stench, to enter the man's living space. 1122's struggle to rise when she entered exhausted him, and it was some time before he was able to respond to his visitor.

"Mesrickmam, you are welcome."

Mesrick acknowledged his greeting. The man's condition brought to the fore all her suppressed sympathies for the slaves. 1122 would soon die, and for Mesrick it would have been an utterly wasted life, without point and without legacy. This appalled her and fed her overarching desire to do something about it.

"I enjoy your stories about earlier times. Particularly I enjoy your stories about how the founders of the city first arrived here."

1122 looked surprised. No woman had ever showed any interest in his tales before.

"They are not stories, Mesrickmam, the founders did come from beyond the distant star and they brought with them everything that we know within the city."

This was still something that was hard for Mesrick to get her mind around.

"But how did they come? If they came from beyond the distant star, how did they get here with all the things that you say they brought with them?"

It never seemed to occur to Mesrick to wonder where they'd come from.

She had no idea how many generations of women had run the city, how many cycles of the distant star had passed since the founders had arrived, but she was aware that with the passage of time there was no evidence to prove that the tales that 1122 and his companions were telling had any truth. Yet she couldn't dismiss them just because of this.

But the straightforward and simple-minded 1122 was convinced by the knowledge he claimed to have.

"They came in a machine that landed near the Edge and that was carried into the forest behind the Edge."

1122 had no idea what this machine looked like, what it was made of, how big it was, why it got carried into the forest, but he was convinced that somewhere behind the Edge, opposite Outer One, the remains of the machine could be found.

In the end it was the clarity of 1122's vision that convinced Mesrick.

She had no fear of what she might find beyond the Edge. The Senate had forbidden anyone from leaving the city. Parties of soldiers had supposedly been sent out to explore but none had been sent out within living memory. The reports, supposedly in the Senate library, all recorded that no one had ever returned from these expeditions.

The practical Mesrick found this hard to believe.

"Anyone who goes beyond the Edge is killed when they return," 1122 said, as if he sensed what Mesrick was thinking.

This was another rumour for which Mesrick knew there would be no evidence.

If anybody had known that they were going…
It didn't take long for a plan to form in her mind.

Being unafraid of what she might find, Mesrick recognised that if she went beyond the Edge in secret and came back in secret, she was unlikely to be killed.

Even as she carefully prepared for the journey, Mesrick wasn't entirely sure why she was making it. Her current life was dreary, pointless and without a future, so exploring beyond the Edge was simply a challenge that she set herself. What she might discover she didn't give too much thought to. And as she would eventually find out, Sorak and her slave had proved without doubt that it was possible to survive beyond the Edge.

* * *

Free of duties and with enough food for seven circuits of the distant star in her backpack, Mesrick set off as the vermillion glare of the first moon faded and the darkest period of the night emerged. The Edge was more than a day's march from the city in the direction she was taking but since the patrols in that area of the plain surrounding the city were infrequent, she knew she could hunker down and sleep in the open, beyond the view from the city walls but still with an equivalent distance to traverse.

In the event her trip was accomplished without incident. It was cold overnight and the return of the distant star welcome as she set off again. It was a long slog over a largely flat, but small, boulder-strewn surface. Hurrying into the forest as the distant star set, she did what Sorak and Nasa had regularly done on their trip beyond the Edge – she slept in a tree.

As she was awakened by the warmth of the distant star falling on her body, Mersick began to take in her surroundings. All she could see were trees and more trees. But that was what she'd expected to see. On the ground she surveyed her surroundings more closely.

"That looks like a track," she muttered to herself.

Mesrick didn't have Sorak and Nasa's knowledge of the creatures that she, and they, would eventually come across, but her instincts were towards extreme caution in a world she had no experience of.

Eating a small portion of the synthetic food that the slaves were fed on, she readied her crossbow and set off along the track that she'd observed. It clearly led further into the forest but, as the track twisted and turned, she became unclear of its general direction.

She knew that if she was to find anything, it would most likely be by luck rather than by any planned exploration, although the apparent track encouraged her. In any event she had no idea what she was looking for, or where to look.

1122 had talked about a machine that had come from beyond the distant star and had crashed into the forest. Crashed... Mesrick wondered where 1122 had got that word from.

But if there was any truth in what the man had said, and since it was information from generations in the past she wasn't very confident that there would be, the machine would have 'crashed' reasonably close to the Edge.

"So, what signs should I be looking for?"

Mesrick had no idea of the lifespan of any of the trees around her, but if the machine had damaged any of them when it came down, surely they would long since have regrown.

As she pondered, she came to her first obstacle. She'd been aware of an increasing noise as she pushed into the forest; then, in a small clearing, she was confronted by a ravine with a fast-flowing stream at the bottom. From where the stream originated she couldn't see, but it seemed to just disappear into the ground again at the extent of her vision. In a scene that Sorak and Nasa would have found familiar, on the other side of the ravine was a mob of frenetically active creatures, a pack of the savage dogs that roamed the forest. They had sensed Mesrick just as readily as she'd observed them.

"Clearly not the place to cross the water," she told herself.

As the distant star was overhead and she'd been walking alongside the ravine for some time, she was attracted by the shadows thrown by some of the trees. At first she thought she could identify what looked like a tunnel, with the stream spluttering out from the arched branches. But there was something else.

"What is it that's different about these trees?" she wondered aloud.

The leaves and branch forms told her that they were the same trees as those in the general location but they were distorted and misshapen, unlike any others she'd seen. As she looked closer she saw that the trees forming what she was beginning to perceive as a tunnel were growing not directly from the ground but from the rotting remains of what had obviously been older trees. As far as she could see, it was only in the area of this tunnel that this was the case. How this could be, she had no idea.

But before she could give it any thought she was distracted.

Mesrick moved into the opening of the apparent tunnel and then stopped, unshipping her crossbow. Something, and she had no idea what, was moving around further into what she was now convinced was definitely a tunnel. It wasn't the dogs she'd seen earlier; they kept up a constant wail of noise.

"There's definitely something moving about!"

Mesrick got the same comfort from talking to herself as Nasa had done.

Cautiously she crept into the shadow of the branches. The noise stopped as she moved and then resumed after awhile, but whatever it was was now moving away from her, that much was obvious.

The ground was hard and dry. Mesrick could see no footprints or any indication of what was making the noise. But as she moved carefully forward she noticed more movements in the branches in front of her... but there was no wind.

With the light increasingly obscured, Mesrick was beginning to get a powerful sense that there was something unnatural about the tunnel she was now walking through. Why did the trees, only in this area, seem to be growing in this odd way? It was a question that she suddenly thought she had the answer to.

"1122 said that the machine crashed in the forest. Would it have hit the trees and stopped? Would it have knocked down the trees that it hit?"

Although she wasn't sure that she believed the old slave's story, its credibility was growing in her mind. Certainly, if there had been a machine all those cycles ago and it had crashed, it would have inevitably destroyed some trees if it was as big as 1122 seemed to think it was.

But suddenly she was in daylight again. The arch of branches had largely given way to another ravine. There was a stream flowing through this ravine too, and from where Mesrick had emerged high on the edge she struggled to see the other side. It was wide and deep.

Curious, she moved along the top of the steep side. Again it was the sort of place Sorak and Nasa would have recognised from their journey back to the city.

"Mother's heart!"

There was something at the bottom of the ravine that told her that 1122's stories were not just stories – exactly as he'd said!

7

When Mesrick returned to the city, over twenty cycles of the distant star previously, the quarry slaves had killed some of their guards and the rest had been withdrawn. The rebellion was underway and her excursion beyond the Edge went largely unreported. Then, as things began to resolve after the initial overthrow of the women's administration, Mesrick was killed. Later, as the turmoil of male administrations that succeeded each other reached its peak, many of the old administration ex-slaves sought refuge with the female soldiers in Sector Four, Chackar being one of them.

What Chackar didn't tell Sorak, because he didn't know, was that the quarters he used, the contents of which he'd appropriated, were those of Mesrick. Mesrick didn't own much but amongst the things Chackar had found were several strange pieces of what he was able to recognise as metal. Where the metal had come from, at the time, Chackar had no idea. But as the rumours and gossip ran rife amongst the old men, his surmise of the metal's origins proved correct.

* * *

Beyond the Edge, as Mesrick's excitement grew, she knew that she'd discovered the answers to the questions that she'd been seeking.

It took her some time to scramble her way down to the base of the ravine. It was only when she began to work her way through the mass of scrub and trees, towards the structure that had attracted her attention, did she recognise that the ravine had taken on an unnatural semi-rounded shape. And the archway, that was beginning to block out the light as she proceeded, was no longer just trees and vegetation.

She'd never seen metal like it before but the collapsed arch that she forced her way into was undoubtedly metal. As she moved forward she could see that her way would be blocked by a shapeless, crumpled mass of twisted metal invaded by trees and creepers the like of which she hadn't seen so far on her journey.

"It has to be the craft from beyond the distant star."

There was little of it discernible but she knew that she was right.

Prevented from moving further into the wreck, she forced her way out sideways. Two things immediately struck her. She was clearly at the front of the craft, and what she could make out amongst the debris was hopelessly compressed. The craft must have slammed into the trees, the ground, and was destroyed beyond recognition.

As she slashed a passage for herself with her sword towards the front of the craft, she came to an area of open ground where the vegetation was stunted. She was confronted by a row of elongated humps, eight, as far as she could see.

There was no mystery here, only final confirmation of the tales from 1122 and the past.

"People were buried here."

All but three of the graves had been dug up, presumably by wild animals soon after burial. The crumbled remains of bones were evident, evidence enough for Mesrick.

Once again she was attracted by signs of movement, augmented now by a feeling of being watched.

But she'd seen what she'd come to see and there was no point in staying any longer. She retraced her steps back to the Edge and then back to the city.

* * *

Sorak and Nasa, as was their custom at the end of the day, talked through their activities together. When Lenrick, the guard commander, finally reported back with information on the second killing, in this case of an unknown newborn baby, and on the evidence that an equally unknown woman was living in the former senior officers' dream-pit in Sector Eight, Sorak's immediate assumption was that this was mother and baby.

Nasa found this link less easy to make.

"But you said Lenrick found no evidence of the birth talking place at the dream-pit."

Sorak acknowledged this, but the death of the baby made no sense if they weren't mother and child.

"And they found the emblem again on the woman's clothing."

This was of more interest to Sorak, as Nasa realised, but they still didn't have any idea what the emblem meant.

* * *

Earlier, as the patrol searched through the main areas of the dream-pit, the woman had waited fearfully in the private room. She hadn't been able to deal with the body of the baby before the patrol had arrived, but it was imperative that she wasn't caught by the soldiers.

Being dark, the soldiers were only able to search a limited area of the old dream-pit. Once they'd departed the woman's priority was to leave as quickly as possible. Not being caught by the soldiers was more important than disposing of the body of the baby, or clearing out her sleeping quarters. She could return and do that later.

But the woman had only been concerned about the patrol returning during the night. That the soldiers might return during daylight hours, privately, never occurred to her. And in fact it was only when she heard voices as she crept back into the dream-pit as the distant star rose in the sky that she became aware that that was what had happened.

And it wasn't just the soldiers of the patrol, but other people whom she didn't know who came and began searching the dream-pit in great detail.

"I'm never going to be able to go back there."

* * *

But the search, when the results were reported back to Sorak, yielded no information to explain the emblem, or who the woman was.

And as it turned out, Sorak and the guard commander never did find out who the woman was. Her having a sword didn't mean she was a soldier or ex-soldier, so the possibility that she was a civilian couldn't be discounted.

* * *

147 was getting worried. His spies had accumulated far more information than he'd expected. It wasn't the information itself that worried him, it was more that he knew he had to share what he'd learned with Sorak, but to do so would alienate some of his sources.

The fact that a white couple had given birth to a black daughter was by now widely known in the city, if not within the administration. It was only a question of time before Sorak heard about it, and 147 knew that it was his duty to tell her before rumour and gossip did. It was what had followed the unexpected birth that was concerning him.

The child had been called Brenan, from a combination of her parents' names. The response within the civilian community where the family lived in Sector Three had initially been hostile, with the baby's life at risk. But the intervention of one of the few brown-skinned women still around had led to an entirely different reaction.

* * *

Anstan was a mangeneer, a contemporary of Lenen's, with whom Sorak had had a love/hate relationship way back before she and Nasa had left the city. Anstan had been destined for great things under the old regime and had been spared the fate of most of the black- and brown-skinned senators and administrators because she'd been seriously ill at the time of the rebellion and had been hidden in part of the more remote burned-out Senate accommodation in Sector One by her slave.

After almost twenty cycles of the distant star, living in secret but supporting the small remaining caucus of women still resisting change, Anstan had at last come out into the open to rally resistance to the present Senate, but more particularly to Sorak. The birth of the black girl to white parents was identified by Anstan as a sign that black and brown women, rather than being vilified, should once again be given a respected place in city society. Except that there were very few such women still alive, no one knew how many, and they were mostly in hiding. Anstan inevitably ignored the existence of black- and brown-skinned men but knew full well that without them her dreams for the future would come to nothing.

How many black- and brown-skinned men there were, no one knew, but what Sorak and the city administration did know was that the number was certainly greater than of black- and brown-skinned women.

Anstan saw it as her mission to reinstate the colour-based order in the city.

147 had been told about Anstan and her ambitions for the future of the city. Whether she'd want to degrade the status of men was the one thing that he didn't know, and the one thing Anstan had had the good sense to keep quiet about. Nonetheless, she undoubtedly would.

* * *

"Sorakmam." Marwek, her assistant, was used to Sorak being lost in thought and had permission to break into these thoughts.

"Sorak, 147 wishes to speak to you. He's here."

Marwek's statement instantly got her attention. 147 never left his secret refuge. Sorak had respected that and had always gone to visit him when they needed to talk.

What can possibly have happened for him to expose himself?

Being Sorak, she didn't speculate; she would find out soon enough.

"147, you are welcome."

"Sorakmam." Sorak made a face; she tolerated Marwek's use of the formal address, it was a part of their relationship, but she discouraged it with everyone else. But old habits died hard with 147.

"A black baby girl has been born to white parents."

This was something Sorak in fact already knew but hadn't told even Nasa, since she was uncertain of the significance of such a birth to the people of the city.

147 was about to tell her.

"Among the ignorant," he said, "there was fear that somehow the old order was reasserting itself. Among the more knowledgeable there was confusion. Such a thing couldn't happen, yet it had."

Sorak was always impatient of 147's rather oblique way of explaining things, but she managed to say nothing.

"Anstan, a mangeneer before the rebellion, one of the few brown-skinned women left, has been stirring up the ignorant, declaring the birth to be a sign that the old ways will return. Since there are still people who would welcome such a return, she's being listened to."

Sorak remembered Anstan. As a consequence she remembered Lenen, and a whole range of feelings surged through her. It took a huge effort for her to concentrate on what 147 was saying.

This wasn't good news, although Nasa had more than once suggested to Sorak that such views were always going to be around; many women felt cheated by the way things had changed, especially ex-soldiers whose entire world seemed to have disappeared.

But 147 had more to say.

"But not everyone wants to look back. There is another group out there dedicated to resisting Anstan's message."

Not for the first time Sorak wondered what 147 truly thought of the society that was being recreated.

147 had no concept of what a cult was, but what he went on to describe as the organisation developing to resist Anstan could readily have been described as such. Secretive, attractive to the more intelligent, it demanded loyalty and discipline.

"The only thing I know for certain is that this organisation is growing and could pose a threat to you and the Senate if it got too powerful."

Sorak was now confused. She could understand why Anstan's movement was a threat, but why would those opposed to her be so too?

Secret societies had always been banned, and Sorak was instinctively against such things, but yet another consequence of the free society that she was trying to build was that she and the Senate were going to have to accept cults, clubs, people coming together for a variety of reasons, if that was what the people wanted.

But 147 didn't give Sorak the time to react or to question what he was telling her. He produced a piece of material with something embroidered on it.

"One of my informants took this from a discarded garment."

Sorak knew what she was looking at. A black arm entwined around a white arm. And thanks to 147, she was beginning to understand what it might mean.

But 147's next statement distracted her.

"There's been fighting between these people and Anstan's followers."

By 'these people' Sorak assumed 147 meant the group that was resisting Anstan's vision for the future.

This was more bad news!

Menar!

* * *

Later, in conversation with Lenrick, the guard commander, Sorak expressed the view that Menar had been killed as a part of the internecine warfare that 147 was suggesting was developing between those who wanted a return to the past and those who didn't.

"And," Lenrick said, "since the dead baby was brown-skinned, can we suppose she was killed as potentially one of the ruling class that Anstan wants to create?"

Sorak was appalled at the thought, but Lenrick's postulation was hard to deny.

"But who was the woman?"

Sorak's initial thought, that the mystery woman was the mother of the dead baby, was looking less certain, notwithstanding that the baby had only seemingly been a few hours' old, just old enough for her pigmentation to begin to appear.

Worrying as all this was to Sorak, once again in late-night conversation with Nasa she was made aware that the situation might be even more confused than she was beginning to understand. It seemed that, according to Nasa's sources, there was more than just the two groups with differing views of how the future of the city should develop. Scattered around Sectors Four to Eight, there were apparently bodies of both women and men with a whole array of views. Sorak's promotion of free thinking was more successful than she realised.

8

The idea that there were still those amongst the women of the city who wanted to go back to the past was no surprise to Sorak, if but a disappointment. Change was always difficult, and she knew from her days as a military officer that the bulk of the lower category soldiers and civilians always held firmly to the rituals and privileges of their existence because they could visualise no other life.

Neither did it surprise her that there were still others who had embraced change and wanted to resist those trying to reverse it. The other shades of opinion Sorak decided to take no account of, since she perceived that self-interest was a more powerful motivator amongst the less intelligent of both genders. The powerful thinkers like Anstan, however, were another matter.

Lenrick, the Senate guard commander, had debated with her patrol leaders whether they should reinstitute the patrols of the city outer walls. There were those for and against. The main issue was resources. They didn't have enough soldiers, and the changes in behaviour in the freer society being created required all the troops they could muster for 'police' duties. Perhaps a more convincing argument was the need to manage the information about the incursion into the city in order not to

53

create anxiety and confusion. Many of the lower orders of both women and men, military and civilian, were easily frightened by the unknown. And as a consequence of Sorak's efforts in developing a free society, anxiety wasn't too far below the surface.

Then, as if the unknown figures who'd stolen the calf had been aware of the decision not to patrol the walls, a second calf was taken from one of the herds. The fact that it was from a different herd quickly got the administration's attention.

But this time it didn't need Nasa to investigate outside the city wall. There was an observer already available.

"We had an aged ex-slave approach a patrol in Sector Three," Lenrick reported to Sorak. "1483, now called Rannah."

In the new scheme of things the amber liquor, once only available at the dream-pits, could now be purchased at the provision centres attached to all of the barracks or civilian residential areas. Not only was it more readily available, it was more potent, and Rannah was very partial to his liquor. Evidence of drunkenness was another manifestation of the greater freedom amongst the citizens.

But Rannah was no irresponsible young man so he knew when to stop drinking and when to take himself home. But sometimes, being used to having had an active life, if the second moon was particularly bright and the second passage particularly long he would take a walk through the sectors before heading for his bed. On this evening, he'd been drinking at a dream-pit in Sector Seven and had headed across the piazza through Sector Two and up onto the city wall. There was a ramp further along that would take him down to his accommodation in Sector Three. It was just the sort of walk that would destroy the effects of the amber liquor.

"Mother's heart!"

Like most ex-slaves Rannah had acquired the habits of his old mistress.

There was movement on the ramp. How could there be?

More curious than frightened, Rannah moved away along the outer wall and crouched down behind a buttress. Why he sought to hide himself, afterwards he wasn't sure. But he was glad that he had. What he saw was totally unexpected.

The movement materialised into a group of figures. Bunched together he wasn't immediately sure how many there were.

Mother's heart, he said again in his head.

As he watched, four figures emerged at the top of the ramp. They moved steadily as a group. At least, all but one did. Again, his vision a little blurred and his brain slowed by the still present dregs of the amber liquor, it took him a moment to realise that the figure on his own was carrying something across his shoulders.

"It was definitely a man," he later told the patrol leader.

But the thing that the man was carrying was clearly a living creature as it was making agitated movements that the man was struggling to control.

"When he put it down I could see that it was a calf."

Rannah had now definitely got the patrol's attention. Knowledge of the calf stealing had been circulated to all patrols, since beasts had now been taken from two herds.

"The group moved to the edge of the wall and hauled something up; I couldn't see what but it was soon clear what they were doing. They lowered the calf down the city wall and then one after another they climbed down."

The patrol leader asked Rannah to repeat his story; she was suspicious of him, his breath smelt foul and it wasn't clear how lucid he was. The repeated story was identical to the first version but with further added detail. That gave the leader confidence.

"I waited. Then I went to look over the city wall, not at the exact spot but nearby. I could see nothing. The moon was waning and the plain was dark."

The patrol leader signalled Rannah to silence and drew her troopers aside. They debated what they'd been told. Clearly the information was very limited and they were sceptical of Rannah since it was evident he'd been drinking. They decided to try and get more information from him.

"So, tell us what these people looked like."

The effort of locating a patrol and telling his story had largely dissipated the last vestiges of the amber liquor from Rannah's brain, but since his experience of anything outside of the ordinary was also limited he wasn't sure what more he could tell the patrol leader; after all, he hadn't really seen that much of the figures close up.

"There were four of them." He indicated the fingers on his right hand.

"They were all men." Again, he reinforced his statement with a gesture signifying flat chests.

The patrol leader encouraged him with raised eyebrows.

"They didn't have clothes like we do. Some of their clothes were hairy, like the dogs that the old desert patrols used to bring in. Their legs were covered with strips of material."

Rannah really couldn't visualise anything more. Never having seen clothes made of animal skins, he didn't know how else to describe them.

"Did they have weapons?"

So far the patrol leader knew that she hadn't heard anything of real interest to the guard commander, or anything that would define who these figures were. She still needed more.

"Two of them carried... ..... poles with sharpened ends."

Rannah had no idea what a spear was; however, the patrol leader did. She'd seen some old weapons in the Senate guardhouse.

"Did they have swords, knives?"

"Not that I saw."

Rannah desperately searched his now almost clear brain. The patrol leader was most interested in whether the figures had weapons. She was a soldier; he supposed that she would be.

That Rannah hadn't seen any didn't mean they were unarmed; but that occurred to the patrol leader rather than to him.

Rannah had nothing more to add. Again the leader made him repeat himself, which again he did accurately; she was satisfied.

The patrol escorted Rannah to his accommodation, as much to know where to find him as for his safety. The patrol leader's report immediately got Lenrick's attention. She was aware that it didn't carry them very far forward but at least gave them clear verification of what had only been suspected before.

* * *

At the end of another long day Sorak was exhausted. In the warmth and comfort of their accommodation she and Nasa ate their evening meal in uncharacteristic silence.

Nasa, knowing Sorak so well, made no effort to force conversation on her, despite his having some exciting news to impart.

And then, having finished their meal, Sorak was ready to talk.

"Lenrick reports another calf being taken, but this time there was a witness."

This immediately got Nasa's attention; this was welcome news.

Sorak told Nasa everything that Lenrick had told her.

"Lenrick has told the patrol, and Rannah, to tell no one of what he saw. We don't want people to get concerned about this until we know more."

"There are people outside of the city," Nasa said.

Sorak sensed that he didn't seem surprised. They both knew that there was some small evidence accumulating that the machine that had brought the founders of the city from beyond the distant star might be somewhere beyond the Edge.

In their new world, such information was no longer suppressed. To Nasa's practical mind, that meant that survivors had to be possible. His and Sorak's experience in finding the other machine trapped in the cleft of the mountain on their original escape from the city told him that if the founders' machine was truly out there, survivors here too had to be possible.

Of course, that raised all manner of additional questions. If the survivors of the crash had come out onto the plain to found the city, why would they leave some of their number behind in the forest? Unknown to Nasa, there were thought to have been at least ten generations of people having lived in the city, perhaps many more. The now lost books and papers from the destroyed Senate library would have recorded the true figure. And if people had left the city to settle beyond the Edge, as he and Sorak had done, why not people from any of the previous generations? The idea of people living happily beyond the Edge was entirely credible to Nasa. The idea of their herd being eroded by wild animals had already been accepted by him.

"Clearly, whoever these people are, they know all about the city and are unafraid of visiting it. So why haven't they made contact?"

"But, Nasa, if they were aware of the way the city had developed, and like the machine we found, the men in their society were equal, why would they want to make contact with the city?"

Nasa had no answer; she was right. His only thought was, how were these people so well informed, yet appeared to be so primitive? He had no answer to that either.

Wearing animal skins doesn't make them primitive!

Nasa admonished himself. The only evidence they had so far suggested people living exactly like he and Sorak and Lenar had done. The only difference from their behaviour was the suggestion of the existence of some sort of community.

"We need to make contact with these people."

Sorak wasn't surprised that Nasa should think this, but once again a whole range of questions and problems filled her mind. She signalled that she wanted to think some more about this latest information they'd acquired.

"Oh," said Nasa, "we had a message from Lenar. Desak is expecting a baby!" All thought of people living beyond the Edge and what it meant was momentarily forgotten.

But not for long!

9

With the news that there appeared to be two warring factions flexing their muscles, seemingly amongst the civilian population, Sorak's interest in the apparent existence of people living beyond the Edge was necessarily minimal. Rannah's evidence seemed credible, and Nasa's further conversations with the other ex-slave Chackar increasingly led him to believe that Mesrick had indeed, all those cycles ago, made a trip into the forest precisely where the calf stealers seemed likely to be headed.

"And, Sorak, if they're stealing our calves, does that not make you think that they have insufficient calves for their needs or, as we experienced, the ferocious beasts of the forest are taking them? And why has it come to such desperate measures now?"

It was this last point that was exercising Nasa's mind.

But with what little time for thought that she was able to give the situation, Sorak's question was still: why had these people, if they existed, not tried to make contact with the people running the city during the cycles of the distant star of the past?

"I think these people have always had equality between women and men, and knew enough about what was going on in the city to not want to have anything to do with a society dominated by just women."

Since this was also his own conclusion, Nasa had been more interested in how these people, and he was convinced that they existed, had apparently known what was going on in the city without ever being detected.

"True as that is, Sorak, how did they... do they... know what's going on in the city?"

The idea that there therefore must have been contact with someone in the city in past times was forming in both of their minds, but Sorak still hadn't got the answer that she was seeking.

"Of more interest to me, Nasa, is: if they've been aware of what's going on in the city, now that we've achieved a more equal society, why have they still not sought to make contact?"

It was the question he was wrestling with too. He found it almost impossible to visualise what these mysterious people might be thinking. Yet the only evidence that they had, suggested they were no different from the people of the city.

Equally, Nasa was clear in his mind that they might never know the answers to these questions, even if they did make contact with these forest people.

"The Senate meets after the next circuit of the distant star to decide what to do about Anstan and the mysterious people with the emblem."

Nasa was concerned because Sorak was concerned, but the more he thought about the calf stealing, about the possibility Mesrick might have met the people beyond the Edge in the past, the more he became obsessed with the idea that they should take the initiative and go and seek them out.

They being me.

Any discussion of this with Sorak would have to await the outcome of the Senate deliberations, but Nasa's mind was already working on a plan.

* * *

"Sorakmam, what evidence do we have?"

Lenrick, the guard commander, had reported all of the information that they had on both Anstan's increasing campaign to re-establish a solely women's administration and the opposition to that by the mysterious organisation characterised by the two-armed emblem.

Sorak wasn't listening to Lenrick. The entire Senate was present. Usually one or two senators were absent but on this occasion this wasn't the case. The level of interest couldn't have been higher.

They're worried, Sorak told herself rather obviously.

But it occurred to her that the worries of some of the senators weren't simply about the threats that Anstan's campaign represented. And as she thought this, another thought pushed into her mind: maybe some of the senators were a part of the two groups they were discussing. If so, that was a complication they didn't need.

In fact, this was indeed the case. Several of the older female senators were either openly now backing Anstan, or at least opposing any action against her.

"We only have the evidence that Lenrick has presented. We need to know more."

Sorak responded to the original question posed by the male senator. Clearly not a supporter of Anstan, the man nonetheless realised that the Senate had to proceed in an open and transparent way.

"All meetings should be reported to the Senate. In the past, citizens weren't allowed to meet without permission and the subject of the meeting had to be approved."

There were murmurs of agreement and dissent. The speaker this time was the oldest female senator present and had always been a reluctant recruit to the new freedoms.

She'd be one of Anstan's disciples.

And the feeling that maybe some of the senators knew more than they'd so far admitted grew a little more in Sorak's mind.

Suddenly, half the senators had something to say and Sorak was hard pressed to keep order. But her experience was that it was best to let everyone who wanted to, have their say, before trying to develop a course of action. The debate got heated, more than ever confirming her thought that at least some of the female senators would support a return to the old ways. The position of most of the male senators was equally clear-cut.

This is going nowhere.

And it was a thought that had occurred to others.

"We need to get inside Anstan's group, go to her meetings, understand what her plans might be."

Again there were murmurs of agreement and dissent, as Lecktan, one of the youngest female senators, finally made herself heard.

The voices of dissent were drowned out by the obvious agreement of the majority of the senators.

* * *

"We noted who disagreed with Lecktan," Lenrick later said. The guard commander had come to the same conclusion as Sorak: Anstan undoubtedly had supporters in the Senate.

Rannah, once fully recovered from his bout of amber liquor drinking, and once he'd thought about the reaction of the patrol to his sighting of the calf theft, was dissatisfied. He wasn't sure that he'd been taken seriously, and he recognised that that was perhaps his own fault, but nonetheless he was clear in his mind of what he'd seen, and like Nasa had a feeling that there were likely to be more thefts.

I must keep watch.

Rannah was an old man and knew that watching was all he could do. But if he was able to report another calf taken, and the patrol recognised he hadn't been drinking the amber liquor, they would have to take him seriously.

But he had a problem; where would he watch – on the wall or with the herds?

Either would be difficult. After the second calf had been taken the herds were now watched throughout each circuit of the distant star. Surely taking another animal would be too risky? Watching at the wall was easier but by then the theft would have taken place and Rannah would have no way of stopping it. Hiding a patrol would be almost impossible; summoning a patrol would be too late. But he had no other real option.

"I must keep watch on the wall."

Rannah had sense enough to realise that it was better to get more information about the people taking the calves before having any thoughts about trying to confront them.

* * *

Rannah wasn't an especially brave man; an administrative slave in the old days he'd had little contact with what Sorak might have called the real world. He more than once had second thoughts as he crouched behind the buttress that had hidden him before. It had been seven circuits of the distant star. He'd been out during the dark hours each night. The last night had been particularly unpleasant. There had been a cycler, one of the torrential rainstorms that afflicted the city occasionally. But when it cleared and the second moon reappeared on its second circuit, Rannah, dripping wet and shivering with cold, found himself in the company of two of the figures, clothed in animal skins, that he recognised as the calf thieves. They had clearly taken advantage of the cycler to climb the city wall.

Mother's heart!

What was he to do now? The two figures, two men, with the taller stature of the women of the city rather than the men, had tried to shelter behind the opposite side of the buttress from where he was hiding. But the cycler had passed through and the sky was clearing.

He tried hard not to panic, but his anxiety levels were rising. Actually meeting up with the calf thieves was something that he'd not envisaged.

The only coherent thought that he was capable of was: where were the two men's companions? Forced to stand up by his aching knees, the water dripping from him, he started to back away. He immediately had his answer as he collided with these other two men. They must have known he was there from when they'd first climbed the wall.

"You must come with us."

Rannah wasn't clear which man had spoken, but it was a statement in his own language, albeit with an odd accent, a statement that he readily understood. He panicked. He was clearly not being given an option.

As Rannah's anxiety levels continued to ratchet up he also realised that no one knew where he was. No one knew he was watching the wall. No one knew he was trying to prove to the patrol leader that he'd been telling the truth, that his thought processes hadn't been incapacitated by the amber liquor.

Why would they want me to go with them?

His next thought was that they would kill him once they were out on the plain, and no one would ever then know what had happened to him.

All he could do was shake his head. But two of the men grasped his arms. They were much stronger than he was and each carried a short sword and a knife in a sheath. They were not to be denied. He sensed that they were nervous, or angry; he wasn't sure which.

Thwarted by the increasing watchfulness of the guardians of the herds, they'd failed to capture another calf. And now they'd been detected. Taking the old man with them was all they could think of to do if they were to protect their entry route into the city.

Rannah was lowered down the outside of the city wall as if he was one of the calves, but he was freed again once on the plain below.

The four men crowded around him as they set off at a pace that left him panting and with rising pains in his chest. His companions were all young men compared with him. As the distant star rose above the horizon, the city was barely visible and the Edge still seemed to Rannah to be no closer. In the gloom the men had clearly not noticed Rannah's physical distress. In the growing light they did.

"We will stop."

As the party settled on the ground surrounding Rannah, he was aware both of the foul body odour of the men and of the tension building amongst them. And it was clear that the tension was about him.

They don't know what to do with me.

Clearly he was a problem to the men. But he was a problem they had to deal with, now they were safely away from the city.

The four of them moved away, and a heated argument began immediately. There was much shaking of fists and even the occasional hand on sword. The oldest man appeared to be the leader and equally appeared to be resisting what the others were urging on him.

If Rannah had been able to hear what was being said he would have had plenty of cause to panic.

"We should kill him," the youngest of the four said.

It was this proposal that the leader was so vehemently opposing.

"We should take him back to the village," another said.

"If we do that we'll have to keep him forever. He couldn't be allowed to go back to the city. The Elders wouldn't permit it. And then people from the city might come looking for him."

Again it was the leader who was raising the objections.

"Then we should leave him in the forest away from the village. If the animals kill him… ….."

The argument raged on. Rannah's misery increased.

The forest people had lived in complete isolation from the city, whilst being aware of it, for many generations. All the men knew this. Their desperation to preserve their herd of beasts had forced them into stealing calves. This inevitably carried the risk of having contact with the people of the city. And this had now happened. The party had no idea why Rannah had been hiding on the wall but killing him was against the culture that underpinned their lives. Only the Elders could approve a killing. Kidnapping wasn't really an option either. Yet the situation of the old man had to be resolved.

But they needed to rest. Settling in a group around Rannah, the men took it in turns to sleep and watch.

As the light from the distant star faded and the party prepared to get underway again, the group leader gave Rannah some fruit and bread. They'd decided what to do about him.

"We will leave you now," he said.

Allowing Rannah to return to the city was the conclusion that the group had come to, in the certain knowledge that contact with the people of the city would now undoubtedly take place.

Such considerations were beyond Rannah as he searched the horizon to determine which route to take back once the distant star returned.

His journey back was uneventful but his anxiety over what to do with the information that he'd acquired was rising towards panic. Men from the forest clad in animal skins?

"Who's going to believe me?"

Unbeknown to him there was one person.

10

Anstan had taken time to decide when a campaign to restore women's rule in the city was likely to be successful. Clearly, during the various male-led administrations the time hadn't been right and the often violent and unforgiving nature of the rule during these periods precluded any efforts on her part. Provoking a backlash from the men would defeat rather than advance the women's cause. Now that Sorak had achieved stability and people could see what life could be like in the future, Anstan perceived that the time had come.

Her particular concern was not to allow Sorak's new freedoms to become too attractive and too entrenched.

"Sorak is allowing people to do whatever they want. Unheard of things are happening; men are taking advantage; the administration is making no effort to manage people's lives."

She was talking to a group of her followers, mainly women in their middle years who'd had positions in the military world before the rebellion.

Anstan worried that she couldn't attract younger women, but she blamed Sorak for that too.

"If Sorak and the Senate won't act, then we must. We must show the women of the city that they can recover what they lost over the last twenty cycles of the distant star. Women can and will rule the city again."

The women that she was talking to needed no convincing. All were ex-soldiers and had formed themselves into a fighting unit committed to dealing with the prominent men and women who opposed their plans to re-establish female domination. Behind them was an indeterminate number of both ex-military and civilians who Anstan knew and who she needed to reach and convince.

Anstan had called together her core group in advance of what she called an operation to remove a running sore. Anstan had two men in her sights: 147 and Nasa. She was determined that they both be killed, by way of example of her group's power, and also as a signal to the main body of women in the city that things were about to revert to their former status. Neither man presented an easy target, so dealing with them she felt would also add to her credentials.

Briefed and armed, the three delegated ex-soldiers set off into the ruined areas of the city in search of the first of their intended victims.

Sorak thought that she was beyond surprises. But when her assistant Marwek and the young senator Lecktan asked to see her, she couldn't believe what they'd come to request of her.

The contrast between Marwek and Lecktan interested her. Her assistant had pale skin and light brown hair; Lecktan, as a result of a past breeding with a black slave, had black hair and faintly brown skin. To Sorak, they represented the diversity that, for her, was so important to the city.

Nasa had always argued that his partner had every reason to hate the black women of the city, yet not only did she not but, to his continuing amazement, she actively sought out anyone who had black ancestry and tried to incorporate them into her vision of the future.

So if Sorak wasn't surprised by what Marwek and Lecktan presented to her, she was certainly bemused.

With her permission two further women were brought into the room.

It was Lecktan who took the lead.

"Meet Pilar and Pelar," she said.

Sorak had never met twins before. Somewhere deep in her brain she recalled that multiple births in the past hadn't been acceptable to the old ruling Senate, although she couldn't remember why. As she recollected that both offspring and parents had traditionally been killed in the old days, a wave of horror and then of curiosity swept over her. It hadn't been like that in recent times, but Sorak was certainly intrigued. So, what did they want of her?

She later recalled that she'd never seen anyone quite as black as these two. But where had they come from? How had they survived?

"You are welcome," she said.

No one spoke for a few moments, giving Sorak the chance to study the two further. Very tall, they were of slight build, and Sorak decided they must be older than her son Lenar but not necessarily a product of the old regime.

But they must have been born before the rebellion.

Clearly, the two young women thought that some explanation was necessary.

"Our mother was a senator and our father a slave of the chairwoman of the Senate."

Whether it was Pilar or Pelar who spoke, Sorak had no way of knowing.

"Our father was killed in the desert outside of the city."

Sorak knew all about slaves being killed on the plain outside the city; somewhere deep in her brain there were bad memories of such things. But she was too fascinated by what she was being told for the thoughts to surface. She was keen to know more.

"But you survived!"

"Yes, Sorakmam," Pilar explained. "Our mother had an old slave who hid us for the first few cycles of our lives in the old buildings behind the Senate library. Even in the old days there were many unused buildings around the Senate. We believe they were once a part of the Senate prison but had been out of use, at least supposedly, for many cycles."

Not for the first time Sorak marvelled at a tale of slave loyalty that ran totally against the spirit of the rebellion. However, she knew that many of the more intelligent slaves who worked for, or had regular contact with, women had always been much more loyal than the old quarry slaves and the like who only saw women as oppressive.

"No one went there because the slaves used it for..." the other twin took up the story.

Sorak was aware, inevitably as a result of her friendship with Lenen in her days as a young military officer, that what the Senate called unnatural sexual relations took place amongst the women. The idea that there was a special place slaves could go to for the same purpose, again when she thought over the conversation later, seemed only to be expected. Having known only the powerful masculinity of Nasa, she couldn't imagine what actually went on there, but she accepted the reality of it. And she accepted the reality that such things would still be going on, but in her new world without the need to hide.

Nonetheless, the conversation stalled.

"But you survived," Sorak finally said again.

"Being twins, our mother probably thought we'd been killed; even in her day it still sometimes happened. She died in the rebellion; we never actually met her."

Sorak noted that there seemed to be no regret in this statement. But then such detachment between children and their parents used to be the norm.

"We grew up like wild animals." Both young women appeared to find this amusing.

Lecktan intervened. For her, the twins' background was no longer important.

"Pilar and Pelar have been reluctant to say where they live, but they have had contact with Anstan and don't like what she's preaching. They believe something has to be done to stop her, and are ready to serve the city, Sorakmam, to help achieve that."

So at last they'd come to the purpose of the twins' visit.

"How?" Sorak asked before she'd really digested what Lecktan was saying.

"Anstan is planning to kill as many men in prominent positions as she can. She has ex-soldiers only too willing to do her work for her. 147 is at risk. So, we believe, is Nasa, Sorakmam."

As if to reinforce what she was saying, she gestured to Pilar to open the jerkin that she was wearing to reveal a well-honed body and the two-armed emblem displayed on the garment beneath.

Marwek and Sorak reacted with surprise. Lecktan had clearly known what to expect.

The conversation then took on an entirely different aspect when it transpired that it was Pilar and Pelar who'd formed the group to oppose Anstan's efforts to reimpose the past. They were careful not to give away anything specific or any detail, but they were clearly expecting support and endorsement of their actions and plans.

There was another pause in the conversation as Sorak and Marwek thought through the implications of what the twins were telling them. Lecktan clearly had no problems with the situation.

"I'm not sure we should know about this," Marwek said, voicing her superior's very thought.

The problems imposed by having two armed groups fighting each other in the shadows was not something Sorak relished; it was too much of a threat to her cherished dreams for the city. The issue for her was, what obligation did knowing about these groups place on her to counter or suppress them? That needed a lot more thought and discussion. However, pretending not to know about them wasn't really a solution.

However, it did register with Sorak that 147 was said to be at risk, and many others, including Nasa. Pilar and Pelar had definitely got her attention.

147 was feeling his age. He was at least sixty cycles of the distant star, but as a former slave no one had ever told him his date of birth. His physical reactions were slowing down but his mental processes were as sharp as ever.

He had more information that he needed to pass on to Sorak and he'd sent a messenger to tell her so. But unlike their previous meeting he'd asked her to come to him. His informants had already been urging caution on him. Attacks on men were sporadic but 147 had a sense that they were increasing and he knew that he was an obvious target.

The message was delivered to Marwek, Sorak's ever-resourceful assistant. The elderly man who'd delivered it, Marwek immediately detected was in a state of high anxiety. She enquired as to whether anything was troubling him.

"I passed some strange women on the way here."

Marwek had no idea what he meant by strange women but his obvious anxiety affected her. She sent the man to the kitchen area, both to refresh himself, and also to give herself time to contact Lenrick, the Senate guard commander. Lenrick was unsurprised that 147 might be a target and ordered precautions to be taken. She also knew that Nasa was likely to be at risk too but didn't presume to take action there; she knew how independent Nasa could be.

Marwek finally got her message to Sorak.

"Sorakmam, 147 wishes to see you. He has something urgent to tell you but is frightened to come here again."

This was something of an overstatement but Marwek had nonetheless sensed that something had changed, and the strange women bothered her. She had pondered on getting Lenrick to send a patrol to accompany 147 to Sorak's office but thought even so that he might just refuse to come.

It was late in the day and Sorak had finished most of her business; the rest could wait.

"Come, Marwek, we will go now."

Marwek didn't mention that Lenrick had sent the patrol to 147's house. Rather to her surprise, Sorak didn't take her usually circuitous route to 147's house.

She knows something isn't right!

Marwek's assessment was correct, although Sorak would probably have been unable to articulate what was motivating her. With her two male bodyguards following closely behind, Sorak and Marwek were soon at 147's house. Marwek had sent the elderly man back to let 147 know that they were coming. There was no sign of Lenrick's patrol but Marwek was hardly expecting it to be openly visible.

"Sorakmam!"

As they approached the house the bodyguards moved in front to make sure it was safe for Sorak. The caution in the man's voice told Sorak and Marwek that something was wrong.

The old man, 147's messenger, lay sprawled against the front wall of the house. His throat had been cut and the killers clearly didn't care whether he was found or not. Four swords were instantly drawn.

"The door, Sorak."

Marwek pointed, her eyes focused on the entrance door of the house; it was hanging half open. As one bodyguard kicked the door fully open, the other, quickly followed by Sorak and Marwek, rushed into the main room. What were they going to find?

"Sorakmam."

A surge of relief flowed through Sorak. 147 was standing rather forlornly against the wall of the room; pale and quivering, he looked a picture of misery. The leader of the patrol sent by Lenrick, who was also there, saluted Sorak, and then he directed his eyes to the crumpled body on the floor in the middle of the room.

Things were happening so quickly Sorak didn't have time to wonder how the patrol had got there.

"Female ex-soldier," Marwek said of the body; the patrol leader nodded his confirmation; her weapons readily identified her.

"When the old man gave me his message, he talked about strange women in the neighbourhood," Marwek then said, "so I asked Lenrick to send a patrol."

"And?"

It was an instruction from Sorak to the patrol leader to explain what had happened. Having now understood why the patrol was there she was relieved and quick to take control of the situation.

The patrol leader took his time, checking that his team were still searching the grounds around 147's house.

"When we arrived there was shouting and screams. We then discovered there'd been three armed women seemingly threatening 147. We found the body of the old man at the door as we approached and made enough noise for two of the soldiers to come out and investigate. Whilst we dealt with these two, Primat and Rankat crept in via the back door and cut down the third woman. We had no idea who the dead man was, or where he'd come from."

Marwek explained about the returning messenger.

"Anstan sent them."

147 spoke almost in a whisper. "She has called on all women to kill any man working with the Senate and with your administration, Sorakmam."

Exactly what Pilar and Pelar told us!

"147, you cannot stay here any longer. We will find you accommodation in the secure housing around the new Senate buildings."

147 offered no objection.

11

Rannah's journey back to the city was challenging for him. Never had he felt his age so keenly as he struggled forward. Moving mainly during the night, to avoid the heat of the day, he could barely see where he was headed and was increasingly concerned that he might travel right passed his destination. Exhausted by the punishing pace that had been forced upon him when they'd earlier crossed the plain, his progress was slow. Aching and footsore he had to stop continually. Hungry and thirsty, the provisions that the leader of the group had given him hardly lasted a day; by the time the distant star went down for a second time he began to despair he would ever make it. But shivering in the night-time cold, he finally arrived at the city wall. If truth were known, he'd walked back along exactly the same route that they'd used when he'd been forced to leave the city.

Entering by the yellow gate, he was immediately stopped by the gate guard. Someone coming back into the city, when there wasn't supposed to be anything outside of it, obviously had something to explain.

The gate guard simply didn't believe Rannah's story. Frustrated, all the old man could do was repeat the description of his trip over and over again.

"We must send him to Lenrick," the gate guard commander, when she was informed, decided.

It was a fortunate decision. Privy to the reports of people secretly stealing calves, once Rannah had explained himself Lenrick immediately had him taken to Nasa.

It was some time before Anstan was able to piece together what had happened at 147's house, or at least piece together what she thought had happened. With her three troopers dead she had no reliable source of information. It took extensive enquiries in the neighbourhood before she could even make sense of the basics. Not knowing that 147 had sent for Sorak, she had no explanation as to how she and her bodyguards had arrived at the ex-slave's house. The earlier arrival of a patrol equally bemused her too.

"How could the patrol have known something was going to happen? Surely we don't have a spy in our midst?"

She made no attempt to explain the reported presence of Sorak at 147's house.

But Anstan was convinced of the loyalty of her small band of followers. Her inner circle had been chosen after much investigation precisely to avoid Sorak or the Senate knowing what was being planned. Paranoid in a way that Sorak wouldn't have understood, Anstan was determined not to make the sorts of mistakes that the male leaders of the city had once made when they'd taken over after the rebellion. Although she was too young to have experienced the extreme secrecy practised by the former women's Senate, she fully understood the reasoning behind their keeping such a tight control of every aspect of city life. And it was this that she was striving to recreate.

"And 147 is no longer living in his old house?"

"No, Anstanmam. We've asked around our contacts in the administration but it's too early for us to have any information on where he might now be."

The speaker was a former officer from the same military unit as Sorak. Having witnessed the process of Sorak's alienation as a young woman, and having no understanding of it, and having lost to her in several fist fights, a prowess for which Sorak had been famous, this aging woman had a hatred for the Senate leader that had burned through her and poisoned her thinking totally. Although contemptuous of her, she was an ideal tool for Anstan.

"So," Anstan said, "we must concentrate on killing Nasa. If anything can defeat Sorak it will be Nasa's death."

Her companion, who'd witnessed the developing relationship between Sorak and 1562/Nasa in her youth, knew this to be true, but she also knew that Nasa would be an infinitely more difficult target than 147.

But at that point what neither of them knew was that they would have to track Nasa through the forest and wilderness beyond the Edge if they wanted to catch up with him in the immediate future.

* * *

Rannah was delivered to Sorak and Nasa's quarters when he'd recovered. Lenrick had decreed that he should be under a form of house arrest so that there was no chance of his divulging what he'd seen and heard during his period of capture by the people from the forest. All were agreed that until much more concrete information was available, the contacts with the people beyond the Edge should be kept secret.

* * *

Sorak hadn't wanted Nasa to go off exploring beyond the Edge. Or at least, being realistic, she wished he'd taken a larger party with him. Pastak, Sorak's ex-soldier friend, had offered to go with him but he was determined that there should be just three of them in the party. Nasa was at his best when in total charge of the action.

"No, I will take only Rannah and Tareck."

Tareck had been one of Sorak's bodyguards but he was too much of a restless spirit to stay in such a limited occupation for very long. Nasa knew him and trusted him.

It was the plan to take Rannah that most irked Sorak. An old man used to a comfortable life within the city's administration, she was concerned that he'd be more of a burden than a help. But his knowledge was too valuable to leave behind.

"He's the only person with experience of the people we'll be looking for, Sorak."

Soral knew this to be true, but she nonetheless considered Rannah's experience to have been brief and of limited use. But she knew that there was no point in arguing.

The trip beyond the Edge was to be the first time in many cycles that Sorak and Nasa had been apart. This troubled both of them, but Sorak, when she could separate her personal feelings from her duties as the chairwoman of the Senate, knew that the question of other inhabitants of the planet could not now be left unresolved.

Like Nasa, she had no fear of what was beyond the Edge, and there was no suggestion that these people were, or might be, hostile, or that they were possessed of greater military capability than the people of the city, but in the interests of the security of the city they needed answers.

The issue of the location of the machine that the founders of the city had arrived in formed no part of Sorak's interest. She and Nasa had talked endlessly about this, but knowing or not knowing about these early people had no bearing on Sorak's perception of her duties. She lived in the present and the past was what they were rejecting in their efforts to establish a viable future.

But what little he could garner from Mesrick's expedition had served only to raise Nasa's curiosity. He acknowledged that his chances of finding what she'd found were very small but, as he told Sorak, that wasn't a reason not to search. Equally, he conceded that such a search was not the primary purpose of the expedition.

Tareck was younger than Nasa and had been born into the fractious world of the earliest male administration, but he was acknowledged as a man of exceptional physical strength and high intelligence. Sorak had rescued him from his military unit and had used him as a bodyguard. He was a part of the expedition as much at Sorak's insistence as at Nasa's own inclination.

* * *

Not wishing anyone to know that they'd left the city, the three members of Nasa's party had let themselves down the outer wall, much as the people that they would be tracking had done. With Tareck's ready help, Rannah made the descent without mishap.

As they set off in the direction Rannah had identified, a whole range of memories flooded into Nasa's mind. Both he and Tareck were burdened with the sort of large backpacks that Sorak had made him carry when they'd first escaped the city. 1562/Nasa was then a physically puny pampered slave born down by the weight of food, Sorak's clothes and other belongings. How things had changed!

It's just food and essential supplies for living in the wild now.

The lessons of those far-off days however, weren't forgotten. Nasa had planned their expedition in as much detail as he could. Just setting off blithely into the unknown was not an option for this trip. Ignorance of what was beyond the Edge was no longer a consideration; Nasa, at least, had a very good idea.

The distant star was setting.

"There's a..." Rannah didn't know what to call it as he gestured with his hand, outlining the depression in the plain that they were entering.

Rannah recognised the place where he and his companions had spent the night on his previous journey. This gave Nasa confidence.

They rested, and as the first vermillion light of the first moon suffused the night Tareck distributed food from his backpack.

"You watch until the second moon's first passage and then wake me," Nasa told Tareck.

Both he and Rannah were soon asleep. But Nasa's slumber didn't last until the appointed time. Tareck placed a hand over his mouth as he gently shook him.

Nasa instantly knew that something was wrong.

"There are people," Tareck said in a low voice, anxious not to awaken Rannah.

Nasa heard the voices. They were receding but neither he nor Tareck could discern in which direction the people were moving. Nor could they discern how many people there might be.

If they're in front of us that could be a problem!

But as the thought formed in his mind, Nasa shrugged it off. They still had almost half the night ahead of them; the time to worry was when the distant star returned. However, there was no chance of his going back to sleep.

And when the distant star did return, as he and Tareck had expected there was nothing. The people that they'd heard in the night had left no signs of their presence, let alone an indication of their numbers or of which direction they'd taken. Neither Nasa nor Tareck mentioned the people in the night to Rannah.

"They headed for the Edge, for a group of trees I could just see in the dim light."

Rannah repeated where the group that had taken him had headed after they abandoned him.

As they set off again across the open plain, the distant star burned down on them. The going was easy and even at Rannah's pace they were in sight of the Edge as the light began to rapidly fade. The group of trees that Rannah had identified was clearly visible and they reached it just before the darkness settled. Since the old man was incapable of climbing into one of the trees, they slept and kept watch from the ground.

Next morning, Tareck, being young and restless, was active before Nasa and Rannah. Taking his crossbow he explored the area around the trees. The ground was firm and dry and, apart from a few strange noises that he assumed were being made by the natural inhabitants of the place, there was nothing to disturb the peace of the morning. Yet something focused his attention just as he was about to return to his companions. He took his time to survey the landscape and the trees, trying to visualise what it was that had attracted his attention.

"The ground is raised in two areas, and although the trees are the same as those growing around there's something odd about the way they've grown curved rather than straight up."

Tareck, having described what he'd seen, led Nasa and Rannah to the area that he'd discovered. The two areas of raised ground, on one of which they were standing, were widely separated but, as Rannah was quick to notice, in the distance ahead of them they seemed to come together.

What they'd stumbled on, although they had no way of knowing it, was the beginning of the malformation of the trees that had attracted Mesrick's attention. It was barely twenty cycles of the distant star since she'd been there, but Nasa sensed, like her, that although what they were looking at had been formed hundreds of cycles earlier it was somehow manmade.

Looking for the remnants of what she supposed was the founders' machine, which Nasa believed Mesrick had found, was very much his second priority for their expedition, yet

Rannah had seemingly led them straight to evidence that couldn't be ignored.

So, the craft from beyond the distant star did land beyond the Edge!

As they moved on, Nasa led the way, clearing a passage through the undergrowth and low-level vegetation with his sword. Tareck followed when he saw what Nasa was doing. He was heading down the line of the two areas of raised ground. And Rannah was correct; as the trees became even more malformed and bent over, the rows came together to eventually form a tunnel. But Rannah had detected something else. Now the silence had been broken, Nasa knew exactly what was making the noise.

12

After their initial meeting with Sorak and Lecktan, Pilar and Pelar were careful to avoid any further observable contact with the administration.

"So, what did we learn from them about this group, the 'Defenders', that they say they've organised?"

Marwek, and the senator Lecktan, had joined Sorak on one of her visits to the various sectors of the city. Sorak hated having to spend too much time sitting around in an office, even if so much of her business had to be conducted from there. She found it hard to remember that she was a soldier and not an administrator. Getting out and about was the only way she could assuage her innermost urges towards doing something active.

For all manner of reasons, Sorak liked to visit Sector Four best. She was always assured of a friendly welcome from the ex-soldiers who largely lived there, and from the new generation of mangeneers who managed the water treatment plant and other essential activities that took place in the sector and between the city walls nearby. And of course, it was the area where she'd once lived and where she'd first owned 1562, the slave who became Nasa, who'd totally changed her life.

And she particularly liked to relax in the old herdsmen's hut under the outer city wall where she and Nasa had spent so much time. It had bad memories as well as good, but for Sorak the past was always the past and its only value was to help them understand the future.

Marwek, having a good understanding of Sorak, saw to it that the old hut was always properly maintained and habitable. It was where they headed.

"Anstan can draw on many ex-soldiers who have no place in the new city society and resent that," Marwek said, "but the Defenders, as far as I could understand from the twins, are almost entirely drawn from the generation born during or after the rebellion and brought up during the worst excesses of the male administrations. All they want is stability and a vision of what the future of the city might look like."

Being of this generation themselves, Marwek and Lecktan, more than Sorak, understood the frustrations that Pilar and Pelar were reflecting.

"And there's unfinished business from the rebellion." Sorak's response surprised Lecktan, although perhaps not Marwek, who obviously knew her principal rather better.

"Yes, that's exactly what they think," the young senator said. "And until the pre-rebellion generation dies out, there will always be those who are afraid of the future and want to go back to the past."

Lecktan watched Sorak carefully for her reaction, since she was of this older generation. Sorak didn't react.

Nonetheless, Sorak would have admitted that she was confused. Sector Four felt safe to her, she was accepted not as the Senate leader but as an old comrade, yet Lecktan was clearly saying that within the body of friendly women now living there, ex-soldiers and civilians, there were still some who didn't accept the current regime of city management. And Anstan was adept at identifying those women who'd lost their place in the new society and deeply resented it.

Sorak would have been surprised to discover how many of these women there were, a significant proportion of whom hadn't really recognised their disenchantment until Anstan had put the situation to them, albeit in an over-simplified and rather biased way.

Anstan had done her best to make her campaign against the Senate and its administration personal. Yet in her turn, Sorak had done her best to incorporate as many of the ex-soldiers into the new military that she'd established as she could. But with the need to also employ men as soldiers there were never going to be enough such places for women, especially as Sorak had also actively tried to reduce the size of the military.

There are always going to be those who resent the changes that have been made.

Sorak knew this had to be true. The original pre-rebellion Senate, determined to allow no divergence from the harsh rule they considered necessary for an ordered society, had had no concept of the submerged resentments that had existed. Yet Nasa had always maintained that the fact that they felt it necessary to have such a large and dominant military machine spoke both for their uncertainty over their own grip on the people of the city and the poverty of their ideas on what sort of society they wanted.

That this was apparent to a slave, albeit a very intelligent one, but not to the senators themselves was a continuing wonder to Sorak.

But her mood of reflection was about to be interrupted.

"Sorakmam."

The tone of Marwek's address immediately got her attention.

The old herdsmen's hut was warm in the midday heat from the distant star; the three of them had been relaxed, enjoying the opportunity to take their ease. But Marwek had been called out of the hut.

When she returned she was accompanied by one of the bodyguards who would not normally have entered the hut unless there was a pressing reason. There clearly was.

As she focused on the man Sorak saw that his tunic was covered in blood and his sword arm was hanging awkwardly by his side.

"Sorakmam," the man said, clearly in great pain, "there are armed women outside. They've killed Merack."

Sorak was now fully in action mode. Merack was the other bodyguard. And as she, Marwek and Lecktan listened to what they were being told, they could hear a rumble of voices outside the hut.

"Come out, or we'll come in and get you!"

The demand was hostile and insistent.

Sorak thought she recognised the voice, but what was more important was how many women there were, and whether they would fulfil their threat. Sorak assumed that Marwek and the bodyguard would know how many women were outside.

"Seven; two wounded," the bodyguard said, reading her thought.

Fours against seven; more like three, as the bodyguard was wounded. Sorak had fought against worse odds when she and Nasa and their son Lenar were returning to the city.

But how good a fighter is Lecktan?

But the women outside didn't wait for an answer from Sorak.

Spurred on by their own anxieties, two of them were forcing their way into the hut. Lecktan was nearest the entrance. She hardly had time to draw her sword before the leading woman attacked her. Moving with youthful ease she quickly sidestepped the flaying sword of the advancing woman, forcing her off balance and causing her to move across in front of her colleague, impeding her ability to join the fray. Then, without waiting to give her a chance to regain her balance, Lecktan stabbed her sword upwards into the woman's chest. She collapsed, dead.

HEDLEY HARRISON

Sorak had her answer. Lecktan was clearly a resourceful fighter; how one so young had got to be so Sorak didn't get a chance to wonder.

The second woman recovered herself and confronted Sorak. Movement behind her suggested that others had followed her into the hut. There was very little room for manoeuvre. As she and Lecktan were immediately faced with three opponents, she was suddenly aware that Marwek and the injured bodyguard were no longer there.

In the confined space of the hut the three women realised that they were only getting in each other's way, but they were each individually reluctant to take on Sorak or the woman with her. But their hesitation wasn't to last.

Screams and clashes of swords told Sorak that Marwek and the bodyguard had exited the hut through the door under the city wall and had come around and attacked the women from behind.

Spilling back out into the area between the city walls, the three women now found themselves seemingly outnumbered; with two dead and two wounded out of the seven, they were confronted by four opponents.

"Lay down your weapons and no harm will come to you," Sorak said.

None of the women made any effort to do so. With the bodyguard injured, the two groups were more evenly matched than it would have appeared at first sight.

"Lay down your weapons!"

It was a new voice. Sorak and Marwek looked startled. The three women who'd attacked them looked confused. Only Lecktan seemed unfazed.

"Lay down your weapons!"

There was serious menace in the voice as the demand was repeated.

No one was very clear where they'd emerged from but the two confronting groups were joined and surrounded by seven

88

or eight young women, all fully armed, threatening them with crossbows. The two linked arms logo on their tunics was all the explanation Sorak needed.

The tension ratcheted up as the three surviving women still made no effort to lay down their weapons. A crossbow bolt, however, fired into the ground just in front of one of the women, finally prompted them to do as ordered.

Sorak and her party lowered their weapons but retained hold of them. The order to disarm was not repeated. It had not been directed at them.

"Sorakmam." The leader of the group of young women who'd rescued them quickly addressed the Senate leader. "We've been following these women as they were following you. Anstan has ordered the death of all prominent men who support the Senate, but we had no knowledge of any plans to attack you. It was just fortunate that we detected them."

Before Sorak could respond, a regular patrol arrived, alerted it seemed by some of the female residents in Sector Four who'd become suspicious of the small group of unknown young women they'd observed acting strangely. As Marwek briefed the patrol leader, the young women, the first contact that Sorak had had with Pilar and Pelar's Defenders in action, melted away. Sorak made no effort to speak further with them or detain them.

With the patrol treating the wounded, leading away the survivors and the injured bodyguard, and carrying away the dead, Sorak, Marwek and Lecktan were left alone.

They were all feeling a little nervous.

And conscious now that, being unprotected, they were vulnerable, Sorak suggested that they return to Sector One and the administration buildings rather than head on into Sector Four. The incident had been salutary. The reality of what 147 had been telling her at last struck home with clarity. The society that she was trying to create, Sorak recognised, was still fragile, still underdeveloped, and still not understood by those with a foot in the past. The incident only made her more determined to press ahead with allowing the city people to develop as they wished. She was conscious nonetheless that there would always be doubters and resisters.

What to do about these doubters and resisters was still an issue, and would be for some time yet.

How can we convince these people? We need our new society to work now, not when all the old pre-rebellion women have died off.

Since she herself was a pre-rebellion woman who'd embraced change, she had little understanding of those who wanted to return to the past.

Back in her quarters in Sector Two, and when Lecktan had left them, Sorak and Marwek reviewed the incident and what it told them. Marwek, Sorak knew, was always good for sensible advice; in many ways she had the same commonsense approach to life as Nasa had. The conversation carried on until well after the distant star had disappeared.

According to Marwek, one of the key things that the events of the day told them was that the young women and young men had to be allowed to flourish. They could no longer be expected to conform mindlessly in the way that they would have been under the old hierarchical regime. Also, they might not have approved of the violence but there had always been aggression amongst the groups in the city for as long as anyone knew, and disagreements had often been sorted out violently.

But as they tried to grapple with the problem of how to move forward, another underlying issue was raised once again. They really had no idea how many women had been born around or after the rebellion. Sorak was continually surprised by the extent of the breeding that had gone on, despite all the upheavals and apparent gender hostility. But she hadn't really grasped the fact that the freedoms she was trying to establish would inevitably lead to the citizens' more basic feelings also being given freedom. And that way led to population growth.

Equally, and more disturbingly, Sorak had no idea how many older women with reactionary views there were.

She shared her thoughts with Marwek. Marwek's response was practical.

"We really need to know how many people there are in the city."

Sorak knew she was right but she was aware that there was a real problem in trying to take any sort of census. Trying to count people might be misunderstood; it was the sort of thing the old women's Senate used to do. And as they'd already discussed, there were still plenty of women who would remember that. She had no wish to do anything that recalled the past.

On her own, Sorak's thoughts were more basic. It was her first hands-on contact with the stresses and strains rumbling below the surface. That depressed her. And with Nasa somewhere beyond the Edge, she had no one to share her anxieties with.

However, never one to dwell too long on her problems, Sorak tried to visualise what Nasa might be doing and what he might have discovered.

13

More memories flooded Nasa's mind as the party approached the ravine and he recognised the noise of the fast-flowing stream that was making conversation so difficult. Both during his and Sorak's original journey away from the city, and when they returned, they'd come across many rivers like the one that they were now contemplating. Both Rannah and Tareck looked in amazement at the turbulent waters cascading through the ravine below them. As city dwellers, they'd never seen anything like the trees that surrounded them, or the river below them.

Unlike on Mesrick's journey, there were no signs of the wildlife Nasa had been expecting to see.

The trees were closely packed and dense and, as they cautiously made their way to the edge of the ravine, the light from the distant star was increasingly obscured.

Much to Nasa and Tareck's amusement, the old man took one look at the scene below him and stepped right back almost in fear. The power of the raging waters was very apparent.

As he surveyed the scene, trying to decide whether they'd need to cross the river, Nasa began to study the trees more closely. There were no signs of the distortions that had been observed before, but nonetheless he was attracted to the point where the river was apparently disgorged from dense undergrowth. The river appeared to come out of the ground. He and Sorak had seen this before; in fact, Nasa, in the past, had been constantly bemused over how the rivers arose, how they were supplied with water and where they eventually disappeared to.

Seeing things with fresh eyes and an open mind, Tareck started to move along the edge of the ravine in the direction of the source of the river. He also was curious as to where it came from.

We need to move on; we can't waste time exploring things that won't lead us to the people we're looking for.

Nasa knew that this was obviously the case, but like Tareck he was inherently curious about things that he hadn't seen before or didn't understand.

Rannah followed Tareck. Clearly, they had to know how much of an obstacle to their journey this ravine and river were going to be. But it was Rannah who brought them back to reality.

The ground along the edge of the ravine at first was rocky and devoid of vegetation but as they progressed this gave way to a softer footing and, as the old man was quick to notice, footprints.

"Nasa!"

Tareck, who'd gone on ahead, recognised the fear in Rannah's voice. He carefully returned and, having seen what the old man had seen, avoided walking on the footprints.

Neither Rannah nor Tareck had seen anything like it but Nasa recognised the pad marks of one of the large predators that he knew roamed the forests and plains of the planet. He'd certainly been expecting to see or hear the rapacious dogs that he and Sorak had encountered several times in the past, but the presence of such a large beast, as this obviously was, in their area would have frightened the dogs away. Nasa's bitter experience in their former home in the hidden valley was that these large killers were very territorial, so they weren't likely to be too far away.

Since in their hidden valley they'd run out of crossbow bolts before the really large predators had appeared he had no idea how effective their weapons would be against them. What he also knew was that these creatures were generally nocturnal and, unless they stumbled upon one of their lairs in the light of the distant star, they were unlikely to come across them directly.

Nasa shared what knowledge he had of the beasts of the forest, avoiding too much graphic detail. Tareck was unlikely to be frightened but Rannah most probably would be. Sorak's concerns about Rannah resurfaced in Nasa's mind.

But not for the first time, Nasa had underestimated the old man. His immediate thought was both sensible and practical.

"There must be a way down to the river," Rannah said. "These animals would have to drink."

He set off along the route that Tareck had begun to take, studying the ground as he followed the animal's footsteps. Nasa wasn't sure what he was expecting to see.

The trees became denser but there were occasional gaps, and with them patches of light still, enabling them to see their way. Nasa let Rannah and Taraek take the lead. It was important that they gained confidence as they penetrated further into the forest.

Clearly the forest people didn't come this way!

Nasa wasn't entirely sure his conclusion was correct; just because they saw no evidence that they had, didn't mean that they hadn't. They needed to stay alert.

Eventually they came to the point where the river disgorged from the ground. And to challenge Nasa's previous thoughts they found themselves following what was clearly a pathway. Rannah noted some places where the bushes appeared to have been broken back, whether by a large beast or by people none of them was willing to speculate.

Suddenly Tareck stopped dead and raised his crossbow.

Nasa pushed Rannah behind them and joined the bodyguard, uncertain what had caused him to stop.

Tareck pointed at the other side of the clearing that they were just about to enter. Just as they'd found the distorted avenue of trees when they first entered the forest, so now Tareck was indicating a similar, but larger, distortion.

The three of them started to cross the clearing. A few paces in, Rannah stumbled. Beneath the undergrowth the floor of the clearing was rutted, and as they moved more carefully forward they discovered increasingly deeper gouges pointing in the direction of the tunnel of distorted trees ahead of them. As they finally approached the edge of the clearing and the tunnel opening, they had to climb down into the huge gouge in order to move forward.

Once again it was Rannah who was first to identify the unexpected.

"What can have made this?"

Nasa realised the old man had made an assumption based on what he was observing. And as they came to an area where there was no vegetation in the gouge, what he was observing was a smooth and clearly mechanically made mark in the ground. What they were standing in Nasa had no idea, but he was instantly convinced that it had to have something to do with the machine that the planet's founders had arrived in. There could be no other explanation. There were no machines in the city that would have been capable of making such a gouge, even supposing there might be a reason why it should have been out there to make it.

It's like the marks on the mountaintop as the other machine crashed into the cleft.

It was, but Nasa quickly realised that the scale of the damage to the forest area was very much larger than that on the mountaintop of their earlier experience.

"We should rest and eat," Tareck said, aware that Rannah was flagging.

But the old man shook his head. There was an excitement about him that surprised both Nasa and Tareck.

Nasa nonetheless signalled that they should rest. In pursuing their interest in the damage to the forest floor, they were far away from where Nasa projected they ought to be in pursuit of the forest dwellers, and with the light fading they'd soon have to consider where they would spend the night. And, as Nasa told himself, they needed to make sure they could get back on track and pursue the real purpose of their visit beyond the Edge.

The distant star had already passed overhead as they rested and ate more of the food that Tareck dispensed from his backpack. Nasa was deep in thought, and it was some time before the others began to fidget to move on.

Tareck, restless as ever, had probed further into the distorted trees. He very soon found that the density of the trees obscured much of the light, but as he cautiously moved forward he both realised that he was walking in the gouge again and that there was obviously another clearing not too far ahead. He reported his findings to Nasa.

"Maybe there will be a place for us to spend the night in the clearing," Nasa said. "But once the distant star returns we must try to move out of the forest and find the people we're looking for."

Tareck didn't disagree, but his curiosity was still getting the better of him.

They set off, Nasa, having settled his course of action in his mind, now leading. The going was surprisingly easy as they found themselves still walking in the gouge, which was getting deeper and wider.

It has to be! It has to be!

Nasa was even more convinced that they'd found the path the founders' machine had taken as it skipped across the edge of the plain and crash-landed in the forest. However, not being a trained soldier and unlike Sorak not having been used to navigating around the plain in the dark, Nasa couldn't have known that the track they were actually following was parallel to and not very far from the edge of the forest. If they'd been able to find a tall tree to use as a lookout this would have immediately become apparent. However, all of the trees around them were misshapen and bent over at the point they'd reached.

Nasa's assumption that the machine must have landed close to the Edge was based on the commonsense acknowledgement that the people and contents of the machine had to have been readily transferable to the middle of the plain in order for the city to have been built. The enormity of this task and the timescale of the development of the city were well beyond Nasa's comprehension.

Rannah stumbled again, or rather he tripped. The gouge they were following had flattened out and become even more rutted in places. Tareck noticed that the trees and foliage to the sides of the gouge were growing, as if their roots had been ripped up and then allowed to re-grow. He said nothing to Nasa since he'd observed that he too had already noticed the same thing. The area around the edge of the gouge had obviously been disturbed at some very distant point back in time. It had been so long ago that neither man could have recognised that the ground had also been scorched.

Rannah was on his knees, exploring what had made him trip.

As Rannah dug at the angular piece of metal that protruded from the ground, Tareck seemed interested in something else. Nasa watched Rannah's labours with interest.

But whatever it was the old man was working on, it was well embedded in the bottom of the gouge and without tools there was no way they could dig it out.

"No matter," said Nasa, "it can only be from the founders' machine, or have been dumped here from the city, but I've never seen metal like this in the city."

And there were to be more surprises.

"Nasa!"

Tareck was holding up two very small metal discs with patterns and figures on their two sides. None of the three of them knew what they were, but for Nasa they were yet more evidence of what they were looking for. Had Sorak seen the metal discs her memories of her youthful days browsing in the old Senate library might have been aroused. The old brown-skinned woman who'd been her guide had shown her something similar. Sorak might even have remembered that they were called coins.

Nonetheless, the light was fading. Nasa hurried them towards the failing patch of light.

"Mother's heart," he said, much to the amusement of Rannah.

As they emerged into what was left of the light, partially shrouded by the misshapen trees they were faced with a metal arch about twice the height of Nasa. It was collapsed and covered in the brown flakes that Nasa recognised as decayed metal from the machine in the cleft of the mountain that he and his son had explored so thoroughly all those cycles ago. But it was quickly too dark to see anything worthwhile or to safely explore any further.

Nasa was exultant. The myths and mysteries might now be explained and what Mesrick had found before she was killed in the rebellion might now be revealed.

They quickly organised a meal and settled for the night. But it wasn't just the cacophony of animal noises that prevented any of them from sleeping soundly!

14

"The old one is with them."

The four unsuccessful calf thieves were meeting after one of their expeditions onto the plain. They weren't very popular; the need for breeding calves for their herd was becoming desperate but as a result of their abortive exploits attempting to steal one again seemed likely to be doomed.

They were equally unpopular because of the belief amongst their friends and colleagues that the people from the city would inevitably come and try and seek them out. They weren't concerned about retribution for the calves successfully stolen, more that they didn't know how relations with the city might develop, or how they would want them to develop.

"We should have killed him and not let him return to the city!"

The youngster in the group stood by his original suggestion.

But they all knew that the Elders wouldn't have countenanced the old man being killed. It was generations since one of their people had killed another. In their society invoking the death penalty was reserved for the Elders and hadn't been used in living memory.

After their failed trip to capture another calf, and after abandoning Rannah to return to the city, the four men had crossed the Edge and re-entered the forest. The route that they'd taken was indicated by the narrow pathway that Nasa and his companions had observed but hadn't followed. The men's disagreement about how they dealt with Rannah, and why they'd captured him in the first place, rumbled on over the circuits of the distant star after they'd returned. They were never likely to resolve the issue.

But they had, however, set out to watch the plain to see if there was any attempt by Rannah or the people from the city to return. They didn't have to wait for long. Nasa's party was quickly observed and their movements monitored.

As Sorak and Nasa had found on their original journey away from the city, the forest eventually gave way to mountains and then more open plain, although on the side of the city Nasa and his party were now exploring the mountains weren't as high as the ones that he'd encountered before. Nasa had nonetheless assumed in his mind that there would be mountains. However, how and where they might make contact with the forest people Nasa had no clear idea as they finally set off to try.

How the forest people might live, Nasa found easier to visualise.

He presumed the forest people would live in some form of shared accommodation, like the barracks blocks in the city. The concept of a compound was unknown to him but would have been recognised readily enough. Situated a safe distance from the edge of the forest the compound where the four calf stealers lived was one of several that had been built, each with access to grazing, running water and a supply of timber. Two things would have immediately struck Nasa. As he'd postulated, there was gender equality. Women and men lived together in harmony, each with an instinctively understood role and each being a part of a family unit. Children were nurtured and protected within these family units. Nothing could have been further from the defunct initial set-up in the city, or closer to what Sorak was trying to establish.

The second thing that Nasa would have eventually observed was that there was no obvious evidence of an overarching controlling function, like the Senate in the city. Age was respected, and a group of Elders met as required to arbitrate, settle disagreements and provide a decision-making forum when matters affecting the whole community needed to be determined. Each Elder represented a compound or group of compounds. However, as Nasa was to discover, the role of these Elders was less benign than it first appeared.

A meeting with the Elders had taken place when the party returned from their latest raid on the city empty-handed.

"The herds have guards with weapons. We didn't dare approach them."

Unwilling to be encumbered with their bows on their expeditions, which were powerful enough to match the crossbows of the city soldiers, they were at a considerable disadvantage. Taking the calves by force in the face of the herds' guardians was not an option.

The leader of the group was still anxious and angry. Although, because of the escalating animal attacks, their herds had been corralled within the compounds, this made feeding them all cycle round much more difficult. They had no means of mass harvesting the grasslands of the plain beyond the forest. If they weren't allowed to roam freely and feed on the plain it was going to be a hard job keeping the herds supplied, particularly in the cold season.

The herds provided both milk and flesh, and hides for clothing. Over the years they had developed methods of trapping the wild beasts that also inhabited the plains, even the much larger predators that were the main source of their problems. Trapping these animals in spiked pits was uncertain, and as their numbers increased controlling them became impossible. But it was the dwindling milk supplies and this effect on the nutrition of the children that was the key problem.

The Elders understood the party's reluctance to become involved with the people of the city. They appeared to have better weapons and an organised body of people to protect them and their belongings; at least, so the men from the forest had observed. That their longbows were not inferior to the crossbows of the city's soldiers, the forest people were too unsophisticated to perceive.

"The old one who was watching you on the city wall… Why didn't you disable him and leave him? He's now brought people from the city to try to find us."

By this time they knew the party was small but that was less important to the Elder than *why* they'd come.

The Elder who asked the question lived in the same compound as the leader of the party. It was he who'd agreed to the raids to steal calves. Because of the risks it hadn't been a universally supported course of action. The Elder was well aware that the doubters would see themselves as justified.

At the time they encountered Rannah, the leader was concerned that the people watching the herds might have seen them, and he assumed, wrongly, that Rannah had therefore been set to watch for them by the city authorities. Knowing that violence was not approved, notwithstanding what the Elder had just said, taking the old man with them was the quickest way to escape the city. That Rannah was a curious but innocent bystander occurred to no one.

The leader said as much.

"But the old one has returned."

The Elder had been made aware that Nasa and his party had entered the forest and were being watched. However, any decision on what to do about the intruders was a matter for all the Elders.

"But it's only a scouting party, and they've not yet moved from the sacred area."

The leader of the calf raiding party's statement caused consternation.

Since the mythology of the people in the forest attributed their origins to the people who'd arrived in the machine from beyond the distant star, the area where it had landed and anything that remained of it was sacred to them. That they had common origins with the people of the city was known only to the Elders and a few learned old men. Hidden in one of the compounds was an ancient and largely unreadable archive, very much smaller but not dissimilar to the one that once existed in the old Senate library.

The leader of the raiding party was dismissed whilst the Elder gathered with his fellows and tried to decide what to do about Rannah and the two people he'd brought with him. There was uncertainty and a greater divergence of views than the Elders were used to. There were those who wanted to make contact, to try and come to terms with the city, and there were those who feared that such contact would only be bad for their people. The unspoken fear was that their power as Elders might be undermined.

But since there were no mystic connotations that reserved the decision to themselves, as was often the case the Elders deferred determining any course of action until each had had a chance to consult with the people they lived with.

The first vermillion moon was high in the sky by the time the Elders had all returned to their compounds. There were nine compounds; the furthest took some time to reach. Each compound comprised four or sometimes five wooden and thatched buildings, each subdivided to accommodate varying numbers of families. There was now a fenced-off grazing area in the middle of each compound. Two additional compounds were being constructed to make room for the increasing numbers of young people coming to adulthood. These compounds were way out across the plain and close to the base of the mountain range that formed its far edge. With the increasing predation of the fierce beasts of the plains, these new compounds were enclosed and equipped like stockades. They represented a newer form of living and one which many of the people in the other compounds found disturbing.

Over the generations the size of families had been restricted by common consent in recognition of the steadily increasing challenges of providing for the expanding population. But the consensus that this was based on was breaking down as the community thrived and the young people could see no need for limiting how many children they had. There was a feeling that the Elders would have wanted to continue to try to control the birth rate but the burgeoning younger community was increasingly inclined to ignore the Elders. It wasn't only the Elders who were concerned about where this increasing fracture in their society would lead them.

Much of the changing attitude was based on the increasing awareness of the city by the forest people. The night patrols from the pre-rebellion days had moved closer and closer to the Edge, and news of the upheavals within the city was brought into the forest by parties that had escaped, and by the knowledge of the horrors of the massacre of the black and brown people on their doorstep. It was true to say that after the rebellion no one in the city knew how many of those who'd escaped had survived and had contacted the forest people.

There had always been rumours within the city that some parties of women, rather than heading in the more favoured direction that Sorak and Nasa had originally taken, had in fact taken the opposite route. But since they never returned there was no way of knowing if the rumours were true and, if they were, what had happened to them. The idea that there might be yet more people separate from the city and forest dwellers, however, appeared to have occurred to no one.

The Elders of the forest people in their turn were aware of these parties but had simply monitored their passage, since they came nowhere near the compounds and posed no threat. Since the parties often only consisted of women, the forest people were at a loss as to why they'd escaped and what they might be seeking. None ever returned, to the knowledge of the Elders.

There were many myths and strange stories about what was beyond the mountains that bordered their settlement but no one ever showed any interest in finding out. Similarly, the Elders showed no interest in either actively seeking relations with the city, or expanding into and beyond the mountains. That the arrival of Nasa and his party heralded a change in their generations-long settled existence was a major concern to the Elders, who felt more threatened by it than the ordinary people.

It was several circuits of the distant star before the Elders reconvened, by which time Nasa and his party were on the move again.

15

All the members of Nasa's party were up and ready as the light from the distant star filtered through the trees surrounding the clearing. Even Rannah seemed eager to get the day started.

Nasa was conscious of a range of feelings. So much of what he was seeing reminded him of his original journey into the unknown whilst still Sorak's slave. But that was many cycles of the distant star ago.

He was curious but at the same time apprehensive, although he couldn't think why. He did, however, have a sense of them not being alone. But if they were to discover what he expected them to, a feeling of the presence of the founders from those hundreds of cycles back was perhaps to be expected. What Nasa would have made of their being watched by the people of the forest, had he been aware, would never be known.

The first thing that was apparent as they approached the collapsed metal arch was that they were looking into the body of the crashed machine. What remained of the body was twisted and degraded. But it was only because Nasa had seen such a machine, albeit very much smaller, before, that allowed recognition.

As they noisily approached, a number of small animals scurried from the interior, and as their eyes became accustomed to the gloom it was clear that the forest had invaded most of the machine.

"There are rooms," Tareck said after a brief period of exploration.

He'd carefully made his way along the outside of the object, cutting back the lush vegetation with his sword and entering through a large hole in the fabric of the machine. He'd come back to report.

"We're unlikely to find anything," Nasa said; "everything would have been taken to the city."

But unlike the machine of old in the cleft of the mountain, they could see the front. The shape of the rounded nose was clear, even amongst the trees and bushes surrounding it, and despite the creepers that had largely filled the inside.

Just about visible was a jumble of what Nasa assumed was the equipment to control the machine, but it was smashed and impossible for him to understand. None of the three of them had seen anything like it.

"So, this is the founders' machine," Tareck said. He sounded disappointed.

Being unable to grasp the extent of time since the machine had crashed, none of them had any concept of what they might have expected. That there was anything at all was a tribute to the generally dry atmosphere of the planet.

"Nasa."

Rannah had made no effort to either walk around the machine or to attempt to see inside. Of the three, he was the least interested in the craft. He'd contented himself with exploring the area away from the wreck.

As Nasa and Tareck joined him they couldn't at first see what had attracted his attention.

He was pointing at seven or eight small mounds, overgrown and barely visible if it hadn't have been for the insects that seemed to be busily scurrying into and out of them. But more particularly, he was pointing at one of the mounds that didn't seem to be subject to the same frantic activity.

Tareck and Nasa pulled off the small bushes and creepers that covered this particular mound and began to scrape away the soil. Suddenly Tareck drew back in surprise. He'd uncovered a section of bone and he recognised it.

"People must have died when the machine crashed," Nasa said. "These are graves."

How he knew what graves were Nasa had no idea; bodies were mostly cremated in the city.

But he and Tareck, just as Mesrick had all those cycles before, realised that some members of the crew hadn't survived the crash-landing. That eight dead appeared to have had no impact on what the founders eventually established, confirmed to Nasa that there must have been a substantial number of people on the craft.

He and Tareck replaced the growth that they'd removed. Tareck saluted as they moved back into the clearing.

"We've seen enough," Nasa said. "We must move on."

Noting the position of the distant star, he gathered up his backpack, urged Tareck to do the same and then led the way around the wreck of the machine and headed for where he believed the forest would thin out.

The party was on full alert as they resumed their search for the forest people.

The trees were dense, and Nasa and Tareck, on occasions, had to cut their way through the undergrowth until they reached yet another clearing, or rather reached an open area that looked out onto the sort of landscape that was familiar to Nasa from his previous travels.

There's not so much water, but otherwise it looks just like the area that we spent so much time finding our way across when we first left the city.

Memories flooded in once again. Memories of time spent in trees warding off the wild animals, and later, when returning to the city, memories of time spent fighting off the soldiers from the male administrations. And then one particular memory surfaced.

"We must find a tree that has orange branches."

Both Rannah and Tareck looked bemused.

"The orange twigs have strange properties," Nasa said.

But although they searched as they began to cross the section of the plain that they'd come to, they found no orange twigs. But they did find signs of activity, of the presence of beasts, although the footprints didn't seem to be recent. However, the light was fading and Nasa urged them towards a group of trees that was growing around a small lake. He recognised it as a good place to spend the night.

Although Rannah was unable to climb into a tree, Nasa nonetheless scrambled up the tallest he could find, to survey the surrounding landscape. He was attracted to an area further round, on the edge of the forest that they'd left, and to what seemed to him to be a faint discolouring of the sky just above the treeline. He thought he knew what it was: smoke. But with the light almost gone he couldn't be sure.

As they set watch and settled for the night, Nasa made no mention of what he'd seen.

It was Tareck who saw them first. It was his turn on watch. Rannah and Nasa were both lost to deep sleep when he became aware of several pairs of eyes just catching the light from the last of the second circuit of the second moon. He armed his crossbow.

Uncertain of what was watching them, man or beast, Tareck was reluctant to fire off a bolt. If whoever, or whatever, it was, was a threat to them it wasn't apparent to him what that threat was. He shuffled himself closer to Nasa and, whilst keeping the pairs of eyes within sight, gently shook him awake. Unlike Sorak, who could awaken quite violently, Nasa's passage from sleep to wakefulness was quick, alert and immobile.

Nasa saw the eyes immediately. He armed his own crossbow but like Tareck saw no justification for firing.

The famous orange twigs came into his mind again. Tossed onto a fire they didn't have, they would have quickly illuminated the whole area and exposed the watchers. He determined to make searching for the twigs a priority when the distant star returned.

But the night wasn't yet over.

So, as it went totally dark as the last vestiges of the second moon's light disappeared, Tareck and Nasa waited. They could hear the snuffling noises that the fierce beasts of the forest made, but in the distance. They braced themselves, each shuffling closer to Rannah to protect him.

And they waited.

The next period of the night was very tense. Then, just as the first signs of the return of the distant star flickered on the horizon, a great wave of sound, screams, growls and the noises of ferocious fighting startled Rannah awake and had Nasa and Tareck on their feet.

"Mother's heart!" cried Rannah.

They waited for more light as the sounds faded into the distance.

"What could that have been?"

The city dwellers, Rannah and Tareck, had no way of visualising what might have been making the hideous noises; not so Nasa.

Expecting to find carnage, Nasa found only the ravaged body of what Sorak had once called a 'leopard', the like of which she'd only ever seen in the old books in the old Senate library until they'd escaped from the city.

There were no signs of what had killed the leopard, or in fact of any other animals.

They readied themselves for their day.

Before they left, unclear about what he thought he'd seen the previous day as the distant star was setting, Nasa scaled the tree again. He'd definitely been seeing smoke.

With better light he took the opportunity to scan the whole area surrounding where they'd spent the night again. At first he saw trees and more trees... and then he saw them.

"There are trees where we can gather the orange twigs," he said when he re-joined Tareck and Rannah. But something had distracted them.

"The forest people are nearby," Rannah announced.

Nasa had no idea how he could know, but Rannah had proved a reliable member of the party so far, so he waited for him to explain. And of course Rannah was the only one of them who'd actually met the forest people.

But Rannah never got to explain. He had no need to. As Nasa and Tareck gathered up the backpacks and prepared to leave, they became aware that they were no longer alone.

Where the single figure had emerged from none of them saw. Both Nasa and Tareck raised their weapons, but Rannah waved them down.

"It's the leader of the party which took me across the plain."

Rannah moved towards the man as he halted in front of the treeline, not far from where they'd spent the night. It was only later that Nasa had time to wonder how he'd got so close without being detected.

When it was clear the man was unarmed, Nasa and Tareck finally lowered their crossbows.

Rannah held out his hand in welcome, and his two companions then placed their weapons on the ground.

"You are welcome. We come to do you no harm."

The expression on the man's face was unfathomable, yet Nasa was sure he saw a fleeting smile. What he didn't see was the man relax. He clearly recognised he had nothing to fear.

Acknowledging that the man was speaking the same language as they did, albeit, as the conversation developed, with an accent that sometimes made understanding difficult, Nasa asked the obvious question.

"Are you alone?"

The trees around them weren't very dense but could nonetheless have easily hidden a small army. It was important to know if the man represented a threat despite his benign appearance.

The man didn't answer Nasa.

"I am Jarson," he said.

16

Pilar and Pelar, as a result of their unusual upbringing, were black-skinned when black women were being persecuted, and had a more intimate knowledge of the byways and nooks and crannies of the city than most people, certainly more than Anstan and even Sorak. They'd survived through all the violence of the male administrations in hiding, and had grown up both streetwise and well-educated. Self-reliant, they knew that whatever future they were likely to have, they'd have to make for themselves.

The twins also had a better understanding than Sorak and the Senate of how many people were in the city; not necessarily in terms of numbers, but certainly by distribution. Equally, they also had a better understanding of the true feelings of most of the people that they came into contact with. Anstan's simplistic view of what the future should be was by no means universally supported, but those who opposed it did so for a wide variety of reasons.

Something that would have surprised Sorak was that, as Pilar and Pelar had discovered, there were a lot more black- and brown-skinned women living out of sight than anyone realised. This was generally regarded as good news amongst both women

113

and men, and it helped to heal one of the outstanding rifts that had hung over from the rebellion and the male administrations.

If asked, most people would have said that the attitudes of the bulk of the women were defined by their age and therefore whether they were alive before the rebellion. With some obvious and notable exceptions, it was Pilar and Pelar's experience that military women born before the rebellion were almost universally in favour of a return to the old women-dominated system. Civilian women of a similar age, and the twins were surprised to find how many there were in the city, seemed to be more accepting of change, provided it didn't prevent them from doing the jobs they'd been trained for. Working with men had always been a part of their lives, and in general that had continued. How much impact the gulf between the views of the older ex-soldiers and the civilians would have on the future, no one knew.

"Working with free men is better," a mangeneer working on the manufacture of weapons had said. "It gives us much more time to do what we were trained for, rather than having to instruct and watch over the men. Now once they learn to understand the job, they just get on with it."

It was a common view amongst mangeneers.

Pilar and Pelar were aware that the problem with the ex-military women was a lack of something to occupy their minds and bodies. They were equally aware that Sorak had reorganised the military, both to employ as many women as possible, and also to remove the mindless and pointless activities that they'd had to undertake in the past. But the key problem was that the military, like all other areas of activity, now needed to have equal numbers of men and women. This was easier to achieve with soldiers than it was with mangeneers, and it would be many cycles of the distant star before there would be a supply of trained male mangeneers, and work for them to do. Sorak and the Senate knew that this had the potential to create problems, but they'd have to be dealt with when they arose.

For Sorak, the disaffected female ex-soldiers were potentially the most challenging problem. That Anstan had realised that this disaffection could be used to her advantage, and was striving to harness it, was a cause of great irritation to Sorak. The Defenders, the group the twins had been steadily building up, was entirely made up of young women, and, since Sorak had insisted that the younger women slowly replace their elders in the city military, increasingly the group was also dominated by soldiers. But they were soldiers committed to a gender equal society.

"One of the night patrols reported that they saw Anstan and a small group of women in Sector Eight. They were headed for a dream-pit that we thought was derelict. It looks as if this is another place we'll need to watch."

Lenrick, the Senate guard commander, was reporting to Sorak as she did regularly. She'd been careful not to identify the source of the information that she was imparting, which told Sorak that it almost certainly came from Pilar and Pelar. Sorak and Lenrick had agreed that they wouldn't admit to the existence of the Defenders officially, in order that they wouldn't have to take action against them for illegal activities.

It had taken Anstan some time to assemble her core group of supporters. Being a civilian, a mangeneer, the former soldiers, especially the officers, were uncertain about what she was trying to achieve and, more particularly, her ability to achieve it. Her stated objective struck a chord with many of them, but an inbred contempt for civilians amongst the officer category was proving difficult to overcome. This suspicion wasn't helped in the post-rebellion world that saw most civilians simply pick up where they'd left off once Sorak and her supporters had established a stable administration. The ex-soldiers, in contrast, had had to struggle for a role, as they weren't generally accepted, because of their age, within the new military.

But Anstan, brown-skinned and a civilian herself, understood only too well that the society she wanted to re-establish couldn't work without civilians but could survive without a large military force. The problem for her was persuading large numbers of civilians of this, whilst not alienating the ex-soldiers.

"We have to increase our patrols during the night in the areas like Sectors Seven and Eight. Since the commercial buildings and most of the accommodation is largely derelict, they make a ready hiding place for those who oppose us."

Sorak didn't need reminding of this.

True to her straightforward approach to her duties, Lenrick didn't make any effort to hide her concerns from Sorak.

"But the Senate has rejected increasing patrols," Sorak said.

Lenrick knew this, but she also knew that Sorak would override or ignore the Senate if she felt it necessary. In this case she suspected that the Senate's position was underwritten by supporters of Anstan. It was one more instance of the Senate's ineffectiveness and one more justification for Sorak to take yet more of the administration from their hands.

The situation typified the dilemma that Sorak was increasingly facing, which she'd discussed at great length with Nasa. By seeking to both establish gender equality and individual freedom of choice, many things that might have been seen as undesirable were surfacing. In Nasa's view this was an inevitable consequence.

Many of the people in the city had no idea how to cope with the freedoms they now had; the three to four cycles of the distant star that they'd had to adapt to this new lifestyle was, for many, simply not long enough. But Sorak was loath to intervene to try to manage the changes taking place.

It's what makes them such easy prey for Anstan!

At least, it did the less intelligent and less motivated of the women, again largely ex-soldiers. It was a thought that Sorak would only have voiced to Nasa.

As Lenrick continued her report, Sorak was aware of just how much she missed Nasa's sage comments when he wasn't there to give them.

"My pardon, Sorakmam." Marwek was exercising her privilege of interrupting her mistress.

Lenrick had gone and Sorak had been left to her troubled thoughts. The guard commander, definitely one of the modern women despite being a cycle or two older than Sorak, was clearly concerned that something was brewing in the areas of the city that had been abandoned as the population had fallen, and which, as a consequence, hadn't been policed.

She had good cause.

Marwek, always calm and measured, waited until she had Sorak's full attention; it was important that she clearly heard what she had to report.

"A number of bodies have been found in Sector Seven. They appear to be ex-soldiers, older women, and the patrol leader who found them believes they're from Anstan's group. He said they'd been keeping an eye on these women as they'd been observed acting aggressively towards a number of young women."

Who were associates of Pilar and Pelar, no doubt.

Sorak wasn't happy; this was something that she'd feared. It seemed like a clash between the two opposing groups slowly emerging from the shadows. So far, Anstan's followers had appeared to be the aggressors, but Sorak's anxiety had been about how long it was going to be before the twins and their followers reacted. The prospect of retaliation horrified her, but it seemed that maybe it had now happened.

But we need more information!

* * *

The vermillion of the first moon had faded and one of the dark periods had commenced. But the young women cautiously making their way out of Sector Four and working their way eventually to Sector Seven weren't worried about the dark. Each of the four carried a military crossbow, although they themselves weren't all soldiers. The two that were took the lead.

Before they'd set out they'd rehearsed what they were planning to do, had discussed what might go wrong and had prepared themselves accordingly. It was this sort of discipline that attracted young women to Pilar and Pelar's group. All born after the rebellion but brought up during the instability that followed, the world that Sorak, and under her guidance the Senate, was trying to create, was all they knew. Nonetheless, they were aware that there were still large numbers of older women for whom the freedom and lack of rigid structure weren't welcome. For many of these women, a return to the past and the controlled existence that they'd known was what they craved. They might not have understood it but the young women certainly acknowledged that this feeling amongst the older women was powerful.

What was now polarising the women of the city was the formation of the movement to actively seek to achieve this return to the past. It would be a world where men were relegated to servitude again; but the young women attracted to Pilar and Pelar had grown used to the interrelations with men and understood that gender equality was the only peaceful future possible.

Although rarely articulated in such precise terms, all of this was why these four young women were creeping into Sector Seven on high alert for both patrols and the group of ex-soldiers that they'd learned were planning to meet in one of the unused buildings.

"The three of them are Anstan's key supporters. It is they who have been recruiting fellow ex-soldiers, and we believe they're also trying to recruit serving soldiers, to Anstan's cause."

It was Pelar providing the background. She and her sister had been approached by an ex-tenant from one of the old military units, one of Sorak's former colleagues as it turned out, who'd joined other disgruntled ex-soldiers in meeting with Anstan, but she hadn't been convinced by what she'd been told. The twins immediately recognised the opportunity being presented to them. Risak had agreed to remain a part of Anstan's group and provide intelligence.

Pelar explained to her troopers how they'd come by the information on the meeting in Sector Seven, without naming their spy.

Moving stealthily, the four Defenders quietly entered the building they'd been told that the three would meet in. Careful to stay below the ventilation openings, the young women crept up the ramp on the side of the building. Although they didn't know on which floor the meeting would be taking place, the sound of voices was all they needed to locate their prey. Having plotted the action they intended to take, they immediately prepared for a confrontation.

By gesture, the two soldiers indicated that the other two should work their way to the entrance to the ramp on the relevant floor, blocking off any escape.

Climbing through a ventilation opening back along the veranda from the ramp entrance, the soldiers moved into the corridor and then paused at the entrance to the room within which they could hear talking.

On nods of agreement they charged in.

The three women were sitting at a table, with a small oil lamp providing light. A second lamp hung from the end wall of the room. Covering the three older women, the soldiers scanned into the dark areas just in case there were bodyguards. They hadn't been expecting any and none were found.

Each of the older women carried a sword, and there was at least one crossbow visible on the floor beside them.

The oldest looking of the women jerked herself to her feet as the other two dived below the level of the table. Shot through the heart, the oldest woman collapsed onto the table. A scream died into a wail as the soldiers moved around the table and the second soldier fired into the back of the woman scrabbling for her weapon. The third woman scurried on her hands and knees for the entrance to the ramp, only to be shot in her turn. It was all over before the two non-soldiers could even get into the room.

The three bodies were thrown from the ramp, to be found later by the patrol.

* * *

Marwek's already pale face took on a sickly hue as she told her tale. Sorak, more used to such violence, nonetheless was equally as horrified at the ruthless way in which the three women had been dealt with. The patrol leader had reconstructed the action for Marwek but even he was appalled by the brutality of the killings.

This is not the future we're working for!

Sorak retreated to her private quarters. Without Nasa to share her anguish with, she didn't reappear until well into the next day.

17

Inevitably, the reactions to the killings were diverse.

Pilar and Pelar were pleased that the action had been completed without any casualties on their side, but nonetheless their reaction was sober and measured. Avoiding violence was always going to be a priority.

Anstan was furious and stormed into the Senate building and into Lenrick's office to demand retribution. The guard commander assured her she would do all she could to find and punish the killers, whilst shutting her ears to Anstan's rant.

"And," as she remarked to Sorak later, "if nothing else, it confirms our view that Anstan is very much involved in the efforts to return to the past."

Sorak could only agree with her.

* * *

The Senate met to hear Lenrick's report on the killings in Sector Seven. The session was demanded by Lecktan, the young senator who'd made sure that Sorak was aware of Pilar and Pelar, without being too explicit about what they were doing.

It was the first time for many circuits of the distant star that all senators had attended a meeting.

Trouble!

Sorak was right.

The atmosphere in the Senate chamber was different from anything that she'd witnessed before. There was a hostility she knew had always been below the surface, but which was now much more evident. It was almost as if the Senate, or at least some of the senators, had at last decided to assert themselves.

"The killers must be brought before the Senate."

It was a predictable response. Lecktan exchanged a look with Sorak. The female senator who'd made the demand was one of the oldest and least supportive of the changes that Sorak and the likes of Lecktan were trying to make. A former capan (a senior military officer), she viewed the increasing role of men and the assumption of equality with uncomprehending horror. Lecktan suspected she was a key supporter of Anstan; she certainly appeared to be in total sympathy with what Anstan was believed to be seeking to achieve. However, for Lenrick, it was her superior military knowledge that was the concern, if the situation was going to turn to violence.

Sorak wasn't unsympathetic to the old senator; she recognised that she'd gone from a position of power and control to a position of unemployed dependence. So had many others. But she'd been elected to the Senate by like-minded older women, basically her ex-colleagues; however, this hadn't given her the renewed power base that she craved. And because of her rigid upbringing and rigid thought processes, she was unable to see the opportunities that even a small amount of mental flexibility would give her. Such close-mindedness saddened Sorak, yet she was increasingly aware that the old capan wasn't one on her own.

If only she and the others would try to see the benefits of what we're seeking to achieve; benefits for them personally.

It was a thought that sprang into Sorak's mind every time one of the older female senators opposed some simple measure that would make the lives of the men better and more equal. But for these people, slaves were slaves, men were slaves; what else could they be? It was a viewpoint that Sorak and the likes of Lecktan and the other one or two younger female senators couldn't relate to.

"And you know who the killers are, Senatormam?" Sorak said with a sweetness that almost covered her exasperation.

The senator retorted instantly.

"Of course we know who the killers are! The so-called 'Defenders' killed these women. And I'm sure Lenrickmam will know who they are."

Lenrick of course did, not by name but by association, but in the world of open justice that she and Sorak were trying to create, that wasn't good enough. In their new society they needed unbiased witnesses, corroboration and proper evidence.

The elderly senator stamped her foot angrily. The niceties of proof and the opportunity to defend one's actions weren't things that she could grasp. If a senior officer, or now senator, had determined guilt, that was enough for her; and she knew very well who was guilty.

As it usually did, the old senator's old-fashioned view of the situation stirred up a heated debate; essentially a women versus men debate. She was known for her blinkered views on the issues of wrongdoing, but they rarely went unchallenged. In fact, as Sorak and Lecktan noted, the older male senators took some delight in goading her to more and more regressive statements. But on this occasion Sorak didn't want the usual rowdy, pointless debate that was about to ensue. They needed to keep focused.

"Senators, Lenrick has the investigation into the killings in hand. The guard commander will ensure that someone is called to account. What is much more important is that we clearly understand what's going on here between the so-called 'Defenders' and the people, like Senator Rossak, who simply don't agree with what we're trying to achieve in the city."

Sorak's statement was greeted with silence, as she knew it would be. Forcing the debate out into the open, something she was keen to do, always had the same effect. The old stagers, used to things being determined behind closed doors, always drew back when it looked like they might be asked to take responsibility. Taking responsibility, of course, was fundamentally what the debate was all about. Getting the Senate as an entity to legislate, even just to decide on something, was an uphill struggle every time, and it was getting even harder. But Sorak knew she had to go through the motions, to force the decisions on them; to simply act on her own would make her no different from the arbitrary regimes of the past. But increasingly this was the prospect facing her.

In the case in point all she wanted was for the Senate to acknowledge that there was an undertone of conflict developing as those who couldn't let go of the past became more and more at odds with those who wanted to move on and develop a new and thriving society in the city. It was a simple enough divergence of views that hid all the dilemmas facing them.

The debate raged, going nowhere, but in the end the Senate was forced to acknowledge that there was a threat posed by the likes of Anstan and those who wanted to undo what had been achieved in the last few cycles of the distant star. And the Senate was also forced to acknowledge that resistance to this reversion was inevitable.

Forcing the debate to an end, Lecktan and the bulk of the male senators carried a motion to allow Sorak and Lenrick to take steps to uncover the identities of the killers of the three women and to investigate the motivation behind them.

* * *

Sorak, Lecktan and Lenrick met after the Senate had completed its business.

"We need to know more about Anstan and exactly what she wants to achieve," Sorak said wearily, "and we need to find a way to oppose it that doesn't involve violence."

The others agreed, but whilst being very much a statement of the obvious they all knew that they, as yet, had no clear control over the situation. Anstan had ensured that the initiative was now in her hands. However, as she thought through the implications of the killings, Sorak realised that with the freedom of action she now had, in the face of the Senate's impotence, she ought to be able to take control and then take action, but still stay within the rationale of the society they were trying to create. However, this realisation didn't make Sorak very happy.

Although I'm not so sure about non-violence!

18

It was a stressful time. Sorak was missing Nasa. She was irritable, and she was short with everyone, including Lenar, her son, when he came to visit her. Even the joy of seeing her grandchild didn't ease her anxieties.

"But Father will be back soon and all the mysteries of the first settlers and the people of the forest will be solved."

Lenar had huge confidence in his father.

Sorak knew this was almost certainly true but her need was physical as well as mental, something Lenar would no doubt have understood, but she was reluctant to share such feelings with him.

But the origins of the city and the existence of people in the forest beyond the Edge were the least of Sorak's concerns.

She needed to be active; moping around without Nasa was no good for her.

"I will go and find Pastak."

* * *

Pastak, her former comrade in arms, and her friend, had retired from active life and gone to live amongst other former soldiers in the barracks in Sector Four. Sorak was aware that some of those women were supporters of Anstan, although she didn't think Pastak was. But if such a visit had risks, Sorak ignored them. She'd visited Pastak many times before; Nasa had actively encouraged her to do so. Whether he might now, was another question.

Sorak always felt at home in Sector Four. Her experience of living in the barracks as a young officer was now a distant memory, and her mind was full of thoughts of more recent events as she arrived at Pastak's door.

"You are welcome, Sorak."

But Pastak was surprised that her friend had come without her bodyguard. Sorak was never foolhardy and didn't appear to seem threatened, but nonetheless Pastak was on the alert. And she quickly noticed a sadness about her that worried her. Sorak had always been so positive. Pastak voiced her thoughts.

"You are worried, my friend?"

Sorak was. The persistent existence of a body of women anxious to return to the old days depressed and saddened her. It was as if she'd achieved nothing since taking over the running of the city, despite the stability that she'd been able to introduce. An end to all the fighting, all the bloodshed, had to count for something, Sorak felt, yet people like Anstan and her followers seemed to regard all that as irrelevant. Their future was always in the past.

Pastak had great respect and great affection for Sorak, although she'd never really understood her feelings for Nasa, and now she was increasingly concerned for her. Part of her anxiety was physical: Sorak's safety amongst the ex-soldiers of the barracks in Sector Four; but it was also about the strength of the movement that she knew was developing in opposition to everything that Sorak was trying to achieve. Pastak had no real idea how many women were supportive of this movement, but she did know that some of them were very influential.

Pastak herself was hugely popular with her former military colleagues, even as they'd split into two factions. Her prowess in defeating the troops of the former male administrations was revered and respected, but her refusal to express any political opinions tended to be taken, by those yearning for the past, as tacit support. It was not.

However, Sorak's decision to pay her a visit at this particular time was about to cause Pastak some discomfort. Sorak's presence in essence forced her to declare for the modernisation and free society Sorak was creating.

"We usually all meet up in the community area after our evening meal."

Pastak was, in effect, inviting Sorak to the gathering, even as she knew it would both expose her own true feelings and potentially create major tensions amongst the women. But Sorak's presence would be known, and she would be expected to join the other women.

Sorak remembered the community area well. The final moments of the last male administration had been played out there as 147, its leader, had accepted Sorak and the other soldiers' plans for gender equality and a free society. The two friends were acutely aware of this.

"It didn't quite work out as we planned," she said to Pastak.

"But there was always going to be those who didn't accept change, those who wanted no part in this new world we wanted to create."

Of course, with hindsight, they both knew it was easy to make such judgements, but at the time, when things were confused and events were moving so quickly, it was inevitable that some women would be left behind. And some women would have had no wish to be carried forward.

"There was always going to be too many soldiers, especially officers," Pastak mused. "The old Senate sought to control so much of our lives; when you remove so many of the controls, a great number of soldiers were always going to have nothing to do. And with so many women used to being in command, there were bound to be problems."

Sorak knew that what her friend was saying was true. With things settling into an entirely different way of life, those who couldn't, or wouldn't, change, needed to be found a place. They were still citizens. But so far, Sorak and the Senate hadn't been able to find a role for the many women who only knew soldiering in the artificial forms it had taken in the previous days. It was the lack of soldiering opportunities, coupled with the need to employ equivalent numbers of men as soldiers, that Anstan was able to exploit.

The two of them sat at a table near the dais that Sorak had cause to remember well. It was noisy, with the sort of background music she hadn't heard for some time. They were served the amber liquor, that was also so much a part of their former existence, by a woman who barely looked at them. So at first they didn't attract any attention.

"We must know who killed them!"

Pastak recognised at least two of the women in the group that had entered the community area, talking loudly amongst themselves. She was immediately on the alert. Sorak sensed her tense up.

Now what?

"We should…" The conversation came to an end as Sorak was recognised.

Trouble! These are Anstan's people!

Pastak's worst fears were beginning to materialise.

"Sorakmam, you are not welcome here!"

Suddenly, in the way of these things, the whole area surrounding Sorak and Pastak went quiet. The group of women formed around the friends' table. The woman who had spoken, a former tenant that Sorak thought she recognised, stood directly in front of her. Her posture was threatening and anything but friendly. Sorak didn't react at first.

"Moonak!"

This was a voice Sorak did recognise. Senator Rossak, who'd challenged Sorak earlier at the fraught Senate meeting, moved through the group milling around Sorak's table. Both she and Pastak had now risen to face the angry Moonak.

"Sorak is our guest!"

There was a tense moment as Moonak turned to confront the senator, but as the other women shuffled away she turned and marched off, her body language shouting her anger. Brave in company, she wasn't prepared to face Sorak on her own.

Senator Rossak remained.

"Moonak is right, Sorakmam; you're not welcome here."

But all three women knew this was an overstatement; Sorak was undoubtedly not welcome by many of the women but she was by others, especially amongst the younger, post-rebellion soldiers. Several of these had begun to move forward as the senator defused the situation.

"Senator, I thank you," Sorak said formally. "I have no wish to cause dissention."

The senator clearly didn't believe her.

"Then either spend your time in Pastak's private quarters, or don't come here at all."

"But Senatormam," Pastak said angrily, "there should be nowhere that the Chair of the Senate cannot go!"

Rossak turned and walked off without replying. She obviously didn't agree.

"I should go," Sorak said.

"I will accompany you," Pastak responded.

Sorak didn't demur. The mood amongst some of the women was clearly hostile, and Pastak feared that someone might take action against her friend once she'd left the barracks. They collected their swords from Pastak's quarters and set off.

Pastak's premonition was justified. Moonak and a number of her colleagues had gathered in the old slaves' quarters at the basement of the barracks and talked each other into deciding to teach Sorak a lesson. Quietly, armed with their swords and knives, but not crossbows, which were forbidden to be carried by non-serving soldiers, they skirted the barracks and made for Sector Five and then Sector Six. Correctly identifying which way that Sorak and Pastak would go, they waited to ambush them outside the closed arena in Sector Six. Moonak, her courage restored by the presence of her friends, drew her sword and made a few passes in anticipation.

Yet another area with bitter memories for Sorak, she and Pastak moved cautiously into the open area in front of the arena. Until they could get across into Sector Two, they would be exposed. In Pastak's mind, this was exactly where she would stage an ambush.

"So, Sorakmam!"

As they emerged onto the piazza that separated Sector Two from Sectors Six and Seven, they were confronted by Moonak and three other women, weapons drawn, as they moved out of the shadows.

"Withdraw," Pastak demanded; "threatening the leader of the Senate will only bring you trouble!"

But as Moonak advanced on Sorak, it was clear that something more than threatening was on her mind. Sorak drew her own sword and prepared to defend herself. And as the other women held Pastak back, Moonak moved to engage Sorak.

But as she aimed her first blow at her opponent she let out a scream and, clutching her leg, collapsed onto the paving of the piazza, all her bravado gone.

"Mother's heart!' Sorak said as she recognised the crossbow bolt sticking out of Moonak's thigh.

There are no patrols due here until much later!

But as this thought occurred to her, the explanation appeared in the form of a group of four young women, each armed with a crossbow and each keeping one of the attacking party covered.

Neither Sorak nor Pastak recognised any of the women in the party. Not a word was spoken. Working only with gestures, Moonak's companions were disarmed, the crossbow bolt pulled from her leg and her party waved away. Supporting Moonak, they hurriedly retreated.

The action was over almost before the two friends had time to understand what was happening.

"Best you don't ask," Pastak said as she sensed the question forming in Sorak's mind.

And then their rescuers were gone, as quickly and as mysteriously as they'd appeared.

* * *

Lecktan, the young senator, came to see Sorak in her office the next day. Never one to dwell on her anxieties, Sorak had already put the attack behind her. Lecktan had received a short message from Pilar and Pelar. Her message for the Senate leader was equally short.

"Better not to visit Sector Four again without a large contingent of bodyguards."

It was enough said. Sorak was now all too aware of the strength of feeling out there amongst those women who wanted to return to the past!

Unspoken, Sorak assumed her rescuers were members of the Defenders, who must have been keeping track of her movements.

19

Nasa, Rannah and Tareck stared at the forest man who'd approached them. His demeanour was confident yet cautious. If he was fearful of them there was no sign of it. Having signalled their friendly intentions by grounding their weapons, Nasa and Tareck both stepped towards the man, still preserving a safe distance. If he was armed, his weapon was well hidden.

The Elders had finally decided that they should make contact with the three people from the city to try to understand their intentions. Choosing the leader of the party who'd raided the city was a risk because of his involvement in those raids, but as he'd already met and interacted with the old man this seemed more important. The visitors' reaction to their man, the Elders reasoned, would give them some idea of their intentions.

Rannah's original description of the forest people, at least the four he'd met, had been minimal and not very informative. The first and obvious thing Nasa noticed was that the man was taller than any of the three of them, taller, Nasa judged, than most women of the city; he was at least a head taller than Tareck, himself the tallest of the city party. Nasa really didn't have time to wonder at the significance of this.

Rannah had also noted that the men had been wearing animal skins. But it was clear on inspection that their visitor's main clothes were of a woven material, with only a jerkin made from a skin. His boots were sturdy, if well-worn and very dirty, much like the military boots of the city; what they were made of wasn't clear. All of Nasa's preconceived ideas, based on Rannah's descriptions, evaporated.

"You are welcome," the man said, much as they might have said to him.

His speech was clear but the accent foreign to them, yet nonetheless comprehensible.

"We thank you, Jarson." Nasa hoped that he'd got the name right.

Jarson, with a gesture, invited them to follow him. Nasa and Tareck slung their crossbows over their backs as a sign of good faith and headed in the direction indicated. Jarson set off at a smart pace and then slowed down when he saw that Rannah was struggling to keep up. They walked in silence.

Nasa was pleased to observe that they were headed towards the horizon where he'd seen what he thought was smoke. That was clearly where their settlement was.

It was much further than the three of them might have imagined and, as a consequence, the journey took longer than Nasa had expected. Rannah had to lean on Tareck's shoulder as they finally breasted the brow of what was an escarpment and began their descent towards the settlements laid out in front of them.

There were several compounds, as Nasa later described them to Sorak; they later discovered there were more in the distance and away out of the forest. As he'd anticipated, the forest ended at the bottom of the escarpment and some of the compounds were built out in the open on the plain. Like the plains he'd seen before, Nasa noted the scattering of trees and the occasional lake. All the dwellings they could see were constructed of natural materials. Jarson immediately set off down the escarpment. They followed more slowly; the going for Rannah was getting very much harder.

No defences!

Nasa was quick to notice that the compounds possessed no physical defences; the only containment seemed to be for the herds that milled around in the middle of each compound. The herds were a surprise, but enlightenment quickly followed for Nasa. The situation was all too familiar. The herds were being attacked by the wild animals, hence the search for new calves, and the only protection that they could offer was to enclose the beasts in the middle of their living quarters. The beasts seemed restless, but the compounds didn't give them too much scope to move around.

Mindful of Rannah's limited capabilities, Jarson slowed right down as he led them along the narrow path towards the settlement. It was slow going and also had the effect of allowing a crowd to gather at the bottom. Nasa noticed Tareck tense. They had no reason to expect a hostile welcome but as they reached the bottom both men noted that, unlike Jarson, most of the men, and even the boys, waiting to greet them, were armed with a knife or short sword.

With so many different new things invading his sight, Nasa only later recognised that the crowd was mixed – men, women and children – and that in general the women were mostly the same height as the men, but rarely taller. Everyone he saw was dressed in homemade garments.

"We must visit the Elders."

It was a friendly enough statement but Nasa knew from the hardening of Jarson's voice that it wasn't an option for them. He and Tareck were undoubtedly better armed than the people crowding around them but they were vastly outnumbered.

Whether by design or just for their own convenience, the Elders were apparently gathered at one of the newer compounds, remote from where they currently were and sited on the open plain area that stretched away from the edge of the forest towards the low mountains in the distance. It was going to be a long walk that Rannah would find difficult.

"We will help the old man," Jarson said.

Wheeled transport didn't exist in the city. The pre-rebellion old female Senate knew about such things from the archives in the Senate library, but saw no need for them, so never allowed them to be developed. With the library and its contents destroyed, Sorak's present administration was never going to know about wheeled transport, let alone introduce it.

At least until now. These people have something to teach us.

It was a rather momentous thought for Nasa, and although he had plenty of time to think about it on the journey to meet the Elders there was too much else going on around him for him to be tempted to do so. But it was something to store in his mind for future reference.

The dwelling houses of the people who still milled around them in the compounds were unlike anything Nasa had seen in the city. Made totally from the products of the forest, each compound had four or five longhouses arranged around the central grazing area. The buildings were tall and the thatched roofs steep, to force the rain that occasionally fell torrentially to run off quickly, with open sides, but with movable partitions that could be closed for privacy.

They all seem to live together in groups – men, women and children, old and young.

This was something new to the three of them. Communal living they were familiar with, but by gender. Communal families were only just beginning to be formed in the city, and there was still resistance to them from some of the older women.

With Rannah sitting rather nervously on a small cart pulled by two of the men from the earlier calf stealing group, they set off. The crowd that had greeted them dispersed; clearly, they weren't expected to accompany them to see the Elders. The journey was as long and as tedious as Nasa had expected. It occurred to him whether this might be by design.

It took them almost half of the period of light from the distant star at its zenith to its beginning to set to reach the meeting place. The pace was governed by how easily the cart in which Rannah was riding could be pulled over the areas of uneven ground between the various compounds. Almost at every point on the journey people from the compounds came out to stare at them. Curiosity seemed to dominate the interests of those who lined their route. But unlike at their first meeting, the people didn't mill around them, or even attempt to come too close.

"They've been warned off," Tareck said, mirroring Nasa's conclusion.

Neither of them could imagine why. There was nothing unfriendly about the demeanour of the people; they were just wary. Again, unlike their first contact, there were no children in evidence. The earlier presence of children had been a surprise to Nasa, who assumed that, like the city, the children should have been spending their day being taught whatever skills were necessary for them to contribute to the forest people's society.

The closer they got to the Elders the more constrained the people seemed to be.

Then finally they arrived.

Even more, Nasa wondered why the Elders had chosen for the meeting the furthest compound from where they'd been met by Jarson.

The compound seemed unoccupied, something else that puzzled and worried Nasa, and they were led through into the open area enclosed by the dwellings. There were four long huts of rather better finish than the ones they'd seen earlier. But here there was no herd of beasts.

The six Elders were seated in one of these long huts, its sides open so they had shade and protection yet could be readily seen by Nasa's party and the men who accompanied them. There was something artificial about the group that immediately put Nasa on alert. It was as if they'd deliberately posed themselves for their visitors.

The six Elders all wore beards. None of the three visitors from the city had ever seen a full beard before. In the pre-rebellion days slaves were required to be clean-shaven. In the current society of the city there was no requirement for men to still be so but it had become a social norm. Nasa recalled the first time Sorak had seen him before he'd shaved, and in their valley home before they'd returned to the city he often had a short stubble, but a growth halfway down the chest was a wonder to him. Tareck and Rannah both stared, until Nasa gestured to them. He had no intention of doing anything to offend the Elders, certainly until they had a better understanding of the forest society.

Silence prevailed.

If there was a senior man amongst the Elders, and they were all men, there was nothing to indicate which one it was. Elderly, muffled up in their robes, Nasa's alert turned to uneasiness. Exactly why they'd been brought to the Elders, other than out of courtesy, he had no idea, but he supposed they'd soon find out.

Rannah was helped from the cart but was offered no chair or bench to allow him to sit down. The leader of the party accompanying them gestured to Nasa and Tareck to unship their crossbows, indicating that they should hand them over to his companions. There was a moment of tension. Neither man made any move to do so.

Jarson, looking ever more anxious, hurried to explain.

"It is forbidden to be armed in the presence of the Elders."

Nasa and Tareck exchanged looks. They would not disarm.

"We mean the Elders no harm. For us it is forbidden to go unarmed in the presence of those we do not know."

Nasa's hurriedly made-up response raised the tension even further. The Elders looked impassively on during this exchange.

Both Nasa and Tareck raised their arms in front of them and opened their hands to indicate no aggressive intent.

Then there was a ripple of movement amongst the Elders, as if by some mechanism they had come to a decision.

"The men from the city are welcome."

None of the city party could have identified the Elder who'd spoken. The tension eased.

A flurry of activity ensued, with signs that there were people in the long hut behind the Elders preparing to come forward.

Chairs were now brought. Nasa, Tareck and Rannah were invited to sit down, aware that the chairs had been deliberately placed so that they were below the level of the Elders. The atmosphere was now more friendly and unthreatening.

"You are welcome."

It was a different voice that repeated the greeting, and none of them were still sure who had spoken.

Jarson and his companions moved to stand discreetly behind the city party. Clearly they knew what would happen next.

Two young women, naked to the waist, emerged from behind the Elders carrying trays of drinks which were first proffered to Rannah, then Nasa and Tareck, before being offered to the Elders. The two women were fair-haired and blue-eyed but at no time did they look at the three or allow any part of their bodies to make contact with them.

But Nasa, for one, had eyes for only one thing.

The two women were wearing slave collars of a type all too familiar to Nasa.

20

Nasa and Rannah exchanged looks as Tareck accepted the drink offered to him, more in surprise at the scanty clothing that the women were wearing than anything else. It was totally out of character with anything they'd seen of the forest people so far. Nasa found it hard to imagine what this apparent evidence of slavery amongst the people presaged.

Jarson, sensing that the tension in their guests was different from before, looked anxiously from Nasa to the Elders in incomprehension. The Elders seemed unaware, and certainly unperturbed, that anything might be wrong. Slavery had been abolished in the city for many cycles of the distant star, but to suddenly apparently find it where it would least have been expected completely unnerved Nasa. Time, he hoped, would provide answers, since future relations with the city would be determined by such things.

Their serving duties complete, the two young women sat at Nasa's and Tareck's feet. Rannah they took no notice of.

What does this mean?

Why the two slave girls had attached themselves to him and Tareck, Nasa had a bad feeling about. In the event, he need not have worried.

"Jarson," Nasa addressed their guide urgently, "there is no slavery in the city; how can there be slavery here?"

He was completely bemused and confused. But as he spoke to the leader of their accompanying party, Nasa was aware that all six Elders were staring intensely at him.

Jarson in his turn shook his head. It was as if the slaves were a surprise to him too. And he got no chance to answer.

The Elders stood up as one and indicated for their visitors to follow them into the building behind. As Jarson moved to follow, the two slave women stood in front of him preventing any such action.

Almost beyond surprise by now, Nasa stared uncomprehendingly at the two women as the three of them in therir turn followed the Elders.

There was no further sign of Jarson and his companions; unbeknown to Nasa they had indeed been escorted back to the forest and their own compounds.

The Elders seemed to have disappeared.

Disappearing and reappearing in their turn, the two women were now fully clothed in knee-length belted tabard-like garments; they were still wearing the slave collars but there was no sign of the deference that they'd displayed before; yet another surprise for the three visitors.

And as they were steered into a large comfortably furnished room, Nasa saw that they'd been joined by other similarly dressed women, none of whom were collared.

Eight.

A quick headcount followed by a closer study of the women alerted Nasa; all eight were dressed so similarly, with identical hairstyles, that they could have been sisters.

Rannah and Tareck were staring too. They too had clearly noted the likeness. Nothing could have been further from the forest women they'd seen earlier.

As his eyes became used to the gloom, Nasa saw that the

room was vast and the Elders had merely disappeared into its vastness. There was very little discernible furniture.

In fact, there were only seats for the Elders and the three of them. The women scattered themselves around the room, but all were within easy reach of Nasa and Tareck. Although he didn't feel threatened, Nasa realised that the women's positioning was defensive. Clearly, the Elders were still suspicious or uncertain about them. Again they took no account of Rannah; this was beginning to irritate Nasa.

"You are welcome."

This time there was no doubt which of the Elders had spoken. And for the first time Nasa noticed that the speaker and at least one other of the Elders was black. So far, they'd seen only white-skinned people, albeit with many shades of hair. Based on the society in the city and how it had evolved and become what it now was, seeing black people raised no curiosity with Nasa. Since their origins were the same, why should there not be black people in the forest?

Nasa nonetheless knew that a response was required of them, the Elder's welcome was a question in reality. But he was distracted.

"They're wearing slave collars," Tareck muttered. It was the first opportunity he'd had to say something.

The two women still were, but as far as he could see it was almost as if there was some status attributed to the wearers as a consequence rather than it being a badge of servitude. Sharing thoughts later, it transpired that Nasa had come to the same conclusion.

Indicating his thanks to the Elders, Nasa gestured to the nearest collar wearer to come to him and pointed to the collar. The woman, after an almost imperceptible nod from the black Elder, removed the collar and handed it to Nasa. He opened it and looked for the engraved number. What the Elders thought of his interest in the symbols of slavery Nasa had no way of knowing.

"297," he said.

"483," the other collared woman said.

Rannah looked almost animated.

"Administration slaves; probably brown-skinned," he said.

Tareck looked surprised. There had been no slavery in his lifetime. Nasa, who knew that Rannah himself had been such a slave, simply nodded.

"Over time there have been many slaves who have come to us from the city."

The Elder's voice was clear and powerful. Memories flooded into Nasa's mind again. He'd been involved in hunting slaves who escaped the city when he himself had been Sorak's slave. But as far as he could recall, they were never found alive and only their collars had been recovered.

But in the pre-rebellion days the women's Senate had always carefully managed the information that was released to the women of the city, and it would have been all too easy to suppress the news of slave escapes. That there had been many didn't seem to be a surprise to Rannah who, in his youth, had been very close to the centre of things in the old administration.

Nasa, nonetheless, had no idea what 'many' meant in terms of escaped slaves. But based on what they'd learned so far there was every reason to suppose that they would have been readily accepted by the forest people.

How much more don't we know about what went on?

Nasa knew he would never get an answer to this question from within the city. All records had been destroyed, and the old senators and administrators were all dead. What could be learned from the forest people and their Elders was yet to be determined.

Oil lamps were brought into the room by the women; the light outside was rapidly failing.

"So, what happens now?" Tareck asked.

Lacking Nasa's broad experience, and unused to inactivity, he was getting increasingly nervous. Nasa, however, was happy to let events take their course. He had long since learned that in situations where he had no control, it was better to let things happen rather than try to force them to happen, particularly when you were in the sort of vulnerable position they were in.

Tareck had perhaps noticed the changing atmosphere more quickly than Nasa. But Rannah was increasingly nervous too.

Everybody seemed to be waiting – the Elders and the women; Nasa wondered what the old men might be expecting of them.

There's something not right here. Why did they want Jarson to leave? What didn't they want him to see?

As they sat there in limbo it was a thought that didn't only occur to him.

"Nasa, these people are evil!"

Finally there was movement. Taking the opportunity of being alone with Nasa as they were shepherded into another large room where a meal was laid out, Rannah voiced his thought.

Nasa indicated that he'd heard but didn't want to respond immediately. Nonetheless, Rannah's statement struck a chord deep in his brain, forcing to the surface his own developing feeling that there was something sinister about the Elders and the hold they appeared to have over the forest people.

Nasa's sense of unease, now clearly also felt by Rannah and Tareck, was further enhanced when they were invited to eat. The Elders withdrew further into the depths of the building, which Nasa realised was undoubtedly much larger than those that they'd seen in the other compounds.

They were invited to help themselves from a variety of dishes containing simple and basic fare. Each of the three of them was surrounded by a group of two or three women and guided to separate tables. On this occasion Rannah was treated equally with Nasa and Tareck.

What's going on here?

Nasa's suspicions were further aroused when the women serving Rannah began pressing him, very much apparently against his will, to drink the beverage they'd been served. Neither Nasa nor Tareck had yet to drink. A quickly suppressed angry cry went up from one of the women as Rannah knocked his drinking vessel over when reaching for more food. It was clearly deliberate.

Rannah thinks there's something wrong with the drink.

Tareck had also become aware of the rising commotion around Rannah. Neither he nor Nasa as a consequence drank the beverage on offer. In reality, none of the three of them ate very much at all.

Where the black Elder had reappeared from none of them saw. He banged the floor with his staff.

"Enough," he said. "We will talk when the distant star reappears."

Like the other things the Elders had said, there was a wealth of meaning behind the statement. In this case it soon became clear. Each of Nasa, Tareck and Rannah were gestured by their women companions into the darkness surrounding the eating area. Out of the full light from the oil lamps a passage was visible. Escorted along the passage, first Rannah, then Tareck and finally Nasa, were each urged into separate rooms.

Nasa protested but the three women with him suddenly appeared unable to understand what he was saying.

The room into which he'd been forced was cramped and contained only a small raised padded area which Nasa presumed was a bed. There was no other furniture.

As the last woman in closed and locked the door, the tension immediately rose. But it was the three women who were tense. The situation was clearly not what they'd been expecting.

It was only afterwards that Nasa realised that the drink that they'd all refused was probably drugged and designed to make them amenable to whatever the women had been ordered by the Elders to do. And it was having to tackle him un-drugged that was causing the women anxiety.

Nasa instinctively stood with his back to the wall, his hand on his sword hilt. He had no time to wonder what was happening to Rannah and Tareck. The three women stood around and in front of him but as distant from him as the small space allowed. It was hardly an ideal place for a battle.

All three women were taller than Nasa, however none of them was armed. But all three were clearly fit and muscular, and equally clearly psyching themselves up for whatever action against Nasa they'd been instructed to take. Their confidence seemed to grow.

"You should hand over your sword."

The middle of the three, blonde-haired and blue-eyed, held out her hand. The other two fidgeted beside her, presumably knowing that, if Nasa didn't comply, they would have to try and take it from him. For Nasa it was an opportunity to draw his weapon.

As the blonde woman stepped forward, expecting to receive the sword, Nasa prodded her in the chest, and a small bloodstain began to spread through her tabard. She stepped back with a yelp. There was a pause whilst they rethought their tactics. They were going to have to grapple with him in order to seize the sword. And he'd clearly shown his willingness to use the weapon.

If they rush me, I might take out two of them, but not three!

They rushed him, or at least appeared to. The blonde-haired woman impaled herself on his sword as she was apparently knocked off balance. Then the other two women were writhing on the floor. It was at this point, almost as an irrelevance, that Nasa noticed that the woman on top, with her hands tightly around her companion's neck, was wearing one of the slave collars.

297!

A vicious jerk and the woman lay still. Covering her with his sword Nasa allowed the collared woman to stand up; she raised her hands in a gesture to signify that she had no intention of attacking him.

She spoke urgently, offering no explanation for her taking his side.

"You must find your companions and get away from here. The Elders wish to obtain information that will allow them to steal more from the city to help us survive. But some of the people don't want to be ruled by the Elders anymore."

Again, it was only later that Nasa recognised just how much information the woman had got into such a brief statement. But before Nasa could respond she had more to say.

"They will have killed the old man. He was useless to them. But the young one they'll want to question. They have means to make you tell them what they want to know."

Nasa, this time, was quick to understand what he was being told.

But a banging on the door interrupted her.

The woman gestured for Nasa to stand behind the door as she opened it. From somewhere she'd retrieved a length of rope that she held between both hands, her intent obvious.

"Shirler!" It was a whisper from the other side of the door.

The woman relaxed but carefully unlocked the door, signalling Nasa to be ready. As she eased the door open, the other collared woman pushed her way in and back-heeled it shut.

483!

Quickly acknowledging Nasa, the two women hurriedly threw the two bodies onto the bed. Then, touching each on the head, they both muttered something in unison in what Nasa assumed was some sort of reverence for the dead.

"The young one is alive. The old one is dead. Only the keepers of the old one are still alive. They're locked in."

In the corridor guarding their route out, Tareck silently saluted Nasa. Led by Shirler they crept back through the room where they'd eaten and out into the compound. The other woman, Merien, rushed on ahead to push aside a pile of rotting vegetation and retrieve the two crossbows and their stocks of bolts. She set off into the darkness. Shirler gestured for Nasa and Tareck to follow. More aware than the men were of the progress of the night, they needed to get to the edge of the forest before the second moon arose for the first time.

Neither Nasa nor Tareck had much time to mourn the death of Rannah, but both were later determined that someone would pay for his killing.

21

The compound that Nasa and Tareck and the two women eventually arrived at was in the forest, well away from the centre of the settlement. The journey had been long and silent. It was still dark, and very cold. Finding an empty room, the four of them attempted to settle for what remained of the night. Shirler shuffled her body close to Nasa's for warmth, but slowly he realised it was more than warmth she was signalling. In his far-off slave days Nasa had slept with many women; it generated no feelings in him; that was something that only Sorak did.

As the gentle noises beside him told him that Tareck and Merien were already engaged, he pulled Shirler towards him.

The rest of the night passed quickly.

The distant star rose and, angered and saddened by the death of Rannah, Nasa was determined to understand what was going on and what the hold was that the Elders had over the forest people.

Aroused and alert, the two women led them into the public room of one of the huts on the other side of the compound. They were joined by a group of men. Nasa wondered how the men had known they'd be there. Their reaction to seeing Nasa and Tareck was both surprise and apprehension.

What is it they fear? Do the Elders have forces that we haven't yet come across?

Shirler seemed to sense Nasa's uncertainty.

"We must talk," she said, gesturing the men away.

She was immediately obeyed – something else that surprised and puzzled Nasa. There were so many mysteries. Nasa knew that they had to solve them quickly and get back to the city. Something was brewing in the back sectors there and he knew Sorak would need his and Tareck's support.

* * *

Pilar and Pelar obviously didn't need to blacken their faces. The other four young women in the group did, and in one case had pulled a heavy black cloth over her almost white hair.

The safest way for such a group to get from the derelict housing area in Sector One to Sector Five was between the city walls, out through the inner green gate and back in through the red gate. The guards were only on the outer gates so they were unlikely to be detected by them. Who they might meet on the way was a risk they'd have to take.

The only sign of any herd of beasts was in the distance; the food gardens were largely overgrown but they saw signs that they were beginning to be cultivated again. Pilar and Pelar noted this with interest. All the evidence pointed to Sectors Seven and Eight being where the followers of Anstan and her campaign for a return to a women-dominated society were gathered. But the feedback that had been intercepted suggested that some sort of resettlement in Sector Five might also be taking place. They needed to know if this was true and whether the resettlement was friendly or hostile.

Sector Five had originally been given over to both military and civilian training schools with associated barracks. The older women like Sorak and Pastak had grown up and been educated in Sector Five, along with the other ex-officers who were edging towards supporting Anstan. It had also been a haven for people escaping the horrors of the earlier male administrations.

"But who's living there now?"

They needed to know.

It was to answer Pilar's question that they were creeping carefully around the inside of the outer city wall.

"There's the hut!"

Pelar was scouting ahead. They were well aware of the old herdsmen's hut. To those who knew, or knew of, Sorak and Nasa, it was a place of legend. But it was also still a good hiding place!

They began to creep forward. Suddenly Pelar threw up her hand in caution. They froze.

"There's someone in there," she mouthed.

Pilar joined her and waved the others to stay where they were.

Pilar knew there was a door into the hut at the back but it was on the opposite side to where they were. Crawling on hands and knees, the two of them passed under the ventilation openings and disappeared around the far side of the hut. Pelar waved the remaining women into a crouching advance, to give them easy access to the front door of the hut when the need arose.

Pausing inside the back door to allow their eyes to become accustomed to the gloom, Pilar and her sister listened hard. There was movement, subdued, and something that they eventually characterised as heavy breathing. An unknown number of people were asleep in the inner room of the hut, but at least one of them was awake.

Being closest, Pelar slowly moved to peer around the partition that protected the back door. Behind her back she counted off her fingers.

"Five," Pilar enumerated.

But she was at a loss as to understand the next signal, as Pelar seemed to be indicating the height off the ground.

There was one oil lamp burning, providing just enough light to see into the inner room, and just enough light for the startled guard to see the twin.

The shout alerted the other advancing women.

"Children," Pilar muttered to Pelar as she rushed in, crossbow at the ready.

There was a chaos of shouts and screams as four small figures were jerked out of sleep and began to lever themselves onto their feet. As they did so, from somewhere one of the women found other oil lamps and lit them. In the now fully lit room the two groups stared at each other in amazement, apprehension, amusement and fear.

It would have been hard to tell which of the two groups was the more surprised. Confronted by a party of black-clad young women had certainly put the children into a panic, but for these black-clad women finding a group of children on their own was totally beyond their expectations.

"What is this?" Pilar asked Pelar without much hope of an explanation.

The city was just beginning to get used to family groups and the concept of it being the parents' responsibility to bring up and educate their children; the idea of feral children was beyond anything anyone could conceive, even if they were as clever as Pilar and Pelar.

In line with their ignorance, none of the women had any idea how old the children might be. But none of them were more than fifteen cycles of the distant star old. The eldest was the girl who was keeping guard. She stood out as the only one seemingly not afraid.

The four children startled from sleep clung to each other as the women grounded their weapons and sat down, instinctively trying not to be intimidating. The only sounds were the shuffling of feet and the sobs of the smallest of the children, a boy who was clearly terrified. For a moment the women seemed uncertain how to proceed.

Then Pelar shrugged herself out of her backpack, hunted inside and offered the frightened boy some food. He grabbed it eagerly, providing the women with yet more useful information; these children were hungry and ill-fed. The other women followed suit, until all in the group were fed. The atmosphere noticeably lightened.

No longer hungry, the children reverted to type and began to allow their curiosity to take over. However, the women were reluctant to allow them to get too close until they understood better what was going on.

"Two girls and three boys," Pilar said to her sister. "How can this be?"

All of the children had clearly been born during the last periods of male administration, when the instability in the city had allowed many abuses. None of the women had a very clear idea of what things were like back then; they themselves had been small children, and they hadn't been born into stable families. Such things were rare then but had now become the norm, thanks to Sorak and the mixed gender Senate, which made the idea of children running wild even more surprising.

As the atmosphere continued to lighten, the children began to settle, but none of them seemed inclined to sleep again. Equally, as things settled the impact of their discovery on their intended activities began to demand the women's attention.

"So," said Pilar quietly, "what are we going to do with these children?"

"Do we have to do anything with them?"

One of the women asked the obvious question: why were they required to do anything?

"They might have been hungry, but they've clearly survived for a long time," the woman said. "If we leave them, no doubt they'll continue to survive."

The twins acknowledged the truth of this.

"But," Pelar asked, "do we want a group of wild children running around the city? How many more groups like this might there be?"

The question pulled them all up short. Since this was the first time they'd come across the phenomenon they had no idea. They'd chanced upon something foreign to the sort of society that was developing in the city, and certainly Pilar and Pelar's instinct was that these children needed to be integrated into that society. But equally, it was neither their job to do it, nor were they equipped at that moment in time to take responsibility for the children.

The older girl who'd been keeping guard perhaps sensed the conversation the women were having. She stood up and moved to join the group of women.

"There used to be more of us." She indicated eight on her fingers. "The women in the school took the others. They do nasty things to them."

She stopped, unclear whether she should have said such a thing to yet more women. A look of fear flashed across her face. What if these women were from the school, looking for more victims?

None of the women had any idea what 'nasty things' might mean, but the children were clearly frightened of the women in Sector Five. For Pilar and Pelar this was confirmation that the rumours about what was going on in the sector were true and that their punitive expedition was justified. The guard patrols had increasingly reported activities in the area which were usually hurriedly suspended when the patrols were detected. Nothing suspicious was ever found.

In another expression of her fear, the girl moved away from the women and huddled together with the other four children.

That told the women as much as they needed to know; they had to get the children to safety.

"We should leave them food, tell them to stay in the hut, and when we've dealt with the women in Sector Five we'll come back and take them with us."

It was the white-haired woman who'd so far said nothing who offered the suggestion. There was no dissent.

Pilar called the girl back over to them.

"We have business with these women in Sector Five. Your information has been very helpful to us. We'll leave you some food, go and deal with these women and then return to take you back to Sector One and safety."

Pilar shouldered her crossbow as if to reinforce her statement.

The girl re-joined her companions once more.

22

Leaving the hut, Pilar and Pelar led their party quickly towards the red gate, hugging the outer city wall. Uncertain what they might find and where, they were on full alert.

"Do you think they'll wait for us?" Pilar asked her sister, of the children they'd just left.

"Who can tell? But we should inform Sorak. If there are more of these groups of children living wild she should know about it."

Neither really knew how to deal with the situation beyond making the children safe. Did they know who their parents were? Had they been abandoned; had they run away? How had they come together? How long had they been living in the hut? The questions flooded into both sisters' minds but the answers were less easy to formulate. The whole situation was beyond their experience, beyond anyone's, they imagined.

But a signal from the woman scouting ahead brought them back to the reality of the action they were undertaking.

"The herd has suddenly become agitated," the white-haired young woman said.

They all tensed. They were too far away for it to be them who'd disturbed the herd. The likelihood of it being one of the ferocious beasts from the forest beyond the plain was remote, although they did sometimes get into the city. The usual thing to disturb the beasts was people.

And so it proved in this case.

As the party formed a tight group to enter the inner red gate, the herd turned and charged towards them.

"They're being driven!" Pelar said. "Whoever it's by must have seen us."

As the party flattened itself against the city wall the herd of beasts thundered past, exposing three poorly dressed women who had clearly been beating the beasts with sticks. All three were armed with swords but didn't appear to have crossbows or any other weapons. They were clearly expecting to find the twins' party.

However, seeing themselves outnumbered, the three women rushed back through the city inner gate and headed into the mass of low buildings that were the remains of the old training schools in Sector Five. The withdrawal was hurried but still left the twins with the feeling that the women wanted them to follow.

But Pilar held her companions back. Chasing the three into this mass of buildings, which they would be familiar with, but which they themselves were not, was not a good idea. This was partly because of the fear of an ambush, but also because Pilar and Pelar had no idea how many women there actually were hiding in Sector Five. Even more caution was required if they were to locate the other children but also provide Sorak with intelligence about the numbers of people living out of sight in the area.

The arrival of the party of young women in Sector Five created panic amongst the residents. Uniformly dressed, but not apparently soldiers, speculation about who they were and why they were there was wild and ill-informed. Were they alone? Were they the vanguard of a larger party? They had no idea.

"We must kill them. They must not be allowed to go back to the city administration."

The group of anxious women were gathered in one of the outbuildings of the old military training school.

The woman who had spoken was younger than the others, better dressed and cleaner. She was their leader, more by force of character than by any special skill or knowledge. Like Anstan, she was a civilian, but briefly a former administrator rather than a mangeneer. The other women were all former common soldiers, aging and in a permanent state of anxiety. Without officers, they'd been unable to cope with the changes that Sorak had been introducing, and with gender equality in the military there was no place for them as older soldiers. With an uncertain future, they and their like were easy prey for Anstan and her supporters.

The group had settled in the old military training school because it was a very complex set of buildings that were easy to defend, and also somewhere they were familiar with. At least it would have been easy to defend if the women had had more skill in creating a defensive position within the maze of classrooms and dormitories. But lacking such skills, the best their leader, Phelan, could do was set up a permanent watch from key points, and send out scouting parties. It was one of these that had detected Pilar, Pelar and their group.

Phelan had escaped from Sector Two after having been sentenced to be executed for killing one of the male senators. Sorak was against such executions and at first was both angry at the ease with which she'd escaped, but also relieved that she wouldn't be put to death. However, it soon became known that Phelan had collected together a group of renegade ex-soldiers and was preying on the city's residents as they went about their business. Sorak's attitude changed and hardened; Phelan and her group were to be hunted down and neutralised.

It was this change of attitude in Sorak that Pilar and Pelar had chosen as a means of giving their followers a chance for some action. They all needed to prove themselves before taking on Anstan and her more experienced body of ex-soldiers.

* * *

The twins gathered their party in the entrance hall of one of the outer buildings of the training school. With so many uncertainties confronting them, they needed to be clear about what they were trying to achieve and how they would achieve it.

"Where would you choose as the safest part of Sector Five?" Pilar asked the others.

It was almost a rhetorical question; since none of the women had been brought up pre-rebellion, none of them had been schooled and trained in Sector Five, and none of them therefore had any idea of the geography of the place. But the white-haired woman, who'd shaken back her black headscarf, signified that she wanted to say something. Heavily scarred, the headscarf was intended to cover more than her fair hair.

In many ways this woman was different from the others. It soon transpired why.

"My mother once brought me here as a child, to meet my father. He was an old slave worker in the water treatment plant. My mother had rescued him from some soldiers who wanted to kill him. But they didn't stay together too long; he was too involved in the resistance to the male administration."

The twins managed to hide their impatience. All of this history must have a point.

"But they met here secretly, and on this one occasion my mother brought me. The military training school, as I remember it, has sets of classrooms connected to a central area, like the Senate offices. That's where I'd hide if I wanted to escape from the city administration."

She gestured around and at the area that they'd just entered.

"And this is the military training school?" Pelar asked.

159

The white-haired woman nodded.

"It has a big open area like the Senate piazza."

Having seen soldiers being drilled, the women knew that they should be looking for a parade ground. It wasn't hard to find. It was adjacent to where they'd taken cover. They walked through to the central area. They found no evidence of habitation at ground level.

The central area opened onto one side of the parade ground. As they studied the layout, two things were obvious. Firstly, they'd have to find a way to skirt around the parade ground if they needed to cross it; to do so directly would be impossible without detection. Secondly, since the central buildings above were four storeys high, and had the outside ramps which were common to most of the public buildings, they'd need to plan their route up the building very carefully. With no knowledge of how many women there might be hiding there, presuming they were in the right place, they'd have to clear as much of each floor as they could as they went up.

The light was failing. But the women knew that moving by moonlight, when any occupants of the building were likely to be asleep, was by far the best time for them.

It was fully dark by the time they'd reconnoitred the whole of the ground floor and found a room they could use as a base to prepare themselves. The room wasn't very big, had very small ventilation spaces and seemed more like a refuse dumping area. This was what made it attractive to the twins; they were unlikely to be disturbed in such a foul place.

The white-haired woman was the first into the room. There was just enough remaining gloom to see that there was no furniture, only a couple of piles of rags and other debris in one corner. The smell was nauseating but they knew that they wouldn't be there for very long. None of them wanted to be contaminated.

Having set a guard and crowded into the room, the women settled and waited for Pilar and Pelar to give their instructions. But the twins didn't get the chance.

"Mother's heart!"

The woman standing next to her white-haired colleague had stepped back onto the pile of rags in the corner, only to be startled, both by it moving and by it uttering a muffled groan. She drew her sword.

Pelar quickly gathered a pile of rubbish and set light to it using her flintlock. The corner was illuminated and something was definitely moving.

"Mother's heart," the woman said again.

As she pulled back the mass of rags, a young boy emerged. Hands bound behind his back, feet tied, with something foul stuffed into his mouth, he was indescribably dirty and smelly. Released, he sat on his heels and struggled to get control of himself, silent tears forging a clean strip down his filthy face. The women let him work off his angst. The guard on the door continually signalled for them to reduce the noise they were making.

As the light from the pile of burning rubbish died away the boy seemed to gather himself. What instinct told him that these particular women meant him no harm he couldn't have said but he eventually sat back calmly and waited.

The other children said that some of them had been taken into Sector Five.

It was a thought that had occurred to both twins but neither could imagine what finding this child, who was, they guessed, around thirteen or fourteen cycles old, signified. It certainly added to their problems.

Acknowledging his safety, the boy seemed ready to talk.

"They will come for me," he said, eyeing the dark-clad women with an unfathomable expression.

"Who will come?" asked Pilar.

He didn't answer directly.

"I don't obey them; they punish me."

Something like pride showed through the boy's voice.

"How many are there?" Pelar wanted to know, anxious to understand as much about the women in the building as possible.

Since they knew that they'd been seen they had to assume that the women of Sector Five would be looking out for them, waiting to attack if they thought they were hostile. The more they knew in advance the better. This time she got an answer.

The boy showed the fingers on his hand three times.

Fifteen against six was serious odds, and the women knew that they'd have to use all of their skill and guile if they were to win out. But they hadn't taken account of the boy. Yet again, they were distracted.

The guard outside the door stiffened. She'd sensed rather than heard someone approaching. And then an oil lamp held by another boy appeared, but it was followed by two scruffy and dirty, but fully armed, women.

The guard slid into the room and the party backed up against the wall in the tiny space. There being no entrance door they'd be noticed as soon as the light illuminated the room. All had weapons in hand. The boy hurriedly lay down and pulled the filthy rags over himself, understanding immediately what was likely to happen.

The second boy carrying the lamp hung back when he reached the door of the room, reluctant to go in. Prodded by a sword thrust into his buttocks he finally did so. Staggering, he dropped, or rather, as Pelar observed, threw down the lamp onto the pile of rubbish in the corner. The first Sector Five woman rushed into the room and raised her sword to angrily strike at the boy as the rubbish flared up. A thrust to her heart from the white-haired woman ensured that the blow never fell.

The second woman lasted no longer. Hemmed in by their rescuers the two boys stared at them, again with expressions that Pilar and Pelar couldn't fathom. But they soon recovered.

"We'll show you the way," the first boy said.

Rapidly, the two lads chattered together. The second boy, who seemed much less intelligent than the first, nodded at whatever he'd been told. The conversation was so rapid that the women had no chance of understanding it. However, it forced the twins to be even more cautious.

Then, stamping out the still smouldering rubbish, Pilar gestured the two boys to lead the way.

"He's fearful," the first lad said. "I tell him you'll kill him if he tries to speak to the women."

It wasn't a statement that gave the twins much confidence but the white-haired woman had taken the second boy by the hand and was holding him tightly as they moved off. She'd clearly recognised that in his fear and panic he might give them away. She hoped she wouldn't have to take action against the poor child.

They were led to the outside ramp and cautiously and silently crept up to the third floor, ducking under the ventilation spaces as they went. There were no signs of habitation on the floors they passed. They paused at each floor, nonetheless, to check; they couldn't afford to leave any hostile women at their rear.

This is going to be a waste of time. This lot aren't likely to be part of Anstan's group.

Both the twins had already realised this but nonetheless Sector Five needed to be checked out; it was too good a hiding place for the women agitating for a return to the past. They also needed to ensure the wellbeing of the feral children.

They'll have to send the patrols in here.

Pilar, as she thought this, knew that Sorak wouldn't be happy. Reducing patrols and allowing people the freedom to do what they liked and go where they liked was so much a part of her philosophy. Having patrols forever watching the citizens was too much like a return to the past that she and they were resisting.

Maybe daytime patrols.

This was something Sorak had allowed in other sectors until she was confident that the people in those areas weren't supporters of Anstan's.

When they reached the third floor their guide led them into the building and headed for a set of rooms that overlooked the parade ground. Smelly and filthy, they needed no telling that this was where the boys lived.

Pilar held up her hand to silently indicate four. The two boys nodded. There was evidence of four piles of rags and the small belongings of the children.

The second boy walked over to two of the piles and, holding his hands open on his chest, gestured breasts. These two children were obviously girls.

Leading from the first room that they'd entered was a second. Gesturing upwards, their guide indicated a hole in the ceiling that clearly allowed access to the top floor. There was a crude platform that allowed the children to climb up into the room above. The twins and the other women didn't have time to wonder why this arrangement was in place. The two boys were getting increasingly agitated.

"We'll go to the women. They'll be expecting us. You climb. There's access to all the rooms along the inside of the building," the first boy said.

Pilar and Pelar acknowledge the information.

Assuming the top floor was like all the others that they'd passed there would be a central corridor that the boy was directing them to use. There were still thirteen women to account for; what they didn't know was where in the rooms above they all were. And they still had to be suspicious of the boys.

The two of them waited until all the women had climbed up into the room above and disappeared into the corridor. They then set off up the ramp, the first lad clasping his hands behind his back as if tied. The second boy led the way, chattering as he went.

Established on the floor above, unshipping and loading their crossbows the six women listened for any sounds of activity. In their black clothing there were barely visible in the gloom; so much so that as a small girl emerged from one of the rooms leading from the corridor she actually bumped into Pelar before she saw her. Fortunately, no sound came from her.

As one of the women grabbed at the girl and put her hand over her mouth she discovered that it was already covered with a band of tight material. She couldn't have cried out if she'd wanted to. Slopping liquid from the pot she was carrying onto the floor, the girl stared at the women in terror. Back down the corridor a light flickered in one of the rooms. Taking the girl with them, they crept to the entrance.

The twins held back but a quick flurry of action ensued as the other four women surged into the room, firing their crossbows as they went. There was a loud crash and a scream and then there was silence again. As they waited for any reaction they counted the bodies.

"Come," Pelar whispered to the girl as she and her sister led her into the room.

The girl would have screamed had she been able.

Nine.

Pilar was mentally counting. The odds were improving.

As the women checked that the four occupants of the room were all dead, and recovered their crossbow bolts, a scuffling came from under the overturned table. A second girl, equally unable to speak, was hauled into the light of the oil lamps.

Like the boys, the two youngsters soon calmed down and the tape was quickly removed from their mouths. They instinctively understood that they had nothing to fear.

"We'll leave you here. You mustn't make a sound," Pilar said.

The girls nodded. The women piled up the bodies of the dead occupants and covered them with what they assumed was bedding.

Back in the corridor they crept towards the low rumble of voices they could hear.

23

Had they known, neither Sorak nor Nasa would have been very happy with the loss of life that was occurring during Pilar and Pelar's expedition to Sector Five; if truth be known, nor were they themselves or the women with them. But the rumours and gossip, particularly around the old soldiers in Sector Four nearby, suggested they were meeting violence with violence. And the appalling treatment of the captured children seemed to bear this out. But the population of the city had declined enough and Sorak, in particular, was anxious to avoid any more killing.

So far, the twins had discovered nothing that was likely to link these women to Anstan and her efforts towards engineering a return to the past. But what they had discovered, nonetheless, they felt justified their action to clear out a group of undesirable women who were living a life in direct contrast to the norms being established in the city. And everyone realised there was likely to be a price to pay for achieving the society that Sorak was seeking.

The two sisters had agreed with the two young boys that they would first check out the area surrounding where the remaining women were known to be. The boys would hold back from presenting themselves, for their own safety, until this had happened. Timing was important but uncertain.

A scream hastened Pilar and Pelar's troops into action.

"They must have made contact with the women."

It could be the only explanation.

Creeping to the top of the ramp, but keeping out of sight until they were confident that their rescuers were in action, the two boys had waited. But the anxiety that the second lad, sent to bring back the first, was feeling was beginning to overwhelm him. Nervously, they prepared themselves for when they judged the twins and their supporters had done their work. Driven by the second boy's anxiety they were a little premature.

The room that the nine renegade women were lounging in was the largest in the building. In the days of the military training school it had been some sort of common room for the older pupils. Sorak would have remembered it well. Phelan, their self-appointed leader, sat apart from the other women. Knowing that Pilar and Pelar's group was out there somewhere, the atmosphere was tense.

The women were scattered around the room. Expecting no hostile visitation, they were relaxed and concentrated on their own small day-to-day activities. Mostly they'd divested themselves of their weapons other than their swords.

From the ramp, the two boys arose at the entrance and walked nervously into the room as Pilar and Pelar and the other four women in their turn began to creep along the corridor.

Although expecting the two boys, it took the Sector Five women some moments to realise that there was no sign of the two women also sent to recover the errant youngster. When they did realise it, they were immediately suspicious.

Phelan, as she usually did, took control of the situation. Striding up to the two boys she towered over them. Even the first boy was intimidated.

Her demand to know where her two troopers were was met with a fearful silence. The blow that struck the second boy, whom she'd been addressing, sent him screaming and slithering across the floor and crashing into the wall. He lay still.

It was Phelan's last action. As she slumped forwards the crossbow bolt in her back was clear to see. The other women, taken by surprise, were slow to react but several managed to recover their own crossbows or draw their swords. But unclear who the enemy was and where they'd come from, they were also too slow to make any response before they were confronted. The first boy hurriedly scurried into a corner away from the action.

"Hold!"

The six black-clad warriors rushed into the room, weapons at the ready. Pelar's injunction had no effect.

The thuds of crossbow bolts were mixed with groans and screams. Four of the women were hit but, following the twins' instructions, their attackers had attempted to aim for limbs rather than vital organs. Two women nonetheless died.

A silent standoff developed. One of the women had attempted to escape onto the outside ramp, only to be tripped by the first boy, emboldened to come out of his corner by the apparent success of the attack. The white-haired woman moved to stand over the prone figure. The remaining Sector Five women, each nervously brandishing a sword, and each facing a crossbow, hesitated and then one by one threw down their weapons.

"He lives!"

The white-haired woman was kneeling over the second boy, who was painfully stirring, blood streaming from his nose. Helped to his feet he rushed into the arms of his companion. But only then did he show any interest in what had been going on.

More screams emerged as the two girls excitedly greeted the boys. Fetched by one of the twins' troopers, the four of them were urged into an adjoining room as Pilar and Pelar began to secure the disarmed Sector Five women. Neither of the two injured women was badly hurt, suffering only flesh wounds which were quickly treated. Only six of the original fifteen women had survived. This gave the sisters no satisfaction.

As a calm settled on the combatants, the twins' need for information became paramount.

"Are there others like you?" Pelar wanted to know of the survivors.

Having no idea how many other groups of such renegades there might be, it was important to gather as much intelligence as possible in order for Sorak and the administration to plan how to deal with them if they proved hostile.

Pelar wasn't sure she'd get an answer. In the face of silence, the eldest of the girls, more a young woman, nodded her to one side.

"There were two groups in the school opposite but they got into a dispute and destroyed each other."

Horrified, Pelar waited to see if the girl had more to say.

"Another group was killed by the older women in..." She gestured vaguely, by which Pelar concluded she meant Sector Four.

That was the limit of her knowledge. Pelar was unable to get any explanation of how or why the old soldiers from Sector Four had intervened. That they might be Anstan's adherents did, however, occur to her.

"We'd be foolish to try to get back to the hut now," Pilar said. "The distant star will soon be gone."

It wasn't a comfortable night for anyone. For the prisoners, restrained, sleeping was impossible; for the children, the excitement of their release kept them awake; and for Pilar and Pelar and the others, constant vigilance was required. All were happy when the distant star returned.

The meagre food supplies the party discovered were hardly sufficient for themselves and the children; the prisoners were forced to march on empty stomachs.

The journey back to the herdsmen's hut was uneventful.

Seeing the hut, the four children ran on ahead despite being cautioned by Pelar. The white-haired woman hurried after them but, unlike the youngsters, didn't rush into the dilapidated building.

Squeals and screams erupted as the two groups were reunited. Then they all spilled out of the hut to greet the rescuing party. The oldest girl to whom they'd spoken before held back.

The twins noticed this. Whilst their friends danced around in the delight of their freedom, Pilar and Pelar approached her.

"The old women came."

The girl was obviously frightened. Pilar gave her a small piece of food from her backpack.

"What old women?"

The sisters realised that they probably knew already.

"The soldiers, that had been soldiers..."

She gestured towards Sector Four.

Pilar and Pelar exchanged looks; this was what they'd thought might happen. The problem was, they didn't know on which side of the divide, Sorak supporters or Anstan supporters, these women were. A rationale for either group leaving the children free until their party returned was easy to construct.

"One was..."

Again, the half sentence, followed by a sweep of the hand, told them all they needed to know. One of the party was black. The only black ex-soldier they knew of, a rare survivor from the old Senate guard, was a vociferous supporter of Anstan, and was noted for not being shy about letting people know how much she yearned for the past.

"We must get away from here quickly. Surely they must be watching us, if nothing else."

Pelar knew that what her sister had said was true, but whilst they remained within the area between the city walls they were both exposed, yet protected, by the open space.

With a group of excited children and the six captives, they were hardly going to make the relatively short journey from the hut to the green inner wall gate without potentially attracting notice.

* * *

Both Sorak and Lenrick were aware of Pilar and Pelar's expedition into Sector Five. In the new society Sorak was trying to create, the women there were entitled to the same freedoms and life choices as all of the other women, provided they didn't indulge in anti-social behaviour. No one in the city would have called it that, but if they did no harm, why should they not be left in peace? Except that there was considerable evidence to suggest that the women in Sector Five weren't interested in anything other than their own selfish pleasures, and weren't too particular how they came by them. The black woman would have been unwelcome to Sorak and Lenrick.

* * *

"Hold!"

The twins were brought back to the reality of their situation, and what they were going to do with the children and prisoners by the challenge of the leader of a patrol which had emerged from the inner green gate as they arrived at it.

The leader of the patrol was unimpressed by Pelar's explanation of their foray into Sector Five and insisted they release the prisoners into their care and accompany them to the Senate building to report to Lenrick. They were happy to do this; Lenrick they trusted.

* * *

The guard commander, who of course was well aware of the expedition, was, however, not very happy to be presented with the six prisoners and only the twins' party's word for their transgressions.

But help was at hand. Once she'd quelled the excited babble of nine children trying to talk at once, with great patience Lenrick was able to construct a story of what had happened and of the terrors the children had been subjected to.

"Enough!"

Lenrick quickly ordered the Sector Five women to the Senate prison, pending their being questioned further by an official from Sorak's administration. A replacement for the old women's Senate's arbitrary justice system was taking time to develop but the women would at least now get a chance to explain themselves. The children posed a more difficult problem.

However, fed and watered and allowed time to relax and play, Lenrick eventually organised safe accommodation for them and the opportunity for the two eldest to explain what had happened to them.

A long-term means of safely caring for orphaned children was another problem, resulting from the changes Sorak was making, that had to be solved. The old pre-rebellion system was considered too impersonal and lacking in any concept of the needs of the children rather than of the administration.

24

The longer he was away the more Sorak missed Nasa, and not just his physical company; his common-sense advice on how to achieve the stability and harmony that she was seeking was equally missed. And things weren't going well with her efforts to introduce her new society. Sorak was conscious that she was 'ageing' and that her vision still wasn't universally accepted. What worried her most was that those still hankering after the old days of the female-dominated past had begun to include a significant number of younger women who couldn't possibly have had any experience of that world.

How can this be possible?

"Anstan and her cohorts seem to be able to sell the past as being much more glamorous than it ever was. And for civilian women, who were always second-class after the military, that's now very attractive."

The civilian world was still something of a mystery to Sorak, but Anstan's understanding of it was slowly emerging as a particular worry.

Lenrick, the Senate guard commander, and increasingly the head of the citizens' protection force, could only agree with Sorak. Closer to everyday life in the city she was even more aware of how things had changed during Sorak's leadership, but also of how many women, in particular, still felt disenfranchised from it. She was aware that this included many lower-grade civilian women, who were being offered a place in society that they hadn't had before and didn't know how to grasp.

Resentment of the prominent roles that the more elite of the ex-slaves had carved out for themselves, and the indulgence of the horde of ex-lower-grade slaves, was rife. It was this that Sorak and the other more thoughtful members of the Senate had begun to recognise was driving many of the less intelligent of the younger women, born after the rebellion, to support the doctrine of Anstan.

* * *

"We can hardly wait until all the old men die; we'll all be dead ourselves by then."

Sorak was sharing a quiet moment with Lecktan, one of the few younger female senators who was fully committed to what her Senate leader was trying to achieve, but was equally fully aware of the growing feeling amongst her age-group that acceptance of men within the natural order of things as equals had still to be universally achieved.

"We need to create more roles for civilian women within the administration, and we need to diversify the roles that men can take within the civilian world."

It was a stark statement that posed a challenge to Sorak's way of thinking. The military had always dominated the city; the generals in the old days had run everything for the Senate. In the new city the military were now just the servants of the people rather than their masters, but Lecktan had increasingly understood that the most outspoken older women, however enlightened, were all ex-soldiers and all thought in the same limited way, even as Sorak did.

She's right, Nasa. When are you coming back? I need you here to help me.

Lecktan took Sorak's nodding as agreement rather than suppressed yearning for her partner. It was both.

But Lecktan also knew her Sorak very well, so she let her comment to her slowly work its way into her subconscious. Past experience told her that that way, Sorak would find a solution and pursue it. That was all Lecktan wanted.

* * *

Nasa, meantime, was equally conscious of how much he was missing Sorak. Having escaped from the stronghold of the Elders of the forest people, and now alone with Tareck and the two women Shirler and Merien in an isolated compound, he resolutely forced all thoughts of his partner from his mind and prepared himself to ask a lot of questions. Tareck, whose anger over the death of Rannah had clearly not abated, looked on uncertainly; the real role of these two women was as unclear to him as it was to Nasa.

What are these two women up to?

After their relations with the two women earlier, both Nasa and Tareck had the feeling they were being used, being brought into supportive sympathy with whatever the women wanted to achieve. But Nasa had no intention of being drawn into local politics.

"We need to return to the city," Nasa said, "but before we go there are questions we'd like answers to."

From their reaction, Shirler and Merien hadn't seemed to expect their visitors to be leaving them. There was a moment of tension. However, both women knew that they were no match for Nasa and Tareck and so couldn't really stop them leaving if they meant to. The other forest people nearby were farmers and the like, and would have been of very little military support.

Nasa came straight to the point.

"Why do the people fear the Elders? What hold do they have over you?"

Shirler, who seemed to be the leader amongst the two of them, gave Nasa a look that he found totally unfathomable. There was certainly fear, and also defiance, but there was something more that he couldn't identify. It determined Nasa to know more.

"The Elders will send after us. They'll hunt us down. And if they find you with us, they'll kill you too."

It was hardly the answer Nasa had been expecting or hoping for, but he'd noticed that Tareck had become very alert. Used to his son Lenar's acute hearing, Nasa immediately recognised that Tareck had heard something that he and the women had not.

"What?"

Faced with what Shirler had just said, Nasa's immediate thought was that they were being approached, stealthily, by unknown forces sent by the Elders. Both he and Tareck armed their crossbows and moved away from the open area and deeper into the shelter of one of the open-sided rooms of the nearest building. The two women followed them, puzzled by their actions; they'd still heard nothing. Then a cry went up, more a scream of pain, followed by a heavy silence. Then, after a brief tense period, one of the fierce creatures that Sorak called 'leopards' crept into the room, dragging a bleeding body with it.

Killed instantly by two crossbow bolts, it was only as the animal collapsed that Nasa saw it was wearing a collar and dragging a chain. The two women reacted with terror.

Rearmed, Nasa and Tareck tracked back along the chain, out of the room and out of the building. The chain ended in a leather loop, clearly a handhold, but there was no sign of whoever had been holding it. At least there wasn't at first.

Whose body it was, Nasa and Tareck, of course, had no idea.

Then a noise in the trees at the edge of the clearing was unmistakable this time. Some sort of violent physical activity, a fight Nasa presumed, was going on and soon spilled out into the clearing.

"Mother's heart," muttered Tareck.

Three young boys were dragging the ugliest old woman that either man had ever seen, by the arms, out into the open. Naked to the waist, the old woman's legs were dressed in the furs of a leopard and her fingernails were almost as long as her fingers; evidence of their potency could be seen on the bodies of the three boys.

As Nasa and Tareck moved towards them, the boys, seeing their raised weapons, dropped the woman onto the ground, uncertain how to proceed. They clearly had no idea that there was anyone in the compound.

It didn't take Nasa long to realise that this old woman was the leopard's keeper. Leaping to her feet with more agility than expected, the woman towered over Nasa and even Tareck. Darting around the boys, she ran for the edge of the clearing, again with more speed and agility than would have been expected of someone seemingly so old. A crossbow bolt through her right calf brought her down into a writhing heap. It was an instinctive shot by Tareck. At no time throughout the whole episode had the woman uttered a sound.

The body that the animal had brought into the compound building turned out to be a young woman. She was still alive, hands bound behind her, and apart from a large bite wound on her left thigh her injuries were largely superficial. Tareck, shrugging off his backpack, produced his medicine kit, quickly staunched the bleeding bite mark and sealed it over with tape. The woman whimpered in pain but otherwise accepted Tareck's ministrations without any other sound.

"She'll recover."

By this time, Shirler and Merien had gathered the three boys together and called back some of the farmers who'd previously been present. Tareck removed the bolt from the old woman's calf, none too gently, and again staunched the bleeding. She shrieked in defiance as Shirler tied her hands behind her back.

The sight of the old woman and the dead leopard caused consternation and then seemingly fear in the farmers. Nasa and Tareck were once again bemused by this latest action amongst the forest people, with no more idea of what was going on than they'd had before. Nasa was even more determined to find out.

But it was the dead leopard that eventually provided the clue. Two of the famers had knelt beside the animal's body and were rocking backwards and forwards uttering a low moaning chant. They seemed to be mourning its death.

An angry shout from Merien caused them to scurry away. They didn't join the other farmers but headed away into the nearby forest.

"The Elders worship the jag-jag," Shirler explained. "The jag-jag women bring punishment if we disobey. This young woman refused to marry the man the Elders wanted her to and she tried to run away. The Elders often force women into marriage if they think they'd be good breeding stock."

Some sort of clarity began to emerge in Nasa's mind. He couldn't grasp the concept of a cult as such, but he recognised its manifestations. Somewhere in the distant past, as the people from the crashed craft from beyond the distant star penetrated the forest and began to build themselves a society, by then completely out of touch with the embryonic city, a powerful leadership had emerged here too. The leadership had perpetuated itself, much as the old women's Senate had, but having lost touch with its sophisticated past their more primitive instincts had prevailed. And as the women in the city had evolved their gender-dominated society, these people had evolved backwards to a society almost pre-historic.

And the leaders, the Elders, kept control by preventing development and using terror to achieve obedience, whilst maintaining the appearance of a happy and contented society.

But as the evidence of Shirler and Merien demonstrated, they hadn't entirely succeeded. But again, Nasa surmised, as the forest people became aware of the breakdown of the rigid control of the women in the city, and of the new freedoms emerging, the Elders' control was inevitably being undermined.

Nasa's reflections were interrupted by yet another scream and with Tareck rushing over to the injured old woman. It seemed to be too late. As he grasped her arm her body went limp.

"She'll have killed herself," Shirler said simply.

How she'd killed herself wasn't immediately obvious.

25

Nasa didn't get the opportunity to consider what this latest strange turn of events might mean for them. Clearly, the leopard and the old woman had some ritual significance, but the bevy of armed women who noisily and unexpectedly surged into the compound as the woman expired were manifestly not interested in rituals.

The ten women were all armed with spears and short swords and were clad in leather armour that protected their upper bodies. Shirler and Merien looked fearful; they obviously knew who these warriors were.

The women forced their way into the room where Shirler, Merien and the two men were.

The leader of the troopers, the tallest woman Nasa had ever seen, gestured for Tareck and himself to leave, signifying that what was about to happen was none of their business.

"I said they would come." Shirler grasped her sword handle nervously.

But Nasa and Tareck had no intention of leaving.

"You should leave," the leader said, reinforcing her previous gesture.

A tense stand-off began when the two men showed no inclination to withdraw.

On later reflection, Nasa found that he could make no sense of what then followed.

The room was very crowded and dimly lit, as the external light was obscured by trees. Several of the women began to move about in the background as if intending to explore the rest of the building. Suddenly a wail went up, similar to the one generated by the two frightened farmers previously. A confusion of discordant noise ensued, during which Nasa and Tareck armed their crossbows and Shirler and Merien drew their weapons. Again, it was only later that they realised the three boys had wisely taken the opportunity to disappear.

Oil lamps were found from somewhere and the leader elbowed her way through the knot of warriors crouching in a corner of the room, where the dead leopard and the body of the old woman had been placed by the boys. There was a momentary silence.

Then, as the four of them, with the injured young woman, watched, all of the women sank to their knees and set up a concerted rhythmic chant. The leader slowly forced the women to back away from the two dead bodies. Then, as an open space was created, the women began to bang the shafts of their spears in a crescendo of dissonant noise.

"Now what?" Nasa asked himself.

"The jag-jag is angry," Shirler said by way of explanation. As with the actions of the two farmers, neither she nor Merien seemed to be affected by the warriors' actions.

Slowly, Nasa began to realise what was going on. The jag-jag was clearly some sort of god or superior being that the Elders worshipped and used to overawe and dominate the forest people. Sorak, again from her earlier experience in the Senate library as a young officer, would have understood the concept of a god and a cult. But it became increasingly apparent that not everybody was in fear of the jag-jag. As he watched, a slow smile of contempt spread across the faces of both Shirler and Merien; for them it was merely theatre.

Then, as suddenly as it had begun, the drumming stopped.

"Tareck!"

Nasa called his colleague to alert, but too late. The leader strode over to the little group and, before Nasa or Tareck could react, grasped the injured young woman and dragged her into the circle of kneeling women.

"They will sacrifice her to placate the jag-jag."

At least that was what Nasa thought Merien said.

The women all now rose up and forced Nasa and Tareck, and Shirler and Merien, out of the room and out of the building into the surrounding compound. They were not to see what was to happen. At least that seemed to be their intention.

The leader threw the young woman to the ground in the centre of the circle and the women began to shuffle around her, silent at first and then began the slow wail. As the circle widened the leader was forced back to the edge of the proceedings, clearly framed in the wide entrance to the building and the room.

As they continued to gyrate around the terrified young woman only the tall leader was standing upright. And then, as Nasa and his companions looked on, she silently pitched forward, the spear that had pierced her heart all too apparent as she collapsed. By the time Nasa grasped what had happened and turned to look, there was no sign of whoever had thrown the spear.

But as Shirler and Merien prepared to attempt a rescue of the injured young woman, the clearing was suddenly full of armed men hurling spears and firing arrows into the Elders' troopers. There was a period of violent mayhem that the four of them could only watch.

"Mother's heart," Tareck exclaimed as the fusillade ended and there was silence and stillness inside the building. He moved to re-enter the building.

As Nasa joined him, Shirler and Merien quickly checked to see if all the women were dead. Sick to his stomach as such unexpected and apparently unprovoked slaughter, it took him a moment to recognise what Tareck was pointing at.

Laying grotesquely on his back, an arrow in the chest, was a man Nasa recognised as the leader of the Elders. When and how he'd arrived no one had any idea.

The startling sight of the dead black man created an immediate silence.

The injured young woman needed Tareck's medical attention again. Her bite wound had been reopened by the rough way that she'd been dragged into the circle. It was only as Shirler and Merien recovered her from the pile of bodies that they realised how lucky she'd been to survive. A graze on her shoulder made by an arrow was the only sign of additional injury.

"We need to get her back to the city," Tareck said; "I don't have the skill to do more than stop the bleeding."

It was a statement that brought Nasa brutally back to a realisation of their situation. Suddenly they were in the middle of a war they didn't understand, against forces that they barely had any knowledge of.

"Three of the Elders have been captured."

Nasa immediately recognised the speaker. Jarson, the calf thief and their original guide, bowed to Shirler and Merien and then greeted Nasa and Tareck with a huge grin.

That Jarson was involved in the apparent uprising didn't come as much of a surprise to the two colleagues; they knew full well that he was an independent spirit.

"They must not be harmed," Nasa said hurriedly.

Jarson's expression once again was unfathomable.

But it was Shirler's look that told Nasa his injunction was probably too late. There was too much fear, too much hatred and too much violent history for any of the Elders to be spared.

Jarson's farmers-turned-warriors were chanting and stamping their feet.

Psyching themselves up.

Nasa recognised what was happening even if he was unaware of the concept itself. It was clear that Jarson was planning to lead the small army to hunt down the remaining Elders and confront whatever the jag-jag was.

"We need to get back to the city," Tareck said, gesturing at the young woman whose condition was worsening.

"We will, we will. But we can't let them slaughter their way through the rest of the Elders and their followers."

Tareck shrugged. He was concerned about the woman but the rest of it he couldn't be bothered with.

Jarson had sent scouts on ahead to reconnoitre the Elders' compound. They reported that only one Elder had been identified but there were up to twenty women soldiers and some older women whose role the scouts had been unclear about.

Quietly the main building in the Elders' compound was surrounded.

"They'll know we're here. The jag-jag sees everything."

It seemed that even Jarson, if not fearing the jag-jag, was nonetheless wary of it.

Suddenly, two of the fierce leopard creatures bounded out of the building and leapt on the first two men they came to, before they had a chance to protect themselves. The initial horrible screams died quickly as the two men died, each having had their throats torn out.

"Mother's heart!"

Nasa's exclamation masked the thuds of both his and Tareck's weapons as the two leopards were shot down.

With wild screams and shrieks, two old women rushed out of the building and started flailing Jarson's soldiers with whips. Then they were silent and still.

"Stay on your feet!"

Jarson's cry halted the motion of many of the men to drop to their knees.

"Kneel!"

The white-haired man, naked to the waist, strode to the edge of the veranda and waved at the mass of people to prostrate themselves. Caught between Jarson and the Elder, nonetheless most stayed upright.

Then mayhem broke out as the women soldiers poured out of the buildings surrounding the clearing and attacked Jarson's men. The women were outnumbered but were trained soldiers; the men were farmers, little used to such fighting. More proficient as archers than swordsmen the fight became one-sided. Even when a woman was isolated and surrounded, she seemed able to beat off the attacks of the men. The toll amongst the men mounted.

"Nasa, we must do something. The women will win!"

Tareck, a trained soldier himself, could see where the battle was going. But Nasa was focused on the veranda and the Elder. He'd been joined by a wizened old woman and the largest of the fierce beasts Nasa had ever seen. Held on a chain, the animal sat next to the Elder, silent but watchful. It was an impressive sight.

"The jag-jag?" Nasa muttered.

Nasa might have been averse to killing people but wild beasts were different. The animal collapsed with a sigh rather than a groan as his bolt entered its chest. The volume of the old woman's screech then exceeded anything that Nasa had ever heard from a living being. Dragging the Elder's short sword from its scabbard she flung herself off the veranda and leapt towards Nasa. Her second shriek was of a different character as she impaled herself on the spear of one of the men surrounding Jarson.

"No, no, no!"

But Nasa's cry was too late. The Elder fell backwards, impelled by the momentum of the many arrows that had struck him.

As the fighting ceased there were only seven female soldiers left alive. Nasa was downcast. Jarson, Shirler and Merien were exultant and couldn't understand why the two men from the city weren't. Violent death had for a long time been a part of the forest people's lives, even if the Elders had supposedly been against taking life. For them, however, it was simply a matter of resources; the concept of the sanctity of life hadn't developed in the forest.

It was all over. Nasa and Tareck looked on as the forest people slowly began to comprehend that their lives of subservience to the Elders and the jag-jag were over. They prepared to depart.

"But you must stay. There will be feasting and dancing; the Elders wouldn't allow dancing."

But Jarson quickly realised that the two men wouldn't be persuaded.

Nasa, however, as keen as he was to get back to Sorak, still spent some time in private conversation with Jarson establishing a means of future communication and offering an open invitation for the forest people to come to the city whenever they wanted. Nasa had no idea if this invitation would ever be accepted or whether he might ever need to seek their help in the future.

The injured young woman, who at last they were told was called Remme, was loaded onto another small cart, and as the distant star passed overhead Nasa and Tareck set off, pulling her carefully across the plain. They were far from confident she would survive the journey.

* * *

The guards at the yellow gate couldn't believe their eyes. Never having seen wheeled transport before, they mustered in force, ready to take any action if this strange thing was to prove hostile. Being pulled by two men, and with a woman apparently lounging in it, whatever it was, it was only as it got up close that they began to understand what they were seeing. Nasa and Tareck were amused and surprised by their reaction.

Nasa called the gate guard commander out, introduced himself and asked for an escort to get the cart and the young woman to the administration buildings adjoining the Senate. The poor state of the young woman was enough to energise the guard commander. Tareck accompanied Remme to the medical facility and continued to spend time with her as she recovered.

* * *

"You are welcome," Sorak said as Nasa joined her in their private quarters. "Much has happened since you went away."

26

Sorak was fascinated by Nasa's description of the forest people and their overthrow of the Elders. Like most people in the city she'd only recently become aware that there were other inhabitants of the planet; inhabitants whose origins must necessarily be the same as their own. Inevitably, she also pondered on whether there might be yet other inhabitants of the planet that they still didn't know about.

As with Nasa, the similarities with what had happened in the city weren't lost on Sorak.

"It seems the rebellion had been building up for some time. We arrived as the final confrontation was about to take place. The Elders claimed not to approve of violence and killing, but they'd created this mystical jag-jag who did the killing for them. A jag-jag was one of the predators from the plain. How they captured the beast and tamed it we couldn't find out. How they were able to get it to breed is another mystery."

Sorak was aware that, as a result of his trip into the forest, Nasa had reacquired the spirit of independence that she hadn't seen for many cycles. She was pleased that he was back to something like his normal self. Having no official role in the city had clearly been a problem for him.

What future relations with the forest people might be, Sorak gave no thought to.

But with a range of problems of her own building up, Sorak was simply happy to have her partner back with her. And for the brief period until the distant star returned she was simply happy to have Nasa within touching distance!

* * *

Sorak as always, was up with the distant star; it was the habit of a lifetime. And as always, Marwek, her assistant, was in her office in the Senate building before her. Outside the office, Lecktan, the young female senator, and Lenrick the guard commander, were in deep conversation, barely conscious of Sorak passing them as she entered. Something was clearly wrong.

She called her two principal supporters into her office.

"Anstan has called for all women who want a return to the old regime to gather in Sector Seven. Pilar and Pelar and their group are planning to infiltrate the gathering," Lenrick reported.

Sorak wasn't sure what was worse – the gathering or the twins' foolhardy plan.

But she'd underestimated the two sisters. All too conscious of their now rather rare blackness, they had no intention of themselves being present in Sector Seven. Unbeknown to Sorak until the meeting, they'd recruited two old ex-soldiers to their group: Risak, who would have been well-known to her, and Sinak, an ex-tenant from the staff of one of the old sector governors. Sinak knew of Sorak, but was unknown to Sorak herself.

That there were older ex-soldiers still loyal to her, Sorak found gratifying, but she wondered just how many there might be. She certainly needed such allies.

But by the time the patrols got wind of the gathering and reported to Lenrick, it was already taking place.

***

"Pastak!"

"Risak!"

The two ex-officers acknowledged each other warily. Keeping to the edge of the main group at the gathering, which was taking place in one of the larger communal areas in Sector Seven, the two women were both clearly surprised to see the other there, and equally clearly concerned to know what their status was in the proceedings. It was a difficult moment for Pastak; known to Risak as a friend of Sorak's, she had no idea what the other woman's affiliations were. That Risak was a former colleague and admirer of Sorak, Pastak was aware, but that didn't necessarily speak for loyalty.

Fortunately, with Anstan newly arrived at the gathering, no one took much notice of the two women or sensed the tension between them. Both knew that they each had to understand the meaning of the other's presence; both would need to recognise that neither was a true supporter of Anstan.

"You are welcome, Pastak."

It was a civilian who interposed herself between the two and addressed the old officer. Clearly not sensing the tension, the civilian even offered an old military salute. Head bowed, the woman didn't catch the fleeting look of distaste that scudded across Pastak's face. Risak did. Not being entirely sure what the expression meant, she nonetheless felt more comfortable about Pastak.

Maybe she's not one of them. Maybe she's like me, here to observe.

"Anstan will need your military knowledge," the civilian said, "if we are to force the Senate to disband the male soldiers and force all the men out of the administration."

Now with eye contact, Pastak's face showed no expression beyond polite interest in what the woman was saying. Grasping the ex-officer's arm she steered her towards the platform at the end of the room where Anstan was addressing the gathering. Risak allowed the movement of the crowd to force her to follow the two of them. Although required to come to the gathering without arms, Risak fingered the dagger hidden reassuringly in the folds of her bulky tunic. Her sense that the meeting could quickly turn hostile kept her on alert.

I need to hear what Anstan is saying but I mustn't lose sight of Pastak. If the civilian were to be suspicious of her…

Risak really didn't want to think about that, but she knew that she'd have to act.

Anstan seemed to have finished her rousing speech in support of the women-run society and, after taking a short break for refreshment, she returned to the edge of the platform. Sensing the mood, she had more to say.

"None of this will happen unless we make it happen. And to make it happen we must overcome the forces of Sorak and the Senate. That is the challenge for us!"

More so even than in her earlier speech, Anstan had the gathering's full attention; they sensed action. Her voice was the only sound in the room. The silence was total.

"We must learn to fight; we must form an army; we must take up arms. Many of you are ex-soldiers. We look to you to form the basis of our army. And we must learn to fight Sorak and the Senate's forces on our terms, not theirs."

If Risak had had any doubts about where Pastak's loyalties lay, they were dispelled by the stiffening of her body as her fellow ex-officer realised what Anstan was proposing. But she was quickly distracted. The silence that had greeted most of Anstan's speech, as she'd elaborated on what she meant by forming an army, gave way to murmurs of conversation. She'd lost her audience as the more experienced of the women, of the ex-soldiers, also began to understand what was being asked of them.

The atmosphere was now charged with uncertainty as well as enthusiasm.

Unable to see who was murmuring, Risak nonetheless presumed that it was more likely to be the ex-officers, with their greater knowledge and experience, than the ex-troopers. She soon found that she was correct.

"Anstanmam, the Senate has…"

Risak was surprised at the supposed number of troops the former aged capan suggested were available to the administration, but she didn't think it entirely unreasonable.

"We don't have that many ex-soldiers. And there are many ex-soldiers not in service who don't support us. Do we have to fight them too?"

Anstan gave the old capan a rather patronising smile. She'd known that there would be resistance; such women as this capan knew far more about fighting than she did. But she had an answer. A mangeneer with a brief period of planning experience, Anstan had done her homework; she knew she'd need to deal with this group of women.

"I said that we must fight them on our terms. We will fight them from the derelict buildings, never in open warfare. That sort of warfare we cannot win. We will train more soldiers from civilian volunteers."

As she continued to outline how she thought they could employ guerrilla tactics, the old capan subsided into silence. Unconvinced, she wanted the old world back as much as anybody else, but her experience told her that what Anstan was proposing was far too risky. They simply didn't have the skills and or resources. Not that she was going to say that in this gathering.

The debate rumbled on. Anstan's impatience began to show. Both Pastak and Risak were quick to recognise that her military knowledge was limited and that her expectations of the ex-soldiers not entirely realistic. But Anstan knew she had to let the women talk themselves out before moving on.

But once again Risak was distracted.

"Pastakmam?"

The civilian who'd accosted the former officer had returned to her side and was urging her towards the front of the crowd and the platform. Pastak had been noted as one of the most competent of the ex-soldiers but Anstan's supporters needed some demonstration of her commitment to the cause. Silence returned.

"Pastakmam, well met!"

A grinning ex-capral with three or four ex-troopers began to surge around Pastak, elbowing the civilian out of the way. The civilian's protests were ignored. Risak edged closer. The capral she recognised as one of Sorak's former subordinates and one of her own fellow caprals once Sorak had left the city. The group was quietly manoeuvring Pastak towards a side door. It was being done so gently that no one apart from Risak seemed to have noticed what was happening.

What's going on here?

Risak was concerned to know but knew that she'd have a better idea of finding out if she didn't get too close to the little group. But what she'd do if the group left the gathering, she had no idea.

They left.

"Risakmam?"

The capral suddenly darted back into the community hall, grabbed Risak by the arm and pulled her out after the group. Risak grasped her dagger under her clothing in readiness for she knew not what.

"Mother's heart!"

How the capral and the troopers had rearmed themselves with crossbows Risak never saw. Equally, where the swords handed to her and Pastak came from she also never saw. But she was instantly distracted by screams and shouts from the community area.

Whatever was going on, the capral clearly intended that they should have no part of it.

Out of the communal building they wove their way around the old derelict barracks and dream-pits and headed eventually for the piazza and Sector Two.

Both Pastak and Risak were panting furiously at the pace of their retreat, much to the amusement of the still super-fit ex-soldiers. All of an age with Sorak, the capral and the troopers had been careful to keep themselves fighting fit.

Why, was yet another of the mysteries bearing down on the two former officers. A further mystery was why the party was headed into the maze of wrecked buildings that had once housed the slaves of the old female senators. It was an area that neither Pastak nor Risak were familiar with.

Recovering her breath as the pace slowed, Pastak finally summoned the energy to ask the question pounding through both her and Risak's heads.

"What's going on here, capral?"

"Pastakmam," the capral said as they worked their way up to the top floor of a small but luxuriously appointed building. "There are many women who don't want to return to the old days, who understand the benefits of having the men as equal partners, but who want to be able to live their lives without interference from the Senate."

It was very much Sorak's basic thesis.

But the capral never got the chance to explain any further.

Pastak and Risak were both aware of there being many factions in the city now, something that they found hard to relate to but which was a consequence of Sorak's changes. However, the idea that the administration itself might be resented, which is what Risak thought that the capral was implying, was almost a thought too far.

"Capralmam!"

One of the troopers who'd been keeping watch from the outside ramp was urgently calling to her leader. A group of shadowy figures was emerging from another derelict building and heading into the mass of accommodation that surrounded the rebuilt Senate building in Sector One. The trooper knew that there should have been no one in the area.

"We must see where they're going," the capral said. "You may come with us or stay here."

There was no chance that Pastak and Risak were going to stay out of the action. The troopers set off down the ramp at a trot, the capral and the two former officers following at a more measured pace.

"That's where Sorak and the senators live," the capral muttered, voicing the underlying concern.

27

Sorak was in pensive mood; not something very common with her. As she sat pondering the impact of the changes that she'd made in the city, a number of feelings niggled at her. She'd told Nasa that things were going well, but they both knew that that wasn't strictly the case. As much as she wanted to ignore the resistance to her changes, Anstan's actions were making this increasingly difficult.

Having freed the people to think for themselves, because of her military background she was increasingly surprised that her fellow citizens were becoming ever more undisciplined. Anstan and the backwards-looking women who wanted a return to the past, she could understand but not relate to. Pilar and Pelar, who supported the concept of gender equality and were prepared to take action to protect it, nonetheless seemed to Sorak to have no guiding philosophy beyond demanding the freedom to do whatever they wanted. And Sorak was also aware that there were women who were happy with gender equality provided it didn't impact on their independence. All of which simply said that the free society was working but the general lack of experience in developing such a world was leading to factions, to stresses and strains, and to incipient resistance to Sorak and the Senate's rule – and to incomprehension on Sorak's part.

Sorak had a sense of ingratitude when people seemed to criticise what she was doing and what she'd achieved. This was also something that she couldn't understand.

"But, Sorak," Nasa said, when in the quiet of their private quarters she expressed her bemusement, "you can't create a world where people are free to think and do what they like, and then be surprised when they think and do what they like."

"But..." Sorak knew Nasa was right but she still couldn't reconcile herself to the apparent lack of discipline that people were showing. She was a soldier by training. She'd always lived an ordered existence. Even in their hidden valley after they'd originally escaped the city, their life and that of their son had been dominated by routines and seasonal tasks that made their lives relaxed and pleasant.

"It'll take time. And while there are still those who recall the former days with regret, there will be a desire to return to those times. Once the pre-rebellion generation has passed, and the next one with memories from that generation, things will settle down."

"But we'll all be long dead by then, Nasa."

Nasa didn't know how to respond. Just as the previous system had developed over generations, so that which was replacing it would have to develop over generations. Based on his own reasoning it all seemed so obvious to Nasa.

Thoughts of the forest people flashed into his mind and he was drawing comparisons before he knew it. The Elders had ruled as the Senate had done, in their own interests, until eventually people could no longer live under their restrictions. More primitive but nonetheless with some sophistication, the forest people were going to have to evolve, much as they were doing in the new situation in the city. How could it be any different?

But Sorak was still troubled, Nasa knew that. But he also knew that she'd have great difficulty in accepting that the freedoms she'd introduced would produce the bad as well as the good. The key thing Nasa understood was that it would take a long time for Sorak's world to develop into the caring, sharing and mature society she was seeking. Nasa didn't know much about idealism as a concept, but he had a sense of it and its absence. The society of the city was never going to be as perfect as the one manufactured by the Senate in the generations prior to the rebellion. And with her background and experience, Sorak was never going to fully understand that!

Marwek charged into Sorak's private quarters without knocking. Her left arm hanging loose and bleeding, she was as pale as someone of her complexion could be. The peace of Sorak's and Nasa's evening was destroyed.

"Sorakmam," Marwek gasped.

Suddenly the small room in Sorak's private quarters was crowded with excited people, with flashing swords and with cries of pain and anger.

Marwek had no time to explain. Lecktan, the young senator, also covered in blood, and Rehack, another of Sorak's bodyguards, staggered through the entranceway, fighting some sort of rearguard action against an as yet unseen foe.

Both Sorak and Nasa hurriedly reached for their weapons and prepared in the confined space to defend themselves.

As Lecktan wilted under the pressure of the black-clad figures attempting to force entry, Nasa moved to take her place beside Rehack.

Who are these people?

It was the sort of nightmare Sorak had often feared. But before she could clarify her thoughts further, Rehack slumped back, fatally wounded. Nasa, thrusting hard into the chest of the assailant who'd struck the bodyguard down, caught the gasp of the figure as she collapsed; definitely a woman.

Another black-clad figure stepped into her space but was hampered by the two fallen bodies and showed more caution than her now dead colleague.

As Nasa prepared for a renewed onslaught he was aware of a sudden agitation amongst the remaining attacking figures, who he assumed were all women, who were trying to push into Sorak's small study.

"Hold!"

More figures appeared to be surging down the nearby corridor towards and into the anteroom to Sorak's quarters. The melee that followed lasted only a few brief moments. The black-clad figures withdrew, the bodies were pulled away and Nasa was confronted with a grinning former capral he didn't know.

"Sorakmam!"

The capral saluted as Sorak tried to focus on her face. Sorak knew the woman but couldn't trawl a name from the depths of her mind.

"Are you unhurt?"

This was a voice she did know. Maybe things would begin to make sense.

"Pastak?! Marwek and Lecktan are hurt. Rehack is dead. What is this?"

Another commotion was taking place in the corridor as Lenrick, the guard commander, and a patrol arrived. The ex-soldiers with Pastak and the capral shouldered their arms to indicate their peaceful intent. Another voice from Sorak's past, Risak, quickly began to organise the small body of troopers who'd saved the day.

With the dead and injured taken care of, at Lenrick's suggestion they retreated to one of the smaller council chambers in the Senate building. The three surviving black-clad women, faces now exposed, were escorted away by the patrol.

A superficial calm settled on the group.

Pastak and Risak let the capral tell their tale.

"We were at a Sector Seven meeting where Anstanmam was urging us ex-soldiers to join her and to help train an army of civilians. She knows she doesn't have enough supporters to attack you and the Senate and the soldiers you have. She's very angry about the male soldiers and has been urging us to kill as many as we can whenever we come across them."

The capral paused, looking for Sorak's reaction. Sorak just nodded for her to continue.

"There has been too much killing. All we want is to live in Sector Seven with our old colleagues and live our lives peacefully. We want to bring the food gardens in Outer Four fully back into production, as the civilians have done in Outer One. No one is getting enough to eat."

It was just what Sorak would have wanted to hear, but whilst Anstan was out there trying to energise her followers there was always going to be a problem and the capral's hope for a peaceful existence was always going to be under threat.

The conversation went over the events again and the situation in Sector Seven. Sorak was far from sure that Anstan's military resources were as poor as the capral was suggesting.

* * *

"So, who sent you?"

The patrol leader wasn't being very patient. The three black-clad women had been stripped naked and fitted with collars and chains in the old Senate prison. Left overnight in the freezing conditions and given the opportunity to reflect on their situation, the patrol leader really only wanted to know one thing. The raid had been well planned and was clearly directed at killing Sorak. This was a new departure in the warfare that was developing. The assumption was that the order had come from Anstan, but they needed confirmation since so far she hadn't attempted such a directly provocative action.

Sensing which of the women was the weakest, the patrol leader laid his whip across the back of the youngest of the women. Not much more than a girl, she screamed as the lash cut into the soft skin of her back. Three more strikes and the young woman collapsed onto her knees, weeping and muttering incoherently. The patrol leader sensed that she might be about to talk. But it was late and well into the night, not that that was apparent from the prison cell, so the leader lashed her again and declared he would expect an answer when the distant star arose again. This was not a good decision.

What he got was a corpse. It wasn't at first apparent how she'd died until one of the male members of the patrol pulled her collar back. It was clear that the chain that had anchored her to the cell wall had been pulled tightly around her neck, throttling her.

I guess she was ready to tell me who'd sent them.

The patrol leader's surmise was correct. Recognising that she was ready to break, the other two women had ensured that no information would be forthcoming. It was an appalling piece of ruthlessness that horrified the patrol leader.

"They will be punished," Lenrick the guard commander, said, "since no one else could have killed her."

And we still don't know for sure that you were sent by Anstan.

Nonetheless, no one had any doubt.

Sorak's new processes of justice were slowly gaining acceptance. But in the case in point the culprits were so obvious even Lenrick had doubts about having the sort of hearing that Sorak had introduced.

When told, Sorak was angry. Yet another wasted life.

Worse still, the incident had alarmed the Senate, or at least those senators who supported Sorak, and the administration.

Recovered from her wounds, Lecktan made it her business to note which senators didn't share the concerns, equating them to Anstan supporters. A purge of the Senate seemed to her like a good idea, but she knew Sorak would never agree. The senators were elected by the citizens as a part of her reforms. A list of names, however, was handed to Lenrick, and the guard commander slowly began to set a watch on these disaffected senators. It was another large drain on her resources but Lenrick accepted that simply arresting the suspected senators was no longer an option in the new society; they needed incontrovertible evidence.

28

Debates in the Senate and decision-making were becoming increasingly fraught. Sorak's proposals were opposed more and more as the senators who supported Anstan became more confident. Sorak was surprised and depressed by how many of the female senators openly or tacitly supported Anstan. Lost to a large extent in her own vision of the future, she couldn't see that progress towards it had slowed down. The advocates for putting time in reverse had realised that citing the indiscipline and disorder of a free society was an argument that won support.

But there were still those clear-sighted people who recognised that Sorak's vision was the only way to a future in the city.

"We must rule by decree," Lecktan the young senator said.

How did she know about that?

Lecktan never ceased to surprise Sorak. She recognised her as one of the cleverest people she knew, although she was perpetually bemused by how, and from where, she got her knowledge. But Lecktan had been shrewd enough from an early age to realise that the old administration slaves, now largely unemployed, were a source of immense knowledge. It was a mark of her intelligence that she also recognised that not everything from the pre-rebellion world was bad. One particular slave, 195 as was, who'd worked with Crenan, the old Senate administrator and erstwhile colleague of Nasa, had provided her with a whole range of insights. And not just insights; he understood the importance of practical help.

"I found this in the rubble of the Senate library," 195 had told Lecktan.

Inevitably, Lecktan had never seen a book before, but the partly burnt and crumbling document that 195 reverentially showed her fascinated her. 195 could read and write, as all such administration slaves could, and had, over the cycles of the distant star since the rebellion, copied out as much of the contents as he was able. 195's instinct that the book contained something of value was rewarded. He also had sufficient insight to recognise Lecktan as the person to share his knowledge with.

Sorak might have recognised the tome. In her youth she'd briefly been allowed to browse the old Senate library, until the senators realised that she was too undisciplined to be allowed access to such knowledge as the library contained. Perhaps more to the point, she might have understood what a Commentary on the Constitution was, as she had at least learned that the world from which their founders had come had been very ordered and had had everything written down for all to access.

"There is much wisdom in this book," Lecktan had said to Sorak when later they discussed the matter.

It was from 195's transpositions that Lecktan learnt what 'rule by decree' meant and what the benefits would be for them if applied in the city.

But Sorak's response to her suggestion had to wait.

* * *

It was several circuits of the distant star since the supposed attempt on Sorak's life. There was a new nervousness running through the administration which, when she heard of it, pleased and encouraged Anstan. Lenrick, the guard commander, had increased patrols in the more remote sectors of the city, and increased surveillance of those senators suspected of supporting Anstan. But as more and more intelligence was gathered it was apparent that Anstan's support, whilst considerable, was by no means universal, and there were several other groups beginning to coalesce around their own visions of the city they wanted to live in. This was just the sort of thing that made Sorak nervous, and which Nasa had tried to convince her was the product of allowing people freedom of choice. To a point, Sorak's nervousness was justified; these groups, factions, were perpetually at each other's throats, and their support for Sorak was uncertain despite largely agreeing with her view of the world.

Why can't people just live in peace?

Sorak could never find an answer to this question. Nasa would have said that there was no answer.

The pre-rebellion Senate had suppressed a whole range of instinctive feelings that had stemmed from the earliest settlers who'd come from beyond the distant star, and which over the generations they'd tried to eliminate. No one, certainly not Sorak, understood what the release of these feelings would lead to if freed from restraint. With no concept of personal property in pre-rebellion days, just taking what an individual felt they wanted posed the first major problem for the Senate and the administration. And with nothing to draw on as experience, they could only react as each problem arose. But inevitably, thievery led to violence.

"Lenrickmam, there are reports of a large body of women fighting in Sector Six around the closed arena. A patrol tried to intervene but both parties turned on them. We've called up all off-duty troopers but need your agreement before we deploy since it's likely they'll be resisted by both groups of fighters.

And since the runner took time to get here we don't know what the present situation might be."

Lenrick took time to digest her deputy's report. Such odd outbreaks of fighting amongst the various groups of women and men who were steadily trying to re-establish life in the various sectors of the city were infrequent but not unknown. For Lenrick, it was more a law and order issue than a part of Anstan's actions to turn the clock back. For Anstan, such violence would not be tolerated in the world she wanted to recreate.

Lenrick's biggest problem was the number of soldiers. The military strength had been markedly reduced and equivalent numbers of men trained up. For the administration this had two problems: insufficient soldiers and too many unemployed ex-soldiers. It was these latter who were the most quarrelsome.

Several parts of the old military headquarters in Sector Six were still habitable. And those parts that had been the quarters of the senior officers, the capans, and at least one general, were desirable residences. Several of the groups of people that were slowly forming around self-appointed leaders had taken up residence, and friction soon emerged over who should occupy the best quarters. In the old days citizens had just lived where they were told to live.

Sorak and the more perceptive of the senators and administrators were slowly beginning to identify both how people were reacting to change but also what the potential difficulties, created in running the city as a result of the freedoms they were trying to introduce, were going to be. So far no effective system had been devised to replace the old Senate's autocratic rule when disputes arose. But the need for a system of justice was steadily being recognised.

But such niceties weren't of much interest to the two groups of women contesting the former top-floor suite of the general who'd once commanded Sector Six.

The group in occupation comprised a mixture of ex-soldiers and civilians. The leader was an aging tenant from one of the former military units responsible for patrolling the plain around the city. Sorak would have known of her, even if she hadn't actually met her. The civilians were largely from the old manufacturing units that lay in ruins around Outer Three. With the destruction of these units, unlike the civilians in other sectors these people had no occupation to go back to, which made them a potent force in the increasingly fractured state of the city.

The group quietly working its way up the outside ramp and carefully checking out each floor, was, again, part soldier, part civilian. The civilians in this case were a small party of ex-warders and prison guards who'd been discharged from the Senate prison by Sorak when she closed the infamous gaol down.

In number terms, the two parties were equally matched. Why the old general's suite was so desirable and worth fighting for, none of the women would have been able to explain. They wanted it, and in Sorak's new society there were as yet no rules to say why they shouldn't have it. Property and ownership were still novelties, still requiring regulation.

The thud of crossbow bolts announced that the attacking party had secured entrance to the old general's suite. As three or four of the women entered from the ramp, firing as they came, their compatriots who'd worked their way up through the inside of the building rushed into what had once been the general's day room.

Screams and cries of pain filled the air, followed by a silence.

But the silence didn't last and was immediately broken by shouts of anger as the occupants, only some of whom had been caught in the initial fire, in their turn stormed into the day room, firing as they too came.

"Hold, hold!"

The aging tenant called a halt. The carnage was as appalling as it was pointless. Seven women lay dead, and five others, including the tenant, were bleeding from wounds. Only six women were uninjured – two from the attackers and four from the occupants of the suite.

It was just the sort of violence that was becoming endemic in the city and which sickened Sorak and Nasa so much, since what they were fighting over didn't seem worth the death toll.

"Patrol!"

As the survivors faced off and sized up the prospects for further fighting, the attacker keeping watch at the entrance from the ramp called the alert. No patrols had been expected, but more patrols had only recently been instituted.

Clearly sensing that something was or had been going on at the top of the building, the patrol carefully made its way up the ramp as the remnants of those involved in the fighting scurried away having navigated around the building to a second ramp.

Discovering the dead, and the injured unable to retreat, the patrol leader soon understood what had taken place and despatched her runner to urge Lenrick to send reinforcements. The leader made no attempt to follow the escaping party; they had little chance of capturing them and would only put themselves at risk.

Lenrick received the message but knew that by the time she'd mustered reinforcements the situation in Sector Six could have changed dramatically.

And it had.

* * *

As Sorak had slowly begun to discover, there was a whole range of groups, small and large, scattered around the city, some known to the patrols and some not. Having never been able to take a census, Sorak and the Senate had only the vaguest of ideas of how many people now lived in the city. This was a constant and growing cause for concern.

"There must be many more men than we know about," Lecktan had said at another of her informal meetings with Sorak.

Nasa, who was present, nodded in agreement. Although he'd originally come from an elite band of breeding slaves, he was well aware of the extent of the slave world of the now distant past.

"There are many quarry and other manual ex-slaves unaccounted for, and there must be many younger men bred by these people in the uncontrolled period after the rebellion."

Lecktan's knowledge was limited but she soon grasped what Nasa was saying; it accorded with her belief also that there had to be many more men than most women thought there were. But Lecktan also suspected that there were many more women than they perhaps realised.

"The question is, where are they, these men and women?"

"They could be anywhere," Sorak said, rather disconsolately. "Sectors Seven and Eight are the obvious places, but there are also plenty of areas in Sector Three, for example, where they could hide if they were determined not to be found."

Sector Three was a civilian area that none of the three of them knew very much about.

"I would reckon more on Sectors Seven and Eight. Very little of the old civilian activity went on there, and the areas around the arenas are ideal for large numbers of people to live undetected."

What Nasa didn't say was that the men in question were the least intelligent of the ex-slaves and wouldn't feel safe in areas where there were likely to be other people, especially civilians, of whom they would have had little experience.

And once again, Nasa was correct.

* * *

The feuding women in the old Sector Six general's accommodation had no idea they were being watched, any more than the patrol did when it arrived.

"Mother's heart, what was that?!"

The patrol members froze at the sound of a distant scream that ended in a groan. Clearly it was someone in their death throes. The injured tenant and her companions reacted in panic.

"They've been attacked!"

That the escaping women had been attacked somewhere nearby seemed obvious to the patrol, but what was not obvious for a brief period was by whom.

Then the general's day room was once again filled with a shouting, screaming mob of people as a body of a dozen, filthy but violently active, men stormed in. In the confined space the patrol had little chance to use their weapons, and they and the remaining women were all soon struck down. With senseless brutality the men decapitated the dead before leaving as precipitously as they'd arrived.

It took twenty of Lenrick's relief troops two days to finally locate the patrol and the two groups of women. The only clue as to what might have happened was the bodies of two aged and grime-covered men, each killed by a sword thrust.

The carnage in Sector Six and the existence of a body of feral ex-quarry slaves was an added complication for Sorak as the pressure from Anstan and her group began to ramp up. Sorak and the administration, in essence, had no idea just how many people, Anstan's group included, they were faced with. And it seemed likely they would only know when battle was joined, which Sorak and Lenrick thought imminent.

* * *

"Are you sure this is a good idea?"

Sorak had called on the Senate to endorse direct rule of the city by the administration, by decree as Lecktan had put it.

They'd agreed.

Nasa was not a happy man!

29

The incident in Sector Six caused great excitement amongst both men and women. No one was very clear as to exactly what had happened, but for Anstan it was a gift.

"They are animals. Giving men their freedom has made the city unsafe; every woman's life is at risk. The men must be forced back into subservience."

It was a considerable overstatement, but since she was preaching to the converted her audience largely agreed with her, and Anstan's analysis of the situation met with no dissenters. And in the way of these things, more and more examples of violent behaviour perpetrated by low-grade ex-slaves were coming to light all the time. And as Sorak and Lenrick, the guard commander, understood, with the relaxation of administration control this was probably inevitable. But Lenrick, unlike Sorak, seemed better able to accept what was happening as an expected consequence of freedom of choice amongst the citizens. Needless to say, Anstan was not.

And just as there was a number of pre-rebellion ex-soldiers still causing Sorak concern, so the same was true of low-grade ex-slaves, and the problems would persist until the entire generation had died off and been forgotten.

But what worried Sorak and the more thoughtful people in the administration was that the younger, post-rebellion men, like many of their female counterparts, were being drawn into the bad behaviour and violence. Since controlled breeding was no longer acceptable, a solution to this problem, in the short term, was hard to formulate, since any such solution had the potential to play into Anstan's hands.

* * *

It was several circuits of the distant star later and Lenrick's troops had failed to locate the hiding place of the renegade men who'd killed the patrol and the feuding women.

"We know they must be in Sector Seven."

One of Lenrick's patrols had captured an elderly ex-quarry slave but had been unable to extract any useful information from him beyond confirmation that his group was somewhere in Sector Seven. The old man, a known troublemaker, was sent to the new Senate prison. Founded on more humane principals, the prison nonetheless was unavoidably increasingly like its predecessor.

"Many more reports of men attacking women are coming in," Lenrick reported to Sorak; "information from Pilar and Pelar's group suggests Anstan is organising the reports. But they say too that, true or false, the reports are causing more women to listen to her."

This made Sorak both angry and concerned. Nasa had said that this would be a likely outcome; she was unhappy that he was proving to be right. Suddenly it looked as if her carefully managed introduction of new freedoms was beginning to unravel.

* * *

Anstan called her principal supporters from the meeting in the Sector Four barracks communal area to her quarters in Sector Five. She'd never revealed where she lived until that moment, well aware that Sorak and the Senate were assumed to have spies everywhere and would be only too happy to see her captured. There were twenty women crammed into the main room.

"The Senate has been suspended. Sorak is running the administration directly."

Four of the old female senators who supported Anstan had made their way to the meeting. Fearful of Sorak, as supporters of Anstan, they'd decided to join her rather than remain in Sector One. Well aware of how the few younger female senators like Lecktan thought, they correctly assumed that once Sorak was ruling by decree, they were likely to be arrested. Their departure to Sector Five was duly noted.

Anstan was as jubilant as anyone of her austere frame of mind was capable of.

"There will never be a better time. The violence of the groups of old men from the quarries has forced many more women to make their choice for the future. Sorak has no way of dealing with them, short of killing them all. And that, within her new way of running things, she can't do. We must ready ourselves."

Many of the surviving ex-military officers who supported Anstan had gathered together such of their former ex-troopers as they could locate and formed them back into fighting units. Equally, aware that ex-officers like Pastak and Risak and several of the caprals either supported Sorak directly or were reluctant to engage in fighting their ex-comrades, Anstan knew that they could well have a major fight on their hands. A civilian, her understanding of warfare and fighting in general was limited, and she was dependent on those around her for guidance. She was apprehensive rather than anxious about the outcome of challenging Sorak. But in the end, a confrontation and a battle seemed unavoidable.

* * *

What Anstan, however, didn't know was that one of the escaping senators, a supporter of Pilar and Pelar's group of free spirits, would report back everything she was now hearing to the twins. How much of the information then made its way to Sorak was another story. There were aspects of Sorak's freedom for all that Pilar and Pelar didn't agree with. For them the men working in the administration of the city had yet to prove themselves worthy of the trust that was necessary for a peaceful future. The role of the men was still an issue even amongst Sorak's supporters, even after several cycles of the distant star.

"So, they're gathering in Sectors Six and Seven to strike at the administration area. The best places to strike at them are from the buildings on the edges of the two arenas. Once they get into the open areas they'll be able to access the piazza in Sector Two directly. They mustn't be allowed to do this."

Pilar knew full well that their group and their allies didn't have the numbers to confront Anstan's forces in the open. In fact, Pilar was unsure whether even Sorak's forces would be enough, if the rumours about Anstan's strength were anything like true. But the twins, like Sorak, were used to fighting against the odds.

"Sorak must know something's going to happen. The patrols will have either been attacked or have become suspicious about being avoided."

Of course, Sorak did know something, but only that Anstan was readying her fighters.

Only when they'd deployed their fighters did Pilar and Pelar send word to Sorak, to report what their spy had learned.

Tension mounted all over the city. No one, woman or man, would be unaffected by the outcome of the events about to unfold.

* * *

Away in the forest, through the mysterious means that Nasa was never able to quite understand, the news that some sort of eruption was imminent in the city was brought to Jarson.

30

The uprising, although expected, took Sorak and the administration by surprise when it actually happened. But since Anstan would always have the initiative, this was perhaps inevitable. The first that Sorak heard of the fighting in Sectors Six and Seven was when the news was reported back that Lenrick and one of the early evening patrols had all been killed.

This was devastating.

"We need to call the Senate together. Our response must be open, public and approved, even by a depleted Senate."

Lecktan, who'd rushed to Sorak's office with a number of other senators, all rather anxious men, knew that her leader was both right and that the time for such action had passed. What was needed now was a show of strength, but Lecktan had real concerns about whether that would be possible.

"All but three of the female senators have left," she said; "I suspect either to join Anstan or to avoid taking any responsibility for what has to be done. We can only rely on a limited number of women. Most of the men in and around the Senate and administration will probably be loyal but we can't rely on even that."

Lecktan knew that they had to be realistic about the support they might get from the men of the city; they were always going to be an unknown quantity.

There was a commotion outside Sorak's door. The guard had been increased, with orders to let no one through to her without specific approval.

"Let them through." Nasa's voice in the background was loud and commanding. Attracted by the commotion, he'd emerged just in time from the private quarters.

The Senate guards fell back, allowing Pastak and Risak to enter the room. Nasa followed.

Risak's jerkin was stained with blood. She had a chest wound; holding her left hand over it she tried to staunch the bleeding. Marwek, Sorak's assistant, also alerted to the excitement, hurried into the room with a medical kit.

"Sorakmam, most of the women in Sector Four have joined Anstan. The increased violence by groups of men in the outer sectors has convinced them that only a return to total women's control will stop the violence. About twenty women who didn't join Anstan…"

Risak stuttered to a halt. Pastak waved her away with Marwek.

"Unfortunately, we don't know how many women are prepared to oppose Anstan," Pastak said. "In reality, I doubt we truly know how many women there are out there in Sectors Five to Eight. But we do know that there are several groups of women who oppose Anstan but don't necessarily oppose women's rule. We don't yet know what Pilar and Pelar's group will do. If large numbers of women stay out of the fight, we could lose, even with every man being loyal… which they won't be."

What a mess.

Sorak's depression increased. This was not the outcome she'd envisaged when she and Nasa had decided to return to the city those few short cycles of the distant star ago.

"So, who's opposing Anstan?"

With no one yet in place to take over from Lenrick, Sorak was unclear who would be organising the action against those she saw as rebels. But Lecktan had already dealt with the problem on her behalf.

"Charlan, Lenrick's deputy, has taken all but the gate guards into Sector Eight. Sector Eight is where many of the ex-officers and troopers have settled, in the old barracks. Charlan reckons that's where we'll eventually have to face Anstan as it's a better base for her than Sector Seven or Five."

But it was Marwek, having dealt with Risak's wounds, who rejoined Sorak and gave her updated information from a runner who'd just arrived. For once, Sorak felt that Pilar and Pelar's reports would have been useful, and was irritated that at this vital moment the twins had disappeared.

* * *

"We have to choose the best place to confront Sorak," the aged capan-turned-senator said.

Anstan knew the old woman was undoubtedly correct. No soldier, she nonetheless knew that a good commander would always seek to choose the best ground for a battle. What she didn't understand was where this 'best place' was likely to be.

"Our forces are gathered in Sector Seven around the closed arena," the capan continued. "We need to seize Sector Eight quickly before Sorak reacts. Sector Eight is a far better operational area than any other sector, both for us, but also for Sorak."

But the new guard commander had already quickly realised this and the rebel women soon found that they were too late. Charlan, having seen the benefits of holding Sector Eight almost immediately, was busily occupying it as Anstan and the capan talked. The old soldiers who'd been living there for the last few cycles of the distant star, without any officers to guide them, allowed themselves to be ejected with very little fight. The question that Charlan had no answer for was how many had then gone to join Anstan in Sector Seven.

The news arrived.

"Anstanmam, Sorak's troops have taken control of Sector Eight. We've ordered our forces to concentrate in Sector Seven. We should try to draw Sorak's forces into the area in and around the open arena where our troops are stationed."

The tenant who made the report was one of the younger women who'd briefly served in one of the Senate's guard companies. What she was proposing was precisely what the capan-cum-senator was trying to avoid. But they had no choice; they'd been outmanoeuvred.

"Charlan has taken over as Senate guard commander, after we killed Lenrick," the tenant continued. "She's a good soldier and a tough fighter. The troops she has embedded in Sector Eight are largely men, younger than many of our troopers but without experience."

Anstan assumed that Sorak putting forward male soldiers was her being deliberately provocative. What she didn't know was that the Senate's forces were significantly outnumbered and that she therefore had an advantage on the ground.

* * *

"We can't stay in the background much longer."

Pilar was much more impetuous that her sister. Pelar was the cautious one. She was all too aware that until they had a better idea of how many women were prepared to fight with Anstan, they would be unwise to commit their forces. Their numbers were small but devoted, but devoted to a free and unconstrained future, not necessarily a future run by a Senate in Sorak's likeness.

Although the numbers of Defenders were indeed small, each one of them was young, enthusiastic and trained to fight in defence of their vision of the future. In fact, it was as a number of young women were secretly training themselves in the lost areas of Sector Eight that the idea of the Defenders emerged. The twins, after a life permanently in the shadows as a result of their being black in the days of the various male administrations, were used to living this hidden life, and used to fending for themselves. This self-reliance was the key feature of the Defenders.

* * *

Charlan, the new guard commander, a young woman herself, specifically chosen as her deputy by Lenrick because of her broader outlook, well understood the mentality of the twins and that seeking to force them into the impending battle was likely to have the opposite effect to the one desired. The Defenders would have to be allowed to join the battles to come when they were satisfied that the outcome would advance their vision for the city.

Sorak would have understood this.

* * *

Tareck, Sorak's most senior bodyguard, and Nasa's former companion in their foray into the forest area, was disturbed by the way things were developing. Unlike Nasa he was in contact with many of the invisible groups of men, and even some of the groups of civilian women, in Sector Six who were desperately trying to keep out of the action.

"I don't think Sorakmam realises how much opposition to her there is out there."

Tareck's statement to Nasa during a casual meeting in the administration offices was rather tentative. He knew he had no right to say such a thing but, as Nasa was quick to recognise, the man was worried about something he could do nothing about and could see no way of resolving.

"I think she's beginning to find out. The problem we have is we don't know how many people, women, are committed to Anstan, how many support her ideas but not her personally, and how many would be prepared to stand up and fight against her and her ideas."

It wasn't the answer Tareck wanted to hear.

* * *

It was as if the herd of beasts knew something important was going on. As they surged around the dilapidated old hut under the city walls, the party of ex-quarry slaves who'd taken it over also knew that something important was going on. Living in permanent fear after their slaughter of the women and the patrol, they were hungry, frightened and desperate for someone to tell them what to do. Old, several injured, there was a hopelessness about them that made them dangerous, but also vulnerable.

"Another patrol!"

Something like panic surged through the dozen or so old men. But the group of women who they detected creeping around between the city walls weren't official soldiers. Part of one of Anstan's groups, they were checking out how easy it would be to move around if they could access the space between the walls from Sector Eight via the green gate. The more experienced of the ex-officers supporting Anstan knew they needed to break out of Sector Eight in order to invade Sector One and the Senate and administration offices. Not only was that where Sorak would be, but it was from where the city was controlled and had to be a target for them. Although the easiest route was via Sector Two, that was also the most readily defended route.

Two parties had left Sector Eight via the green gate. Heading around the outside of Sector One and in via the yellow gate was the quickest route but again also the most heavily defended. Tracking the other way and accessing Sector Three via the blue gate and then to Sector Two was where the party disturbing the herd were headed. They never made it.

Approaching the wall-side hut, the party leader observed a filthy man lying in the doorway of the building, fast asleep. Despatched by a crossbow bolt but observed by his companions, the ensuing fracas left two men and all the women dead.

When they subsequently learned who the women were who'd attacked them, Sorak acquired a significant number of dirty, hungry and angry new supporters. But in practical terms, she acquired effective control of the areas between the walls.

31

Anstan had two key objectives in starting military action: she needed to neutralise Sorak; and she needed to prevent her major supporters in the administration, in particularly Nasa and maybe 147, the last male leader, from rallying the disparate groups of ex-military and civilians who opposed a return to women's rule. But most of all, she knew she had to overcome the resistance of the Defenders organised by the twins Pilar and Pelar. Whereas she, or at least her supporters, had a good idea how many troops Sorak might be able to muster, she had no idea of the strength of the twins' organisation.

"We believe we can capture all but the yellow gate without too much of a struggle. The yellow gate guards have a strong history of support for Pastak, their commander in the old days and a lifelong friend of Sorak's."

Nisak was a former tenant of the Reds, one of the military units long since disbanded, and a fellow officer of Sorak's from their youth. Sorak had always bested her in the fistfights the pre-rebellion Senate had approved of as a means of releasing the women's energies, as they carried limited risk of serious injury. Over the cycles of the distant star Nisak's animosity had matured into a deep hatred. And in essence, she'd become

225

Anstan's military commander, trusted much more by her than the old capan-turned-senator.

"So," asked Anstan, "how do we get to kill Sorak?"

* * *

In the quiet of her own quarters, certainly in the absence of Nasa, Sorak had contemplated her death more than once. She was basically a soldier; death was a military hazard. The violence that had always been endemic in the city and that she'd tried to suppress was a factor she knew she had to continually take into account as the situation began to deteriorate. And despite Nasa's optimism, in her heart Sorak knew that the situation in the city was deteriorating. There were still too many women looking to the past for it to be otherwise.

"We can rely on Pilar and Pelar, and their followers, but how many more women can we rely on?"

Sorak, like Nasa, was prone to talking to herself when stressed, and she certainly felt herself to be stressed. Nasa had recently returned from both a reconnaissance trip and a visit to their son Lenar and his partner Desak and their grandchild. They'd settled in an old civilian house in Sector Three, much to Sorak and Nasa's relief. What the future held for their grandchild, and all of the young children, was a major part of Sorak's concerns. They were the future of the city; and all of Sorak's efforts were directed at creating a worthwhile society for them to live in.

With the Senate largely dispersed and essentially only the male senators still fully in place, Sorak was now in effect a dictator. It was a concept foreign to all that she believed in and all she was trying to establish, and was something that worried her even more. Yet someone had to guide the city and oppose those who wanted to put the clock back.

"It's important you're seen to be active in combating Anstan and her vision for the future."

The speaker was one of the young male senators who'd rapidly gained confidence as the situation began to worsen and had become very forthright with his views. Lecktan, Sorak's main female supporter in the Senate, was wary of Keltan but recognised that he could be a powerful influence on the men of the city. Out of either ignorance or reluctance, the various groups of men in the city were generally disorganised and incoherent. The only seeming exception, worryingly, were groups of renegade ex-quarry slaves, and the like, who had both created mindless mayhem but also antagonised Anstan. But Keltan, like Sorak and Lecktan, was well aware that the main problem with managing the men of the city was this predominance of low-grade, ex-manual slaves. The more intelligent ex-administration and personal slaves were few in number and reluctant to put themselves forward.

What Keltan meant in his statement was that Sorak needed to be seen in the more remote corners of the city, where many of the people lived, often in communities of varying make-up, and often being civilians with unknown views on the future of society in the city. Nothing since the rebellion had been done to bridge the gulf between the ex-military and the civilians. Keltan believed that they were in danger of losing these people to Anstan by default by not attempting to recruit them to Sorak's view of the future, particularly as Anstan herself was a civilian.

But what none of Anstan, Sorak, Lecktan or Keltan knew was exactly how many committed supporters amongst these disparate groups the various factions really had. Nonetheless, the main concern for Lecktan and Keltan appeared to be that Anstan was beginning to gain increasing access to an expanding number of ex-soldiers, and was actively courting the support of the largely passive civilian women who'd never been involved in politics.

* * *

"There's someone to see you, Nasa."

Nasa was in his and Sorak's quarters when the messenger was brought in to see him, a gate guard from the yellow gate. Nasa was surprised to find her so far from her post. But that was soon explained.

"The guard commander ordered me to come. She didn't want to draw any attention."

Nasa was intrigued. He indicated that the gate guard should explain her commander's caution.

"A man appeared at the gate asking for you. He claimed to have come from beyond the Edge. He's certainly one of the forest people."

The yellow gate guards, as a result of Nasa's expedition into the forest using their gate, were amongst the few of the city's inhabitants who knew anything about the forest people. It was the first time that such a person had openly come to the gate. The guard commander, who had been privy to the expedition that Nasa and Tareck had made, once aware of what the man wanted, immediately sent for Nasa.

"He says his name is Jarson. He says he knows you," the gate guard explained.

Nasa acknowledged that he did indeed know Jarson, and hurriedly set off with the guard to the yellow gate.

The two men met in the guard commander's quarters at the gate. The conversation between them was wide-ranging and clearly reflected Jarson's concerns. In essence, what he said was that things had settled down in the forest community after Nasa's visit but there was concern about rumours of violence developing in the city. Once again, Nasa was astonished at how much Jarson knew, and irritated at his own ignorance of how he'd come to know it. Equally, he was unclear as to what the forest man was truly worried about and why. Clearly Jarson was looking to have closer contact with the people of the city but was worried, as he always had been, about being contaminated by the less attractive features of city life. Nasa tried to reassure his friend.

Finally the conversation turned to more personal matters as Nasa asked after the various people whom he'd met.

"We must continue to keep in contact," Jarson said.

Nasa could only agree.

Arrangements were made for more organised communications. Nasa made no mention of Jarson's visit to Sorak; she had enough to worry about and he saw no way that it could have any bearing on what was developing in the city. Although Jarson and the forest people's desire to have more contact with the city continued to niggle at Nasa, he realised he'd probably never know why, and all he could do was take the forest people at face value and if more contact made sense, they would make it.

* * *

The first serious clashes between Anstan's main group of ex-soldiers and the troops of the administration occurred in the area around the open arena, a familiar battleground. The fighting was inconclusive but instructive. The younger troopers under Charlan's command, when on equal terms, were always going to win over the older ex-soldiers. The lesson for Anstan, and more particularly Nisak, was to always have superiority in numbers. And as things began to develop, it became clear that she already did have this superiority in numbers.

The lesson for Charlan, again, not that she needed to be told it, was to avoid any staged combat and to concentrate on both guerrilla tactics and their efforts to capture or neutralise Anstan.

"Anstan is no general," Charlan said in reporting back to Sorak, "but she's certainly getting military advice. And one of the old tenants who was with us at the open arena said she thought she recognised Nisak, a fellow former officer, in the background during the fighting."

Sorak, of course, knew who Nisak was, and identified her to Charlan.

"Well, we knew there were always going to be some good soldiers in Anstan's camp," the guard commander said; "we'll be looking out for her!"

Charlan knew that Sorak wouldn't approve of deliberately seeking out Nisak to kill her, but she equally knew that on the battlefield there would opportunities enough to do so.

32

"There's news of heavy fighting in Sector Eight."

Marwek, Sorak's young assistant, made the report as soon as the information came in from one of the patrols that had been carefully scouting in the area.

"None of our troops are involved."

"So, who's fighting?" Sorak wanted to know.

Marwek had no definitive answer.

* * *

Pilar and Pelar had called the main body of the Defenders together in the still derelict buildings in Sector Two. Much of this area had been used by the administrators of the pre-rebellion women's Senate, and had been substantially destroyed as a consequence. The Defenders were deliberately avoiding Sector Eight until they were ready for action and were assured of achieving their objectives. With the yellow gate in Sorak and the administration's hands, they had freedom of movement right around the city via the areas between the walls that could be accessed from that gate. The twins were adept at using this freedom of movement. With their limited numbers they needed to be.

The twins had also heard about the fighting in Sector Eight. But unlike Marwek and Sorak, they knew that it was between a group of women who, whilst supporting a return to women's rule, did not however support Anstan, and one of the diminishing groups of ex-quarry slaves who simply resisted any manifestation of women's rule. It was the sort of pointless warfare Sorak had been unable to suppress.

"Best let them fight it out," one of the Defenders said.

It wasn't a universally supported view. More and more people were becoming aware that the erosion of numbers within the city, particularly of men, because of all the fighting, was increasingly threatening its entire future. Only Anstan, it seemed, and her most immediate clique, didn't see this as a problem.

"We must occupy Sector Eight," Pilar said. "And we must get control of the area around the open arena."

Like Sorak and the military officers in the administration, the twins were aware of the importance of not allowing Anstan's troops to establish a firm base in Sectors Seven or Eight from which to operate. The increasing fighting between the seemingly ever-increasing number of small factions was a worry for them as well as Sorak, but they knew they mustn't be deflected from the main enemy, Anstan.

Having spent most of their early life in hiding as black people, Pilar and Pelar had a far better knowledge of the obscure parts of the city than people like Sorak. They were beginning to put this knowledge to good use.

The Defenders had gathered in Sector Two in order to consolidate their forces before they got into any serious fighting. Sorak and the forces of the administration were doing the same in Sector One. Both parties were aware of their inferiority in numbers compared with Anstan's gathering army. Both also knew that there were unknown numbers of both men and women under arms whose loyalty was uncertain and maybe even fickle. It was these unknown numbers of potential opponents that were causing both the administration and the Defenders to be so cautious.

As a result of this caution, the Defenders split themselves into a number of smaller parties, both to disguise their strength and to make it easy to pass between the walls.

As the first of these parties moved out through the inner yellow gate and around between the walls, the twins knew that their first challenge would be at the blue gate. They had no idea of the status of the gate's defenders or where their loyalties might lie.

But they were in for a surprise.

"Male soldiers are holding the gate," the scout sent forward to reconnoitre had reported back. This was unexpected.

But as they edged forward what they saw was a small knot of dirty, scruffy ex-quarry slaves, fully armed but not apparently threatening. These it turned out were the ex-quarry slaves who'd allied themselves to Sorak and the administration and who were only interested in the fighting stopping and their being able to live a peaceful and unstressful life again. Contact was friendly when the ex-quarrymen understood that the Defenders were also supporters of Sorak.

The subsequent parties of the twins' troops set off at intervals, heading into the area between the walls.

* * *

Sorak and Charlan recognised that the future of the city wasn't going to be decided by one cataclysmic head-on battle. Anstan and Nisak, however, felt that it could be, and certainly would have welcomed such a battle. They were justifiably confident that they would win. Reluctantly, because they were less than confident of success, Sorak and Charlan, in their turn, recognised that such a battle had to be avoided. Guerrilla warfare was, for them, the only solution. But none of these four principals knew how the situation was, in the end, going to be resolved. It was this uncertainty that was determining their actions.

* * *

In the same way, neither Anstan nor Sorak had ever heard of Merlak. In fact, when they each first heard of Merlak neither of them knew if it was a man or a woman.

But if Anstan and Sorak didn't know who Merlak was, Merlak certainly knew who they were. Merlak was a very knowledgeable man. However, being a black man, since the rebellion he'd kept out of sight of anyone who'd had anything to do with the administration. This was a sensible precaution after the massacre of the black and brown women of the Senate and administration in the early days of the rebellion. Black and brown people in the public gaze had consequently become rather rare.

Nonetheless, as Pilar and Pelar were witness to, in reality there were rather more black and brown people in and around the city than Anstan and Sorak realised.

* * *

As much to satisfy themselves that there were no groups of women or men hiding between the city walls, the Defenders went backwards around between the walls to Sector Eight, heading past the blue and red gates rather than more directly via the yellow gate and then the green gate. Until they got to the old herdsmen's hut the only evidence of people was in Sector Four at the water treatment plant.

"Someone's got the plant going again," Pilar said.

Fundamental to the operation of the city this was inevitable. The twins assumed it had been the civilians who'd formerly operated the water treatment plant who had returned. This was a worry, as the loyalties of many civilians were unknown. The Defenders had to pass right alongside the plant.

"How can they work here?"

Pelar couldn't stop her disgust showing, yet the foul area through which Sorak and Nasa/1562 had escaped all those cycles ago was obviously being managed, and managed far better than in previous times. Without the ex-slaves to do the most menial of the work, the civilians had had to modify the plant and develop more efficient ways of operating it. Nonetheless, it was still a foul place.

As they moved cautiously through the area they saw evidence of the people who'd been there, but where they now were they had no idea. Wary and watchful, the civilians working in the water treatment plant, hearing the approach of an unknown band of women, had headed into the old barracks area of Sector Four, but avoiding the ex-soldiers also living there.

The Defenders moved on.

The guards at the blue gate had proved friendly, and Pilar and Pelar had taken the opportunity to rest their troops there and to talk though their next moves before approaching the water treatment plant and heading on. They realised that as they got closer to Sectors Seven and Eight it would be more difficult to disguise such a large body of troops, even split into small parties.

But they still had to deal with one more obstacle.

Things were different at the red gate when the first party reached it. At first there appeared to be no signs of the guards, but they knew they had to be there.

Eventually, as they approached right up to the inner gate, they were challenged by the guards who'd stationed themselves on the inner wall gate. The outer gate appeared to be closed and without a guard. Pelar, splitting the small party again into two groups, went with the smaller group to confront the guards on the wall. The guards hurried down the ramp to meet them. Would they try to confront the Defenders? They would, and did.

With the gate guard distracted, the larger group managed to get past unnoticed as the guard took Pelar and her four companions into the gatehouse to interrogate them. However, the guard, also only being five in number, seemed disinclined to take issue with the Defenders, recognising that they were probably the superior fighters. They soon let them go.

The groups recombined when out of sight of the red gate and crept cautiously through the open herd area, keeping close to the outer wall until they moved towards the herdsmen's hut. In their turn the following parties also passed by the red gate. Seeing such large numbers of troops, the gate guards hid themselves away.

"Someone's working the food gardens by the gate," Pilar said.

Again the evidence of people, but with no physical signs of them, put the women on their guard.

There were no signs of the herds between them and the hut as they moved forward, which was probably a good thing as such a large body of troops gathering would have sent them into a frenzy that would have alerted the women in Sectors Four and Five.

Pilar sent a scout forward to check out the hut as she waited for the final parties to join them.

"There are people in the hut," the returned scout reported.

The twins decided to wait until they were at full strength before investigating further. They were planning to rest at the hut as their next destination was going to be the green gate and then into Sector Eight. That was when the real action was likely to begin.

* * *

Merlak knew about the hut, amongst the many other things that he also knew about in the sectors between the red and green gates. And as he stood in the shadows at the top of a ramp on the former military headquarters in Sector Six, where he'd been living, he recalled two things: he'd once been abused by a black senator in the far-off days before the rebellion in the very building where he was standing; and he'd been helped to escape the woman's clutches by a slave of the Senate administrator, 1562. 1562 seemed to have had a charmed life in those days, very much as a result of Crenan the administrator's favour.

And now 1562 is called Nasa and is the most powerful man in the city.

Merlak knew he had to contact Nasa and share his knowledge of the byways of the city with him. Merlak also knew he needed to do this because he was aware that Anstan's forces were larger than those of the administration and seemed to be growing as she managed to inveigle more and more civilians into her way of thinking.

For Merlak, Anstan was the worst thing to have had happened to the city in his lifetime, worse than the rebellion.

"But you won't win!" he shouted aloud.

There was no one to hear him.

33

Whilst Pilar and Pelar assembled their full body of Defenders outside the herdsmen's hut, Nisak was urging Anstan to go on the offensive.

Anstan was cautious; Nisak couldn't understand why.

"We have more troops," she was saying. "Sorak's forces are dispersed. The so-called Defenders seem to have disappeared. And the fighting between the various groups of women and men in the outer sectors can only mean that Sorak has to keep her troops dispersed. We must get into Sector Eight."

Getting into Sector Eight was a constant theme for Nisak. Anstan understood the military logic for this but some of the ex-officers from Sector Four were pressing instead for them to head straight for Sector Two and then into Sector One and the Senate and administration buildings. Nervous of Sorak's resilience and general toughness, they wanted to confront her and defeat her as quickly as possible. The longer they waited the more certain it was that Sorak would be able to enhance her capabilities.

Anstan inevitably was torn. And being a civilian, the ex-officers were rather in contempt of her understanding of military imperatives. But they were also concerned by Nisak's apparent hold over Anstan and the indecision she was showing at a time when decisiveness was required.

Unfortunately, Sorak was unaware of the fractured views amongst Anstan's supporters.

* * *

"Welcome."

Anstan had gathered the people she considered most important to the conduct of her campaign to her quarters in Sector Five. She was aware of the undertone of dissent amongst her followers and knew she needed to take command of the situation.

"We're getting messages of large troop movements between the city walls."

The twins would no doubt have been delighted to have their Defenders defined as a large troop movement.

"We must finalise our plans. Do we concentrate on Sector Eight first, or do we head straight for Sector Two?"

Anstan knew that this was the key issue that had to be decided.

But identifying the options was as far as Anstan got.

Screams and cries of pain, accompanied by all the other signs of combat, invaded the room where they were meeting.

There was consternation. No one had any idea what could be happening.

Nisak, who was at the meeting reluctantly, drew her sword and carefully eased the door open. A wild-eyed man, clearly an ex-quarry slave, or the like, thrust at her with a crude spear. Anstan was almost in need of a new military commander.

Struck down from behind, Nisak was astonished to see that her saviour was Pastak, friend of Sorak and sworn enemy of Anstan and herself.

And behind Pastak the surly features of Risak appeared, sword covered in blood and panting from the exertion.

The fighting outside the room continued but the sounds of battle were diminishing as the assailants were forced away for Anstan's quarters.

Anstan, to Nisak's disgust, had retreated further into the back rooms of these quarters.

"Pastak, Risak, you are welcome."

On hearing Nisak's greeting, Anstan returned. Her smile was a little nervous; the reality of what she was proposing, forcing the city to return to the past, had suddenly taken on a rather different aspect for her. The violence she was calling for was no longer remote and theoretical; suddenly it was very real.

"Pastak, Risak, you are indeed welcome."

Anstan had clearly interpreted the intervention of Pastak, Risak and their troops as support. Nisak, more intuitive, searched the faces of the two old soldiers. Her sense was that there was something other than support for Anstan behind the action that had just taken place. Of course, she was right.

* * *

Pastak and Risak had continued to live in the barracks in Sector Four but had had nothing to do with the body of women, young and old, providing Anstan with her military muscle. Respected, even revered, the two women were left to themselves but were tolerated rather than welcomed. And as Nisak had gathered as many of the Sector Four ex-soldiers as were willing for a move into Sector Eight, Sector Four had become depleted, under-resourced and vulnerable.

It was the arrival of two groups of warring ex-quarry slaves, looking as much for loot as for accommodation, that had changed the situation for Pastak and Risak.

Uncertain as to how many men there actually were, Pastak gathered such of her own followers as she could safely locate and waited to see how the running battle between the two groups of men would work out.

"If they kill themselves off, so much the better."

Pastak was only too aware that such an outcome wouldn't have been approved of by Sorak, but she wasn't there.

In the end the killing was minimal. The smaller group of men, those unlikely supporters of Sorak, withdrew, preferring to preserve their numbers rather than fight to the death. Elated with their victory and finding very little to loot in Sector Four, the remaining party, now reduced to seven, headed off towards Sector Five. Detecting activity, and attacking any women they came across, they arrived at Anstan's quarters just after Nisak and her companions. Suspicious, and with a similar number of soldiers, Pastak and Risak had followed. They arrived very much in good time.

* * *

"So," said Anstan, attempting to hide her anxieties by continuing her meeting, "we were about to decide where to gather our troops."

Nisak immediately intervened. She turned to the two ex-officers.

"Before that," she said, "are you now with us?"

Pastak and Risak realised it was an obvious question to ask them.

"The men were trying to break into the Sector Four barracks. We chased them away and followed them when they headed in this direction. We had no idea you were here until it was apparent that the men were about to attack you. Not knowing how many of you there were, how well-armed, we drove the men off."

Pastak was rather stretching the truth. She'd known Anstan was using Sector Five but didn't want to alienate her and her followers unnecessarily. Equally, she had no intention of joining them.

Nisak didn't get the answer she might perhaps have been hoping for. But her question was probably better answered by the fact of the two women and their troopers immediately withdrawing.

It was only much later, when Pastak was talking through various aspects of the action that subsequently unfolded, that she acknowledged she might have helped Sorak's cause better by staying and listening in on Anstan's planning. But Pastak was too straightforward a person to practise such a deceit.

* * *

"Rather than Sector Eight, we should gather our forces in Sector Seven and then access Sector Two with as many troops as we can."

Anstan, her confidence restored, announced her decision, a compromise, but in her mind the best way to bring the administration forces to battle.

Foreknowledge would have been a benefit to Sorak and the administration but Anstan's assumption that she and her followers had control of the situation was not well founded.

* * *

From his vantage point at the top of the old military headquarters in Sector Six, Merlak watched the stream of armed women head through and around Sector Six into Sector Seven. Not being a military man, but being very intelligent and knowledgeable, it was obvious to him why the troops were gathering.

It was at this point that he declared that Anstan and her forces wouldn't win.

* * *

"Where would you attack, in Anstan's position?"

Sorak's rather sleepy question to Nasa as they settled for the night was more about her uncertainty of Anstan's thinking than any real military interest. Charlan would have prepared plans for all eventualities.

Nasa didn't respond.

34

As Merlak looked on, and Anstan's forces gathered in Sector Seven, the Defenders crowded around the battered herdsmen's hut under the outer city wall. There was a sense of anticipation; the hut was another part of the city's mythology.

Pelar signalled for silence.

Faint noises emerged. There was clearly some sort of subdued activity inside the hut. Aware that cycles ago the hut had been used by Sorak and Nasa during the defeat of the old male administrations, and then later by a group of feral children, the twins nonetheless had no idea who might now be inside. What they did know, however, was that such a large party as they were couldn't fail to have been observed by the hut's occupants.

By quick gesture Pelar instructed a few of their soldiers to the back door and another group to the front entrance; the rest to await instructions. With Pilar she led the way cautiously into the hut.

Dimly lit, at first they couldn't see what had been making the noises they'd heard. Piles of animal skins and other bedding littered the place, piles that in some cases appeared to be alive and moving. The troopers covered the bundles with their weapons.

"We mean you no harm," Pilar said loudly.

Nothing happened at first.

Then an elderly woman struggled from under one of the skin piles at the back of the hut. As she moved into the dim light of the only oil lamp burning she stopped, looked shocked and then retreated.

"A black woman," she muttered. It wasn't a response anyone had been expecting!

"Show yourselves!"

Pilar was losing patience. If all that there was were other old women like this one, all they needed to do was ensure that they posed no threat. And as five other such women struggled from under the piles of bedding, she knew that that had to be the case. These aged women were manifestly no warriors and never had been. But the question remained of what they were doing there.

An answer soon emerged.

A muttered conversation between a couple of the Defenders clarified the situation. One of the women had been recognised as a civilian mangeneer who'd once been in charge of managing the food gardens in Outer One.

It then transpired that all of the women were civilians. They'd all worked in areas now either occupied by administration forces or more recently by Anstan's troops. They'd all originally lived in Sector Three, an area virtually deserted after the rebellion until groups of lawless women and men began contesting for the living space. And when the administration soldiers had driven these people out, they'd then made the accommodation uninhabitable, without regard to the women who'd once lived there. It was another example of the gulf between the military and the civilians.

"We have nowhere to go. The soldiers took over our work areas and then destroyed our homes."

The woman's petulant whine irritated Pelar.

Typical useless civilians.

This of course was unfair and untrue, but Pelar was more focused on the need to confront Anstan's forces in a favourable situation for the Defenders; they didn't need this diversion. But clearly the situation needed to be dealt with in order to protect their rear as they moved towards Sector Eight.

One of the other women, less haggard-looking and more alert, interrupted the conversation. She was more alive to the presence of the armed band and why they might be there. And she was probably the youngest of the women they'd discovered.

And it was what she said that got Pilar and Pelar's instant attention.

"Anstan is a coward. She'll only fight if she can be sure she'll win. The more you attack her, the less likely she is to attack you."

Obviously the woman had no knowledge of Nisak's existence and of her influence on Anstan, but it was an unexpected insight into the mangeneer leader. Notwithstanding, the twins had no time to respond. There was a ripple of agitation amongst the women, all of whom had now fully shown themselves.

The woman who'd first spoken to them, and whom the twins assumed to be the boldest of the women if not exactly their leader, elbowed the other younger woman aside. Her gestures seemed to suggest that her companion had mental health problems, not that such a concept existed amongst the city people. However, since she seemed perfectly lucid to Pelar, her suspicions were aroused; but then the unexpected happened yet again.

A new voice, powerful and cultured, made itself heard.

"We believe Anstan's main forces are gathered in either Sector Eight or, more likely, Sector Seven. We also believe they will then head into Sector Two, and then Sector One."

An ancient white-haired but light brown-skinned woman hobbled out of the group and pulled herself upright in front of

Pelar. She was clearly confident in what she was saying. In her jumbled mixture of clothes Pelar couldn't be sure whether she was military or civilian, but what she said made sense and was useful intelligence to confirm what the twins had learned from other sources.

"Coward or not," the woman continued, "she'll have people with her who are not cowards and are good fighters. How else is she going to confront the Senate? But she'll not fight when the first moon goes pale. She's fearful of the time when the first moon loses its vermillion."

The planet's first moon was slow-moving and made only one circuit each night, unlike the second moon that made two. And the first moon's colour cycled from a full rich vermillion to a dull pale watery pink in a rotation that defined one cycle of the distant star into thirteen repeating periods.

Superstition wasn't something the people of the city had a name for either, but it was something they well understood. That Anstan was superstitious about the first moon on the wane, something else that the people of the city had no name for, wasn't unusual. They were just as inclined to attribute powers to things they didn't understand as any other species in the universe, and just as inclined to be fearful of them. Clearly, Anstan was no exception. But for an intelligent and practical woman it was a surprise to the twins.

Pilar and Pelar exchanged looks. The slave who'd saved them and nurtured them as children in the hidden backblocks of Sectors Six to Eight would never leave his bed during the bright period of the second moon's second rotation. As children, the twins had simply accepted this, so Anstan's foible didn't surprise them but it did set some interesting trains of thought in motion.

This is something to be exploited.

Being close twins, the fact that this thought occurred to both of them simultaneously was not unusual.

HEDLEY HARRISON

But they needed to move on. What they might do to take advantage of Anstan's weakness was something for the future. And both twins were also well aware that the whole thing might just be based on rumours and be nonsense. And so it later proved to be.

"We'll leave you some food. It would be sensible to remain in this hut until the fighting is over."

Pilar could feel the question: *When will that be?*; but of course she had no answer.

The Defenders left the women in better spirits than they'd found them in! But the encounter did nothing for their own spirits; they still had a difficult job to do.

Working back through the inner green gate, they established their base on the edge of Sector Eight closest to Sector Seven, using one of the derelict dream-pits for cover. Pelar sent out scouts to try to identify where Anstan's army was and where Sorak's troops might be.

The Defenders rested. Battle was imminent; everybody felt it.

35

"Nasa?"

Nasa was making his way carefully through the derelict buildings adjacent to the rebuilt Senate and administration offices. With no official role, and Sorak increasingly taken up with her military commanders, Nasa had taken to wandering around between the city walls. For him these were the city's most vulnerable and least defensible areas, something he wouldn't have been surprised to find that Pilar and Pelar had also already appreciated and exploited.

The woman addressing him was wearing a battered and filthy ex-ordinary soldier's jerkin, some sort of short dress or skirt and the sort of tall boots worn by the Senate guard in the pre-rebellion days. It was this mixed-up garb, rather than the voice, that attracted his attention.

In the dim light of the fading second circuit of the second moon, Nasa had a sense of familiarity as the woman's shining eyes caught what little light there was.

"I thought I would come and find you!"

Shirler? How can this be?

Recognition came in a rush.

Nasa remembered Shirler both as a fierce warrior fighting

249

to defeat the fearsome Elders in the forest, but also as the compliant young woman in his bed during the time they'd been making their way to the safety of Jarson's compound. But nothing stirred in Nasa's brain.

"You are welcome," he said almost mechanically.

Often a slow thinker, Nasa took his time to get to grips with the woman's presence, and more especially what she'd meant when she said she'd come to find him. His first thought was that more trouble had erupted within the forest compounds as the remnants of the followers of the Elders tried to reassert themselves.

But as Shirler came up to him and threw her arms around his neck, he knew that his first thought was utterly wrong. But repelled as much by her rank body odour as by her show of affection, he gently grasped her arms at the elbow and pulled them down from his neck.

"Shirler," he said softly, "why did you want to find me?"

As realisation began to dawn, asking the question made Nasa feel even more uncomfortable.

Sorak would have been amused and surprised by his uncertainty. Nasa the decisive had disappeared; Nasa the indecisive had taken his place. But Sorak would perhaps have been less amused, if still surprised, had she known what was going on in Shirler's mind.

Shirler, who'd crept across the plain and into the city via the green gate two circuits of the distant star previously, had had time to orient herself and to observe the comings and goings of the people in what was Sector One before setting out to find Nasa. Although she was unaware of it, she'd also seen Sorak and her retinue. Based on the intelligence that got back to the forest, and that so bemused Nasa, Shirler had a good idea who Sorak might be, but of course she had no idea she was Nasa's partner.

Finding Nasa so quickly, as a result of his habit of wandering around the byways of the city, delighted Shirler.

In his slave days, Nasa had had intercourse with many women as a good breeding slave, but also with Crenan the old Senate Administrator, where he learned to enjoy the sexual act for itself. But with his feelings for Sorak so powerful, his brief dalliance with Shirler had passed from his mind as a pleasant but meaningless diversion. But as he was now beginning to realise, this was not the case with Shirler. For her, her whole being had been engaged, and she'd thought of nothing else since he'd left.

Nasa needed time to think; as the sounds of a patrol or some other group of people began to emerge, he pulled Shirler off the street and into the building they'd been standing in front of. As he did so, he realised he was drawing her into what had been his old mistress Crenan's private quarters. He couldn't have chosen a worse place.

Much of the luxury still remained, although the rooms were cold and damp.

Shirler followed Nasa into the depths of the apartment, excited by what she misinterpreted as his intentions.

The sight of the washing station, and there was seemingly still water connected, sent Nasa's mind way back to his days as 1562, but the all-pervading stink that Shirler was giving off overrode the nostalgia.

What am I doing? If I get her to wash she'll expect…

The thought was overtaken by the reality of Shirler stripping off her clothes and quickly understanding what the washing station was for. Turning on the water, as Nasa had done for Sorak in the past, she plunged in.

Just go along with it!

The old pragmatic Nasa showed itself, albeit rather fretfully.

But Nasa knew that her just washing her body wasn't going to deal with the smell; it was coming mostly from her clothes. More in hope than expectation, he took off deep into Crenan's quarters to see if any of her garments had survived the predations of male administrations and marauding groups of both women and men. Amazingly he was able to find some undergarments and the sort of tabard the elite women used to wear. Since her military jerkin and boots, if cleaned, would no longer smell, he was satisfied. He set about cleaning them with what little materials he could find.

Why am I doing this?

Shirler emerged from the washing station no longer smelling but shuddering from the cold of the night. The clothes Nasa had found for her lay on the sleeping couch.

But Shirler made no effort to dress, cold as she obviously was. She walked up to Nasa and again flung her arms around his neck. And once again, since he wasn't expecting such a display of affection, he was taken by surprise.

"I came to find you," she said once again.

Such wanton behaviour was unknown amongst the people of the city until only the last few cycles of the distant star, and it took time for Nasa to understand what Shirler was really saying to him. When he finally grasped that she wanted to have intercourse with him again, he was confused, then angry, and finally unsure of how to react to the young woman.

At least, his brain was uncertain; he was aware as his erection grew that his body had a good idea what to do.

"Shirler…" he started to say, but she was kissing him on the mouth now and his protest was cut off.

How he got onto his back on the sleeping couch, with Shirler riding down on top of him, he later preferred not to think about. But he was suffused with pleasure that, to his horror and humiliation, he did remember.

"Nasa!"

There was alarm in her voice as she threw herself off him and scrabbled for some of the clothes that had now been scattered around the room. Then he heard what she had heard. They were no longer alone in Crenan's old house.

Nasa leapt off the couch, adjusted his clothing and drew his sword. He had no idea who might be searching their way through the rooms, but he did know he didn't want to be recognised. But that rather depended on who was out there.

"Nasa?" Shirler whispered again.

He signalled her to be silent and into a corner where the light from the oil lamp he'd found didn't penetrate.

Two women, as dirty and scruffy as Shirler had been, shuffled cautiously into the sleeping chamber. One of them had an injured leg and a chest wound bound with bloodstained strips of material. Not expecting there to be anyone in the room, she headed straight in and immediately laid down on the couch. She was obviously in a very bad way.

"Ahhr!"

The cry of alarm from the second woman indicated that she'd seen Nasa. She raised her sword. Without a tip, and badly damaged, the weapon was no match for Nasa's military weapon. But she made an attempt to engage with him. Clearly frightened and confused, her thought processes were painfully slow.

"Ahhr!"

Her second exclamation followed Shirler's appearance from the shadows and her approach to the dying woman on the couch. Pausing for a moment, Shirler's reaction then suggested that the woman was in fact now dead. Sensing this, the other woman set up a wail that Nasa violently suppressed by striking her across the face.

Typical of many encounters in and around the city, as the basis for Sorak's control began to break down, Nasa's reaction was now to try to get away from the house as quickly as possible before other less friendly people might appear.

There was nothing they could do about the dead woman. Grabbing Shirler, Nasa hurried her out of the building and into the area behind the Senate buildings whilst he tried to think what to do about her. He didn't have time to decide. Forcing her out of sight into another doorway, he stepped from the shadows and stopped the patrol that he heard approaching. A quick discussion with the patrol leader directed them into Crenan's house and the two women. The patrol leader, who recognised Nasa, asked no questions.

When they were alone again, Nasa hurried Shirler to the green gate, hoping the gate guards wouldn't interfere. They didn't. He then accompanied her well out onto the plain before leaving her. He needed her to return to the forest. Frightened by his sudden fierceness, she went, the tears streaming down her face causing Nasa some anguish, but he had no other choice; she couldn't remain in the city.

36

Having seen a tearful and clearly unhappy Shirler set off across the plain, Nasa decided that he needed to do something vigorous to distract himself and to help him deal with what had just happened.

The idea that the forest woman had developed feelings for him took time to register. But now it had, at least she knew he had a partner and could have no place in his life. But try as he might, Nasa was never going to be able to dismiss Shirler completely from his mind. And on occasions in the future, he had vague premonitions that he would see her again.

It had been still dark when he'd seen her off but he'd climbed the outer city wall just as the distant star began to rise over the horizon. As he looked out over the route that Shirler would have taken, he thought he saw movement in the distance but knew that it was probably his imagination. Since the wild beasts of the planet almost never came out onto the plain, he had no concerns for her safety.

"Come on, move yourself!"

With nothing planned for his day he decided to circumnavigate the city, travelling along the outer wall. It was a journey that would take him all day. Until he got to Sector Six onwards, he didn't expect to see anything.

Passing over the yellow gate and overlooking the now abandoned quarries, the distant star had passed overhead by the time he traversed the blue gate and found himself looking down on the water treatment plant. Memories stirred again from his deep past, but thoughts of Sorak still generated the feeling of discomfort that his dalliance with Shirler had created. Feeling disloyal to Sorak all over again he was about to move on when he became aware of movement in and out of the buildings of the treatment plant.

"If it's working, there will be people operating it," he told himself. And he knew that it had to be working otherwise there would have been problems all over the city.

But as two men, he suspected from their dirty appearance to be ex-quarry slaves, appeared, dragging a young girl, his attention was fully engaged. He hurried to the top of the ramp that led down to the plant, to get a better view. The girl's screams now became frantic. It was all too clear what was about to happen. It was only after the action was over that he realised the girl was pale brown-skinned, another unknown survivor.

"Hold!"

Aware that there might be more men about, Nasa nonetheless ran down the ramp, sword unsheathed.

Since one of the men was already trying to force himself into the girl, Nasa was initially confronted with only one opponent. His determination not to kill was lost in the heat of the moment and the sight of the violence he was trying to prevent angering him. Nasa ducked away from the man's wild slash with his short sword and thrust his own into his chest.

"Mother's heart," he muttered when he realised what he'd done.

But he didn't have time for self-reproaches. Desperately clawing up his lower garments the second man lunged at him as he kicked the girl aside. Angered again by such gratuitous violence he parried the wild swing and again thrust his sword at the man's chest. But although encumbered by his disorganised clothes, this second man was a far better fighter than his colleague and pulled back to avoid Nasa's blow.

Standing back to sort himself out, the man then awaited Nasa's attack. But Nasa wasn't interested in any more killing. He lowered his sword to signify he had no intention of engaging the man. But as he watched, the man crumpled forward, a crossbow bolt buried in his back.

"Mother's heart!" Nasa muttered again, uncertain as to where the bolt had come from.

"Merlak!"

As Nasa moved to assist the young girl, he was aware of the silent arrival of the former slave. But if he'd fired the crossbow, he'd abandoned it before approaching. Nasa didn't have time to think that this was odd; the girl's retching cries of fear and anguish drew him to her.

It took Nasa some time to reassure the girl and to convince her that neither he nor Merlak meant her any harm.

Still alert for the possibility of other men being about, the three of them eventually sat quietly on the ramp as Nasa pondered on what they should do next.

The two women whom he'd encountered before, and the violence offered the young girl now weeping silently beside him, gave him food for even more thought. He was aware of what Sorak was trying to do, but as he saw more and more examples of the people of the city behaving in violent and cruel ways, he was niggled by thoughts forming in the depths of his mind.

There's no way we can go back to the past; women and men must be equal, but the harsh discipline of the old women's Senate certainly saw to it that there were no such incidents as we just interrupted.

Nasa couldn't believe he'd just thought that, but equally he couldn't find any strong arguments against it. The idea that the people of the city were somehow imperfect was almost a thought too far for someone brought up in the old rigidities. But that was what was very obviously emerging.

Maybe Sorak is expecting too much from people. In the old days people knew how they should behave. Giving them freedom of choice maybe isn't the answer, if the strong are to overcome the weak.

Nasa hadn't spoken out loud, but Merlak was looking at him as if he had.

But they had more practical considerations to deal with.

"So, where did you come from?"

It was Merlak who started to question the young girl. Giving her time to compose herself even more, he gently probed at her presence in the area and what had brought her there.

"There are many people who live in Sector Five and Sector Six."

Both men were surprised that she seemed to understand the geography of the city at her young age. But as they listened, they were introduced to a world that Nasa at least didn't know existed. What Merlak knew of the world that was described, Nasa had no idea.

The girl, who they found was called Thrillak, had been living with a group of ex-soldiers, officers as Nasa deduced from her description, one of whom she named as Nisak. It was a name Nasa knew of from Sorak, which put him on even greater alert. So much so that Merlak seemed to realise that Nasa's attitude had changed. Merlak himself was well aware that Nisak was Anstan's favoured military commander.

"Do you know who Anstan is?" was the next question.

Both men were surprised by Thrillak's response to Nasa's question.

She clearly did know who Anstan was. Her body stiffened, her face clouded over and neither Nasa nor Merlak could understand the fierce mutterings she then embarked on.

"Hold, hold!" Merlak said.

But by then she was crying loudly and with heart-rending cries of anguish. The men watched her unbelievingly. No one in Nasa's experience had ever reacted to Anstan in this way.

"Anstan!" she almost spat out. "Anstan killed my mother!"

Silence! Nasa knew what the concept of mother meant; he wasn't sure whether Merlak did. But it didn't matter. The floodgates just opened as Thrillak began to speak in a low voice.

"My mother was a mangeneer, just like Anstan. She worked in an office in Sector Three. Weapons manufacture; she was very important. Anstan worked there too. I don't know what she did, but my mother definitely knew her.

"It was after the rebellion. The men were in charge. They could do anything. And one of the office slaves, former office slaves, having worked for her for many cycles, apparently had feelings for my mother. My mother didn't object and they did what people were then beginning to do. And then there was me. Anstan was furious. It was none of her business, but she was always on about the days when women were in sole charge. My mother and the former slave, whom Anstan didn't even know, doing what they did was exactly the sort of thing that Anstan opposed.

"When I was born my mother wanted to go back to work. People were given rewards, money, for working; she needed it for me. But Anstan tried to prevent her from working, and then one day they found her body in a pit in one of the old quarries. The former slave said that Anstan had arranged for my mother to be killed; he was certain of it. Then he disappeared; went into hiding to avoid Anstan's killers. I eventually found out that he lived in Sector Five, that's why I went there, but Anstan and her followers had got there before me so I had to hide. The water treatment plant seemed to be the best place, but there were bad men there!"

As the girl slumped, exhausted, the two men were both lost in their own thoughts. Merlak asked a few more questions that

Nasa didn't take much notice of but which elicited information that told Merlak who Thrillak's father was, and that he'd known him.

Nasa's thoughts were more about the different side of Anstan's character that Thrillak's story revealed. It somehow made Nasa feel better about opposing Anstan's desire to return to the past.

Nevertheless, it transpired that Thrillak's father had survived and was living safely in Sector Five.

"We should take her back to Sector Five and hand her over to her father."

Merlak was very clear that this was what they had to do. Whilst Nasa agreed with him, he was less than happy about being recognised in Sector Five. With a battle between Anstan's forces and those of Sorak and the administration pending, he was justifiably fearful for his safety.

Merlak was shrewd enough to perceive Nasa's problem. He addressed the girl quietly and reassuringly.

"I will take you to find your father, but first I must talk to my friend here."

But before the conversation could get underway two men appeared from the water treatment plant area; clean, tidy and obviously acquainted with Merlak, they were clearly working with him. One of them was carrying a crossbow that answered a raft of questions in Nasa's mind.

"We've been observing Anstan and her forces from Sector Six," Merlak said; "there are things you should know."

Ignoring Thrillak, it took Merlak some time to explain the dispositions of Anstan's troops that they'd observed and to discuss with Nasa what they might mean. However, in the end, one thing was clear, Anstan, or rather Nisak, was planning to confront Sorak's forces in the area around the open arena, with the obvious intention of then pushing through into Sector Two. It was what Nasa would have done.

"From contacts my friends here also have, it seems that Anstan and Nisak want to keep engaging the administration's troops as much as possible until they've destroyed as many of them as they can, and then they'll have the overwhelming force they need to ensure they can re-enslave the male population."

To Nasa it all seemed plausible. He was certain Sorak didn't have enough troops, and that was without taking account of other hostile groups, numbers unknown. Anstan appeared to have the advantage.

If only we knew how many of the other groups in and around the city would support us, things would be easier.

But this of course was both the big unknown and the main thing Anstan and Nisak believed gave them the edge.

Delivering Thrillak to her father was easily achieved, as the old man, anxious about her safety, was on the lookout for her.

* * *

Tareck, Sorak's bodyguard and Nasa's companion on his travels to the forest people, sought Nasa out once he'd returned to Sorak's quarters.

Tareck had heard about the mysterious woman who'd sought Nasa out. Secrets were impossible in the close society of the city. The guardsman had guessed correctly who the visitor was.

As Tareck quizzed him about Shirler and talked about the forest people, he said something that grabbed Nasa's attention.

"We could use a few of those bowmen!"

Both men had been impressed by how effective the farmer bowmen had been when the fanatical supporters of the Elders had tried to suppress the uprising. And it was a thought that had stayed with them.

Nasa's next meeting with Tareck was brief, secret, and took place just before the distant star disappeared and the city gates were closed. He didn't report this conversation to Sorak.

37

As Anstan's real character began to emerge, Sorak, and Nasa in particular, were increasingly determined to bring what they saw as yet another rebellion to a successful conclusion. That was not to say that they didn't understand the difficulties this was going to involve. Their major concern, inevitably, was how to do this when the forces ranged against them outnumbered them.

"We shouldn't have to abandon whole areas of the city, but that's what we'll have to do if we are to defeat Anstan, and even then it isn't certain we'll be able to."

Sorak found Charlan the guard commander's analysis depressing, if realistic. Nasa had nothing to say.

* * *

Sector Eight was a complicated area of the city, seemingly having been abandoned for many cycles of the distant star. Very little of the area was residential but that wasn't to say that people didn't live there. The old dream-pits, the Senate-approved pleasure areas from the old pre-rebellion days, although neglected and in poor condition, still provided homes for significant numbers of people, albeit with a continuously changing population of both genders determined not to be discovered.

"In fact," Nisak, Anstan's military commander, said, much as Sorak might have done, "we really don't know how many people actually live there."

Anstan's ordered mangeneer's brain found this hard to believe. Nor did she fully understand Nisak's concerns over the uncertainties that this ignorance introduced.

What they were discussing was an outbreak of fighting or, more accurately, an outbreak of attacks on isolated groups of their soldiers in the derelict buildings of Sector Eight. Quick and clinical, a small number of attackers would fire on one of Nisak's patrols, wounding rather than killing, but still taking a slowly increasing number of their troopers out of action.

"The Defenders?"

Nisak wasn't so sure, although she knew Anstan had a particular dislike of the twins and their private army.

"At least two of the wounded troopers reported men amongst the attackers. Dirty, smelly, ex-quarry slaves seemingly."

Sorak, if she'd known of these guerrilla attacks, might have recognised the small group of men involved.

But for Nisak, it all added to the confusion; confusion at a time when clarity was the thing that they needed most.

"We must find these men and kill them."

Anstan's disregard for male life was well known to Nisak, whose adherence to her cause was as much driven by his hatred of Sorak as by a genuine desire for a return to the past. If the truth were known, Nisak was happy enough with the world that Sorak was trying to create; it was the woman creating it that was her problem. If there had been another way of getting rid of Sorak, Nisak would not have been so keen to support Anstan.

And for Nisak, just killing off anyone who interfered with Anstan's pursuit of the past was not a solution likely to achieve a stable future.

"More importantly, we need to know if they're working for Sorak and the administration."

Nisak suspected they were freelancing, but saw the men's efforts to disable rather than kill as reflecting Sorak's influence. Needless to say, she didn't share this thought with Anstan.

But the debate, as so often happened, got no further.

"Nisakmam, you should come to the open arena. We've captured a body of administration soldiers. Quilik, Formack and some of the older women want to kill them. But you said no unnecessary killings."

Quilik and Formack, as Anstan knew, were tenants from one of the former military units. They were proving to be the most aggressive of her commanders and were often at odds with Nisak's more measured approach to combating Sorak and the administration. And this was just the sort of situation that exposed the differences between Anstan and her commander.

"No unnecessary killing?" Anstan queried. "Surely the only way we'll be able to make the changes we want is by removing the opposition completely."

This was Anstan's philosophy, but Nisak believed that such an objective wasn't achievable and in the end a compromise would be necessary, a compromise that wouldn't deplete the numbers of citizens any more than necessary.

Nisak ignored her leader's question by heading out with the capral who'd brought the news from the open arena.

And at the open arena there was a complex standoff. The platoon of Senate guards, as the captured troops turned out to be, were gathered defensively against the outside wall of the arena, whilst an argument between what they recognised as some of the older women, and a group formed around one of the younger tenants, raged.

"We should kill them," Quilik was saying, but the younger women were contesting her proposal.

"Nisak has said that we shouldn't kill anyone unless it's completely unavoidable."

But Quilik was impatient; Nisak's approach made no sense to her.

But Nisak and the capral didn't make it to the open arena. As they attempted to cross over the open area in front of it, first the capral and then Nisak were struck down from behind by crossbow bolts.

Neither was killed, but both were disabled. Nisak, tearing the bolt from her thigh, and bleeding heavily, shuffled painfully towards and then into the arena. The argument about what to do about the Senate guard was still raging, and the wounded Nisak was right in their midst before she was noticed.

"Nisak!" Quilik was alarmed.

A few brief words and a number of the women from Anstan's army were despatched to try to locate whoever had fired on Nisak. Drawn away from the arena into the depths of Sector Eight, none of these women returned.

The fact that Nisak had been attacked and seriously injured with impunity was not lost on Anstan, but having no idea who'd attacked her or where to find them, there was nothing she could do.

"Mother's heart!"

Quilik's anguished exclamation followed a hail of crossbow bolts that flew into Anstan's gathered forces. They were being attacked from outside the arena but with no idea by whom. Galvanised, the captured Senate guard patrol also set about attacking the remaining women. With those incapacitated by the crossbow bolts, the guards now outnumbered Quilik and Formack's troops, and quickly disarmed them. The attackers from outside the arena simply faded away once the battle ended, without revealing themselves.

Bleeding heavily, Nisak eventually succumbed to her wound.

Killed, injured and captured, Anstan's forces had sustained significant losses but still comprised more soldiers than Sorak had available.

* * *

"Merlak, you are welcome."

Pilar, Pelar and the Defenders had retreated after effecting the release of the Senate guard from the open arena without revealing themselves. Merlak and his two followers, having engineered the elimination of Nisak, were happy to join forces with the twins. Merlak then shared with them the same intelligence of Anstan's dispositions that he'd given Nasa.

Without Nisak's restraining hand, Anstan was even more determined to take on Sorak's forces in the area surrounding the open arena, and ordered all of her troops to gather there.

Pilar and Pelar, observing the gathering of Anstan's army, made their own dispositions but with some apprehension. A final battle was pending but they were far from confident of the outcome. If Anstan were to break through into the piazza and Sector Two, it would be impossible to contain her.

* * *

In the quiet of her quarters and the comforting arms of Nasa, Sorak knew that a new phase of the struggle to establish a future for the city had opened. Anstan seemed to have the initiative, as well as the superior resources, but having faced overwhelming odds for much of her life Sorak pushed her anxieties away, as she always did, in favour of searching for a way to turn events to her advantage.

38

Egged on by Quilik and Formack, Anstan gathered her forces initially within the barracks and unused dream-pits of Sector Eight. The plan was to then move into Sector Seven, in and around the open arena, and thence across to the piazza in Sector Two. It was a predictable strategy that Sorak, and Charlan the guard commander, had already anticipated. Notwithstanding their limited resources, they made what defensive preparations they could.

"It's important that Sorak doesn't know how many people we have."

Whilst Quilik, who'd effectively taken over Nisak's role, agreed that deception was necessary, she didn't agree with Anstan's overall view. In her opinion, the sooner Sorak realised the difficulty of her position the better; anything to minimise the actual fighting.

Just killing off as many of Sorak's troops as possible would leave the city denuded of people to keep order, and there will still be many who don't want a return to the past even when the administration is defeated.

But she'll have to know in the end, since we have to engage all of her forces, and that will require all of ours.

Quilik, however, unlike Nisak, was unwilling to confront Anstan and kept her thoughts to herself.

* * *

Guided by Merlak, the twins and the Defenders, in their turn, gathered in Sector Six, hiding in the closed arena until the distant star disappeared below the horizon. Attacking in darkness was proving a more successful means of confronting Anstan than facing her forces in the light.

The sounds of fighting, the thuds of crossbow bolts and the screams of pain formed a background. The Defenders' patrols were intercepting Anstan's gathering forces whenever they could. The attrition of their soldiery was small but increasing; this worried Quilik more than it did Anstan.

Just as in the wilderness beyond the plain surrounding the city the noises of death filled the night, so increasingly did they in and around Sectors Six and Seven. As the vermillion light of the first moon suffused the atmosphere, the gathering soldiers making their way from Sector Four came within rage of the Defenders' weapons and those of several other groups, mainly men, whom the fighting had drawn from their hiding places. The order to 'disable not kill' wasn't always adhered to by these men but, recognising Pilar and Pelar's warriors by the clicking noise that they made through their teeth, they largely abided by the twins' rules. Later, Sorak and Nasa marvelled at this.

The atmosphere was tense and getting more so as the night wore on. But frustration was the biggest feature of the night for the twins.

"Anstan's troops will all be in place by morning. Despite our efforts we've hardly reduced their numbers."

Pelar knew that what her sister said was true. Sector Four was almost devoid of the ex-soldiers, mainly ex-officers, who'd taken up residence there. Those remaining, like Pastak and

Risak and any others who opposed Anstan, were insufficient in strength to achieve anything significant. And their numbers were so small that Nisak, and now Quilik, didn't see any point in wasting troops guarding them.

"Mostly those left behind are too old to be of much use."

Pilar wasn't sure that her twin's comment would have been much appreciated by the old soldiers!

* * *

Intelligence coming in to Sorak and the administration confirmed that Anstan's army was slowly concentrating in Sector Seven. And despite her commanders' efforts, although hidden away in the open arena, Sorak was soon well aware of what they appeared to be planning. She and Charlan and the other Senate military leaders had drawn up their plans accordingly but, unspoken, their confidence wasn't high as they knew they were still significantly outnumbered, even including the Defenders.

Remembering back a few cycles of the distant star to a similar battle between her invading forces and those of the last self-imposed male administration, Sorak ordered the construction of barricades across the back of the piazza in Sector Two. On that previous occasion, the male administration's forces, commanded by a renegade female officer, the first Marwek, were also outnumbered, but Sorak recalled how effective the barricade had been. The ensuing confrontation on that occasion didn't result in a battle, but she saw no prospect of one being avoided this time.

Marwek, how we could use you now!

However, Sorak's nostalgia was short-lived. Her principal assistant, herself named for the legendary warrior, was awaiting her leader's instructions. They needed to brief their waiting troops. Sorak knew she had to take control of the situation.

"We should move to the piazza," she said.

She, Charlan the guard commander, Nasa, and the youthful assistant Marwek, had been meeting in Sorak's office in the administration buildings in Sector One. But she knew that it was essential she be seen by her troops and by as many other citizens as possible. There were still large elements of the civilian population who were uncommitted, and any apparent inaction was in danger of handing the initiative to Anstan.

But aware of their inferior numbers, Sorak was uncertain of the best strategy, offensive or defensive?

She need not have worried. Anstan was impatient to bring things to a conclusion.

Nonetheless, the first phase of the battle was inconclusive.

* * *

Quilik, lacking Anstan's over-confidence, was reluctant to commit too many of their troops until Sorak's strength and depositions were clearer. A few crossbow bolts were exchanged as Sorak's defenders were enticed out from behind the barricades, but very little harm was done to either side, and the only impression Quilik got was one of determination and professionalism.

Her troops seem to be a lot younger than ours. How can that be?

But of course, Quilik knew the answer. Anstan had attracted all the older women who wanted to live in the past, whilst Sorak had attracted all the younger women who wanted to live in the future.

The conclusive battle had still yet to be fought.

39

There was so much movement around the outer sectors of the city as preparations for the final battle were made that no one was very clear who was stationed where and who was facing whom.

As Pilar, Pelar and the Defenders moved cautiously into Sector Six, each group leader making the clicking noise that the ex-quarry slaves had noticed as a signal of both their presence and their potential belligerence; they were surprised to see how many groups of both women and men, and in one case mixed, emerged on their fringes. None of these groups appeared hostile but none of them advertised their affiliations. What their intentions were, were equally unclear.

"Where's Merlak?"

With their troops ensconced in both the military and civilian headquarters in Sector Six, awaiting orders to move forward, Pelar realised that the old slave was no longer with them.

Both twins were still suspicious of the man but had too much else to think about to worry where the man and his two companions might have gone. There weren't that many options in any case if they weren't to be caught up with Anstan's forces.

But Merlak hadn't deserted them. At least, he hadn't deserted them in spirit. But in body he'd worked his way through the military headquarters and out into the area where the commercial Sector Three met up with the piazza. He left one of his companions in the entranceway to the military headquarters and the other in one of the civilian offices in Sector Three. He needed a communication route to the twins for when he reached Sorak and Nasa. For an aging ex-slave he'd suddenly become very active.

* * *

Relations in Anstan's camp were becoming ever more strained. With limited military knowledge and understanding, Anstan couldn't grasp why Quilik was so reluctant to simply confront the administration troops in the piazza head-on.

"We have the numbers; why do you not attack?"

But Quilik and the other former officers knew full well that a direct assault on the barricades that Sorak had erected would only result in the loss of many more soldiers and had no certainty of success. They weren't prepared to risk that. And worse, from their point of view, they had no clear idea where the twins and the Defenders now were.

"We must wait until all our troops have arrived," Quilik said.

It was an excuse, and Anstan recognised it as such; Quilik's refusal to attack frustrated her still.

The conversation was interrupted again by the arrival of an elderly former tenant. She was panting from her exertions, and her military jerkin was covered in congealed blood, although where she'd been wounded wasn't obvious.

A former tenant in the old pre-rebellion red platoon and, like Nisak, an old colleague of Sorak's, the ex-tenant was not only exhausted by the running battle that she'd been involved in, she was also having second thoughts about the support she was giving to Anstan. More sensitive than her leader, Quilik instinctively understood the tenant's concerns.

"We were attacked by a mixed group of old quarry slaves and three or four young women. They were well-armed and knew what they were doing."

It was typical of the disordered state of the outer sectors of the city and the problems that would manifest themselves if Sorak were to be defeated.

As Anstan's supporters began to gather, first in the old Sector Four barracks, and then to form into units and head first for Sector Six and then Sector Seven, it was clear that not only were their movements being watched but they were also increasingly subject to attack. Several of the older and more experienced of the former officers recognised that these attacks were being orchestrated. And of course, they all knew that the Defenders were out there somewhere.

"We had no idea who was attacking us at first," the tenant reported to Quilik.

At least two of the groups of women, as they moved into Sector Five en route for Sector Six and onwards, were attacked as they made their way through the complex of buildings that Sorak would have remembered as the training school where she'd spent much of her early young life.

The buildings were interlinked, with many rooms and long internal corridors. The women from Sector Four had been reluctant to pass around the outside of the buildings as there were many open areas that were totally overlooked by the buildings and ideal for ambush.

But as the first group passed along the inside of the old military training school, they were set upon by assailants who emerged from the multitude of old classrooms and other internal spaces. Firing a limited number of crossbow bolts, the attackers faded out of sight before any opportunity for retaliation was possible.

"We barely saw who was firing at us. It was mostly men. We hadn't expected that."

But as Anstan's troops worked their way through Sector Five, they were confronted again by a body of dirty, scruffy men, with a number of younger women in the background. Armed with swords and short spears, the fighting changed in character. It was now to be hand-to-hand.

"The women were all younger than any of us. Even our ordinary soldiers are in their middle years. We're all out of practice in this sort of warfare."

The groups quickly separated into fighting pairs, or in some cases trios. The former soldiers were more skilled, certainly in defence, but the ex-quarry slaves, albeit of a similar age, were more wiry, more used to demanding physical activity, and slowly they began to prevail. As the blows fell, the cries of anguish and pain, and the occasional scream, filled the air. With the first group to be embroiled in the fighting with the women falling back, injured or, increasingly, disinclined to risk their lives, the younger women weighed into the action.

As this second sprawl of fighting bodies closed onto the first, the leader of the younger women suddenly stepped back from the slashing and thrusting bodies.

"Hold!" she yelled.

The clash of metal on metal stopped; the background noise of groans and cries of pain diminished.

"Hold!" she yelled again.

As a wary calm settled on the ten or twelve fighters, none of whom was uninjured, swords were lowered and the two groups separated and coalesced on opposite sides of the classroom within which they were battling.

The tenant of the old red platoon, who'd been a part of the second group which had joined the fighting, stepped forward.

"I was one of the least wounded."

But as she began to seek out the leader of the fighters who'd attacked them, she realised that they'd all melted away the moment the fighting had ceased.

"In the middle of the fighting none of us had the opportunity to really see who we were actually fighting with. Certainly there were men, we could smell them, but who the young women were we had no idea."

Quilik was puzzled, but she was also concerned. Less than half of the fighters from Sector Four had subsequently made it with her to Sector Five and then Sector Six. The wastage of Anstan's forces continued.

Worse, from Quilik's point of view, since these attacks continued to occur, was that she had no way of knowing both how many more soldiers she should expect to join her force, and how long it would take for them to arrive. There seemed to be nothing organised about these attacks; they were opportunistic, by the men in particular, simply taking advantage of the chaos to take revenge.

And Anstan still wants to attack Sorak, even now as our forces are decreasing.

But Quilik hadn't heard the whole of it.

More straggling bodies of soldiers arrived, many of them injured, as the marauding groups in the outer sectors continued to nibble away at Anstan's army. News of these depredations was slow to get to Sorak; and much as any reduction of the forces opposing her might be welcome, Anstan still retained her superiority of numbers.

"We should attack Sorak's forces," Anstan repeated.

Quilik's reluctance persisted but she knew that Anstan would soon simply override her advice.

* * *

The attacking groups weren't part of the Defenders, any more than they were a part of Sorak and the administration's military strength. The twins knew this, but from experience they also knew that attempting to take control of all these disparate minor armies would cause problems they didn't need.

The uncertainties of having such freelance action mixed up with what they were trying to achieve worried them but there wasn't anything they could sensibly do about it.

"At least it also creates uncertainty for Anstan!"

And even as the twins were discussing the situation, another confrontation within the complex of training area buildings in Sector Five was developing.

This time there seemed to be no chance that the Defenders wouldn't be drawn in.

* * *

Quilik's reluctance to fight until she was ready was founded on the uncertainty of the whereabouts of what was probably one of the best groups of soldiers Anstan didn't know that she had. Billeted in the old wall-guard barracks at the edge of Sector Four, they included at least four of the old Senate guard, black soldiers who'd been in hiding for most of the time since the original rebellion. Hated and hunted by both the male administrations and subsequently by Sorak's soldiers, they were feared by both sides.

They were aware that they should be mustering with Anstan's main body of troops in Sector Six, ready to move into the final battle area with Sorak, but equally they knew that when they left Sector Four the whole of the outer areas would be denuded of soldiers and exposed to attack by Sorak. Their concerns seemed justified when they detected a large body of the Defenders in Sector Five.

One of the fiercest engagements so far between Anstan's and Sorak's supporters ensued when the two groups encountered each other in an open area between two of the training schools in Sector Five.

* * *

"They're all dead," Pelar finally said, her voice hoarse from shouting orders to the Defenders.

The battle had been bloody; killing not disabling was all that was possible. In the end, Anstan was short of twenty-odd crack troops, and the Defenders' strength was reduced by half.

"We must join Sorak," Pilar responded.

Not exactly a spent force, the twins' contribution to the impending battle was much reduced, and the Defenders were no longer capable of independent action.

It was only when all the fighting was over and mature thought was applied to the events that had taken place that Nasa, for one, recognised the importance of this particular encounter. Outnumbered, Sorak's forces would have a difficult enough job defeating Anstan without having to contend with such a body of ex-Senate guards and other highly experienced fighters.

40

The barricade that Sorak had constructed to reach across the piazza in Sector Two wasn't as substantial as it appeared. Mainly made from old furniture and unused timber from the manufacturing plant, Sorak was less than clear how long it might last if seriously attacked. But the guard commander had more confidence than she did. It wasn't physical strength that was important, more it was the barrier that it represented, and the hard fighting that it would require to breach it.

"They'll have to get through our troops first," Charlan said, "and they'll have to get *to* our troops even before that."

She was right. The barricade was well back, leaving a large area of piazza for Anstan's forces to cross before they reached it. They would be totally exposed and vulnerable. This was a tactic that had worked very well in the post-rebellion period during the final confrontation with the last male administration, and one which Sorak and Nasa were confident would work again. It needed to!

And still with uncertainty, both about how many soldiers were ranged against them, and the attitude that some of the civilians were beginning to show, Sorak and Nasa needed all the confidence they could generate.

The news of the mauling the Defenders had received finally reached Sorak with the arrival of the twins and the remnants of their force. Sorak and the administration could ill afford the loss of such experienced warriors, but it had happened, and they would have to make the best of it. It wasn't all bad news.

"We at least accounted for some of their fighters," Pelar said ruefully.

As the distant star rose, there was an ominous silence in and around Sectors Seven and Eight. Apart from small patrols occasionally appearing, Sorak's scouts saw almost no signs of the bulk of Anstan's forces, yet they knew that they were definitely there.

"We must wait for them to attack."

Agreeing with Sorak, Charlan certainly had no intention of seeking out Anstan's troops wherever they were congregating. They had too few soldiers; they couldn't afford the risk of dispersing them anymore than they already were.

The standoff lasted until the distant star began to fade over the horizon. There was an unreality about the situation, with the administration's forces waiting for an enemy that they couldn't see but who they knew was watching them closely. It was an anxious and exhausting time.

"Surely they aren't going to attack in the dark!"

Charlan was incredulous. With only the light from the two moons, even with Anstan's superiority in numbers that would have been foolhardy. But whatever Anstan might have been advocating, Quilik was too cautious to take such a risk.

But there was certainly activity. And as the vermillion light of the first moon lit the piazza and the open areas in Sectors Seven and Eight, it was clear that Anstan's troopers had at last been moved into the open but out of crossbow range from the barricade.

"We must hold our positions," Nasa said to the guard commander; "we mustn't be drawn into a battle in the dark."

Charlan had no such intention. Nasa's injunction seemed to be more a sign of the nervousness pervading Sorak's forces.

* * *

"But, Anstanmam, our advantage in numbers will soon disappear if we allow Sorak the opportunity to disperse our soldiers."

It seemed to Quilik that she was in permanent dispute with Anstan. And every time she found herself having to argue the mangeneer out of a course of action, the niggles in her mind over Sorak and why she was opposing her got more strident.

Why am I doing this? Sorak isn't going to live forever. And it's Nasa I fear most.

"We'll attack after the second moon fades finally, just as the distant star begins to rise."

For Quilik, it was the most sensible thing that Anstan had said for some time.

* * *

As night came without battle, Sorak was beginning to get seriously concerned. She was glad to have Nasa with her now, as well as Charlan and the other officers, but since no one could offer her an explanation as to why Anstan and her troops were holding off, all manner of scenarios began to form in her mind.

The Sorak of old wouldn't have worried like she was now, but the Sorak of old hadn't had the sort of responsibilities that she now had.

But of course, just because no action was visible didn't mean that there was none.

* * *

Many of the old women from Sector Four, the old officers who knew Sorak well and knew her capabilities, were clear on what they wanted to achieve but were increasingly concerned about Anstan's ability to both achieve a return to the past but, more specifically, to then run the city, as they would want it to be, when she had.

Hidden in the old dream-pit quarters in Sector Seven, as they waited for the command to move forward to attack Sorak's forces, six or seven of these old officers had gathered. Quilik, who knew of the meeting and would have dearly liked to have been there, understood the anxieties only too well.

"They don't like change, yet it's change they want," Quilik told herself.

One of the few capans still alive had joined the meeting. Sentack, who'd been attached to the pre-rebellion office of the governor of Sector Six, and who knew Mesrick and Sorak, was the first to voice her feelings.

"What does Anstan know about running the city? A mangeneer! Will she call up all the other civilians? Will we still have control of the military once she's in command?"

The murmurs of assent told Sentack that her companions were equally concerned. She knew that they could rely on Quilik, but she was only one.

"We should move to Anstan's quarters. We should— Ahhr!"

Missek was one of the younger tenants; she'd just joined the old green platoon for one patrol on the plain before the rebellion broke out. Her experience of the old regime was limited.

The other officers watched in horror as Missek clutched at her chest and at the crossbow bolt that had pierced her heart. As she pitched forward, a tangle of the old women ensued as the others struggled to their feet and to draw their weapons. But nothing more happened. But in the main hall of the dream-pit, screams and shouts began to fill the night. Whoever had fired the crossbow bolt had done so from back along the corridor towards the main hall.

Sentack gestured the other women to silence. Edging carefully through the entranceway of the room they were in, she crept silently towards the open area. A number of the ordinary soldiers who'd joined Anstan's party were anxiously treating the wounds of a number of their colleagues.

Sentack gestured the other women forward.

Two bodies were being ignored. Both were men and both had been almost decapitated by sword blows. Smelly and dirty, Sorak once again would have known who they were.

More shouting filled the dream-pit. Another body of ordinary soldiers flooded the room.

"We are ordered to the piazza." An aged capral saluted Sentack and made her report.

"We are to attack as the distant star rises over the city walls."

At last the fighting amongst the various groups of women and men lost in the outer sectors would stop through want of opponents as Anstan's troopers concentrated on facing Sorak.

Sentack, the old capan, felt both relief and anticipation. A former friend of Sorak's old capan, she knew that the task ahead of them was going to be tough. Anstan had repeatedly said that they were bound to win because they had more troops than the administration. Sentack, like Quilik, didn't share her confidence. She was well aware that it wasn't just about numbers on the ground.

A stream of women soldiers, none of them young, moved from the area adjoining the dream-pit and across into the area in front of the open arena to join those already gathered there. It was the first time that anyone had seen the totality of Anstan's forces.

Across the open area and across the piazza into Sector Two, the barricade was clear to see. Quilik was quick to notice that it had been further reinforced and now blocked any opportunity to enter either that sector or those adjoining it.

As their troops gathered, defenders appeared on the top of the barricade, ready to fire down on them; but also, protected entrances, which would allow Sorak's forces to sally out to confront the attackers, had been constructed. The barricade was now a formidable defensive barrier.

* * *

"Mother's heart," muttered Sorak from her vantage point on the roof of the old derelict Senate prison.

Both she and Charlan understood the problem that confronted them. As in the previous confrontation against the last male administration, they would have to face their opponents in the open in front of the barricade. There was no other way that they could meet. The preponderance of Anstan's forces undoubtedly favoured them. The protected entrances allowed them to fall back through the barricade into the safety of Sector Two. Both Sorak and Charlan were aware that that would also invite the attackers to follow them through.

If they're brave enough!

Somehow, Sorak thought that they would be!

* * *

"We'll have to close with them quickly before the crossbows shoot down too many of our troops."

Quilik gave the orders. Sorak's tactics were obvious and simple.

With the front rank protecting themselves with wooden shields, Anstan's first body of troopers moved forward. Crossbow bolts rained down on them but were mostly taken on the shields.

As Sorak's defenders poured out through their protected entrances, the scene suddenly froze. The moment of battle had arrived.

41

With the front rank holding their wooden shields to cover as much of their bodies as they could, and the second rank holding their shields over their own and the heads of the front row, there was virtually no target for Sorak's soldiers to aim at.

It was an attacking formation that somehow seemed familiar to Sorak.

As a young officer, and before her streak of independence had come to the notice of her superiors, Sorak had been allowed to browse, under supervision, in the now destroyed Senate library.

"It was in one of the old books."

No one was listening; there was too much to concentrate on down in the piazza. But in an aged book that had dealt with the ancient past of the planet beyond the distant star from which the people of the city were supposed to have come, there was a picture showing just such a formation. The formation even had a name, after an animal that Sorak of course had never heard of. The soldiers were wearing metal garments, which was mainly why she remembered it.

"How could Anstan have known about it?"

Of course she hadn't; it was the product of Quilik's fertile imagination.

The formation moved slowly forward at a measured pace. The line of administration troops that had emerged from behind the barricade, also with wooden shields, waited nervously.

"Let them come to you!" Charlan shouted.

Next to Sorak overlooking the piazza, Nasa was talking urgently to one of the Senate guard tenants. Sorak's troops needed a plan of action as their opponents steadily approached them, otherwise they would simply be pushing at each other futilely.

"Aim for their legs; aim below the shields. There's no point in just firing bolts into their shields."

The tenant immediately understood what Nasa was ordering and rushed off to give the necessary instructions.

The formation came to a halt, within crossbow range but not sword range. They would need to form up differently to push through an attack on the waiting defenders and to force their way through the protected entrances. But they didn't get the opportunity. A barrage of crossbow bolts striking the thighs and legs of the advancing soldiers produced chaos. Injured women, staggering, crawling, broke ranks, exposing themselves and those behind them. More bolts rained down and the formation then broke up completely and raced back out of range.

There was a ragged cheer from Sorak's troops.

But Quilik was beside herself. About a third of Anstan's soldiers had been injured, although many had sustained only superficial wounds and were still able to fight, not a single bolt, or spear, had landed on Sorak's forces.

The standoff began again.

Charlan was deep in conversation with her commanders. She had a problem. Even by recovering crossbows bolts that had been fired at them, she was being told that they only had sufficient missiles for maybe two more assaults.

When told, Sorak found it hard to contain her anxiety. To her surprise, Nasa didn't seem concerned, yet she was sure that he fully understood the situation.

Nasa's more measured response to the initial attack by Anstan's forces stemmed from two things: Merlak, the old slave, had come secretly to him to tell him the make-up of Anstan's army that he'd gathered from his observations in Sectors Six and Seven; it was the same information that Merlak had given the twins.

"Most are old patrol troops, used to long marches out on the plain but with very little fighting experience. The ordinary soldiers are sticking to their caprals, and only do what the officers tell them if the caprals agree. And there are too many officers all giving Anstan different advice. Fortunately, or maybe unfortunately, Quilik seems to know what she's doing."

Apart from the last point, Nasa was happy with what he was hearing. But with all the ex-officers around, there was bound to be a high level of military expertise.

Nasa's second point of confidence was that the twins and the Defenders had quietly regrouped and, by a tortuous route, had set off to restart their campaign of harassment at Anstan's rear.

"Why don't they disperse? It makes no sense to attack across the piazza."

Nasa didn't expect Merlak to have an answer; he was simply thinking aloud.

"They don't trust Anstan," the old man said, following his own line of thought. "And the ordinary soldiers don't trust the officers. For them the old ways of running the city were the good times, and few of Anstan's supporters can visualise how it will be in the future. That worries these ordinary soldiers. And very few of them think the men can be forced back into slavery."

So what are they fighting for?

But Nasa didn't have time to try to understand what was motivating Anstan's followers. The piazza was beginning to fill with her troops again.

As both Nasa and Sorak had thought likely, the formation was much smaller, more concentrated, and almost impregnable behind its barrier of shields.

"Where are the rest of them?"

Charlan's question was the obvious one. Her worry was that Anstan's more straightforward approach and limited military view had been replaced by Quilik's more imaginative form of soldiering.

And of course it had.

Within the tight formation there was clearly a body of crossbow women. And they adopted Nasa's tactics when they got the opportunity to fire. But the defenders only emerged from behind the barricade in small numbers, forming small mobile groups, leaving little of their bodies exposed. The result was that Anstan's troops were able to get much closer to the barricade, but again, as Quilik had anticipated, when they were drawn into close-quarters combat, more of the administration soldiers poured out from behind the barricade.

Nonetheless, Sorak's forces were still in danger of being overwhelmed.

* * *

Pelar ordered a brief rest period to allow the remaining Defenders time to recover their breath and to form into a coherent fighting force again. Their journey through Sector Three and then Sector Six had been largely uneventful. They'd seen no signs of any of Anstan's troops and had been able to work their way through the old military headquarters in Sector Six very quickly. It had seemed to be all too easy.

"We're being watched. I'm sure we're being watched."

Pelar didn't disagree with her sister; she had the same sense as her. But who was watching them, neither was very bothered about, as they knew that the final phase of the battle was about to unfold. They just needed to get into place for it.

Moving from Sector Six to Sector Seven was potentially likely to be much more hazardous. As they silently crept into the back of the largest of the dream-pits, there was no doubt that there were people there. Who were they?

"Wounded?"

As one of the scouts returned, she explained that the dream-pit was being used as a medical centre treating soldiers presumably injured in the first assault on the barricade. They were more in number than the Defenders' party and many were still capable of fighting.

The twins were in a quandary. To move forward into Sector Seven with a body of troops at their rear wasn't sensible but, short of pausing to kill all the wounded, it was a risk they had to take. Sorak's 'no unnecessary deaths' order had to prevail.

Gathering quickly in the closed arena, the Defenders once again arranged themselves into their fighting formation before moving into the open area surrounding the arena. This took them straight into the rear of the troops attacking the barricade. They were still heavily outnumbered.

As they emerged, a fierce battle was raging. The pressure of the attackers against the barricade had forced Charlan to commit more and more of her troops to the fray. Equally outnumbered, and with no reserves left, the administration's situation was becoming desperate. All that they could do was stand and fight.

"Mother's heart!"

The exclamation came from both Sorak and Pilar from their separate viewpoints.

As they watched, a body of warriors, dressed in animal skins and other unfamiliar garments, moved quickly into the gap between the fighting mass and the emerging remainder of Anstan's forces. The action froze. Armed with their long spears, and with a body of bowmen taking station on both edges of the piazza, the intentions of the forest people, for such they were, were clear. With sufficient numbers, they were challenging Anstan's forces to cease their attack.

* * *

"Mother's heart."

This time it was Quilik who mouthed the exclamation. Unlike Sorak and Nasa, she'd never heard of, let alone seen, the forest people.

"Drive them away!"

But Quilik knew that carrying out Anstan's frantic order wasn't possible. Whilst she had no idea who these new warriors were, or where they'd come from, what she immediately realised was that any attempt on their part to attack them was bound to end in disaster. Aware of the body of bowmen overlooking them, even if she'd never seen such a bow before their intent was clear enough; they could all be struck down before having the opportunity to return fire.

This is madness. It has to stop!

Quilik sheathed her sword, insisted that Anstan and the others did the same, and gave the signal for their forces to stop fighting. She waited for her order to be carried out. Then she walked out into the small remaining space at the edge of the piazza with her hands held in the air.

Charlan gestured her troops to lower their arms but she remained cautious; the unexpected change in the situation bemused her. She had no idea what was happening.

Tareck, and Jarson with bow in hand, moved to meet Quilik, while Anstan screamed incoherent invective in the background. No one took any notice of her as the tension eased.

42

Mother's heart, what's she doing here?

Sorak looked questioningly at Nasa as he suddenly stiffened at the sight of the slight figure of Shirler standing at the edge of the piazza. Following the direction of his gaze Sorak saw the small group of forest women. Having no special knowledge of Shirler at the time, she simply saw the group and supposed that Nasa's surprise was just at seeing the women there in the thick of what could have been a desperate battle. Nasa's descriptions of the forest people had told Sorak that their relationships were different from theirs, and it was usually the men who took the lead in such things as warfare. Why were the women there?

"Nasa?"

Sorak was uncertain. Nasa had never seen her so uncertain. If he'd had time to think about it, he wouldn't have supposed that it was Shirler who was disturbing his partner. The situation had dramatically changed; it was this that was disquieting Sorak. That Nasa had engineered the change by sending Tareck to seek the forest people's help, wasn't something that Sorak was yet aware of. For her, what seemed likely to have been the decisive battle to shape the future of the city had been interrupted by a totally unexpected intervention. But the situation still had to be resolved. How to achieve this resolution was far from clear.

The initiative was still with Anstan and her forces.

* * *

These forces had now fully emerged from Sector Seven and had deployed themselves ready to resume battle immediately on Quilik's command. Mindful of the fact that they themselves were now significantly outnumbered, and confronted by a mass of weaponry, the caprals and officers were nervous and uncertain in their turn. The sudden reversal of their fortunes had disconcerted them all.

"Attack, Klanncurs!" Anstan was shrieking, using an expression that neither Sorak nor Nasa had heard for many cycles of the distant star.

But no one was taking any notice. Anstan was hysterical and beyond reason.

"Sorakmam?"

It was a question from Quilik because within the mass of forest people and administration troops she could see no leader. Where was Sorak?

Charlan was there, carefully shielding herself within the front ranks of her troopers until she understood what was happening. Seeing Tareck, and knowing him to have been close to Nasa, enlightenment began to dawn for her.

It was Nasa who called these people out of the forest!

"Sorakmam!"

Quilik's tone changed as the Senate leader and her small party of bodyguards and advisers slipped through the cordon of soldiers and out into the open.

"Kill her, Quilik, kill her!"

The incoherent screech from Anstan caused Sorak to pause and her party to coalesce around her.

291

Quilik, who'd been advancing towards Sorak and her supporters, stopped in her tracks. She had no intention of obeying Anstan's strident demand. Then, very slowly, she unbuckled her sword belt, let it drop and stepped out of it. A ripple went around the bowmen as they relaxed and eased back their bowstrings.

The forest men's action ended a display of readiness that wasn't lost on Quilik and the two other officers who, unarmed, had come to join her.

Sorak knew that it was up to her to both defuse the situation and seek a compromise that would meet the aspirations of both Anstan and her diehards, and those who were fully committed to gender equality. What she also instinctively suspected was that amongst Anstan's supporters were those for whom a return to the past was a return to a life that they understood, but who nonetheless didn't see it as a cause to die for. How much influence these people had she had no idea. There was only one way to find out. She needed to force the pace of a resolution.

"Anstan, you are welcome!"

Sorak offered the traditional greeting to the mangeneer by shouting it into the mass of subdued noise and movement into which Anstan's forces had now degenerated. Where Anstan actually was, wasn't immediately clear to her. Finding her was paramount.

But by now, Sorak, Charlan, Nasa and several of the administration's more senior officials had gathered in a highly visible group in front of the barricade. The bulk of the administration forces had pulled back behind the barricade once Quilik had signalled that they had no intention of attacking. Similarly, small groups of Anstan's soldiers began to fade away into Sector Seven and, ultimately, to Sector Four for the officers, and Sector Eight and other less obvious quarters for the ordinary soldiers. For many, having to retreat was a bitter experience; for others it was a relief. Certainly Anstan was no longer in control of her supporters.

"Anstanmam?"

Quilik was getting anxious again. As the area began to depopulate there was no sign of the leader of the uprising. But it was important that she be part of the negotiations that Quilik hoped would now take place. Finding her was a priority.

Sorak, in her turn, was relieved that once again a major confrontation between two parties holding opposing visions of the future of the city had been defused. She recalled the previous situation a few cycles back when the last male administration was crumbling and the city had been invaded by another group of women intent on putting the clock back. But now, as then, bloodshed had been avoided and a compromise that established the concept of gender equality had apparently then been accepted by everybody.

Well, clearly not quite everybody.

That the yearning for the past was resurrected by a civilian was beyond Sorak's comprehension, but the problem now was how to accommodate the aspirations of those who felt like Anstan, without disrupting the imperfect but thriving society that was now entirely based on gender equality. And for the first time, Sorak began to recognise that any solution had to be acceptable to not only the former military population and but also to the civilians. These latter, in the past, had simply been assumed to have accepted what the soldiers determined. This was manifestly no longer the case.

"Sorakmam?"

The situation was drifting; the ever practical Charlan needed authority to deal with the remaining body of Anstan's troops and to offer hospitality to the forest people before encouraging them to return to their own territory.

But as Sorak and the other leaders of the administration joined up with Quilik and others of Anstan's supporters, notwithstanding their various different interests the sense of expectation was palpable. But what was going to happen next was still unclear.

But as Charlan, still nervous of the military situation, quietly redeployed administration troops back out onto the piazza, this sense of expectation amongst the remnants of Anstan's forces turned to a tension that soon affected all but the forest people.

Anstan had reappeared.

Calm, all signs of her fury at being thwarted having disappeared, it was some time before Nasa and Charlan identified her hidden in a small party of ex-officers positioned back at the edge of Sector Eight.

Now what?

Nasa, concerned, and fearful at the same time of Anstan's hatred of Sorak, was at a loss as to know how to resolve the situation. Clearly Anstan needed to be punished for the uprising that she'd engineered, but he knew that to be too provocative would simply restart the fighting. This was clearly something that no one wanted.

But Anstan's calmness was misleading; her self-control was overriding her anger. She was seething at Sorak and the administration, but it was now Quilik who'd attracted her ire. Quilik's caution and common sense she saw as either cowardice or a deliberate attempt to undermine her and prevent her from achieving a return to the past. At the back of the remaining group of her most loyal supporters, on the edge of the open arena, as she worked through her anger, it was her erstwhile military commander on whom her fury was now totally focused.

"We must gather our troops in the dream-pits," she demanded.

The dream-pits in Sectors Seven and Eight were where she'd mustered her forces before. But a major part of these forces had now dispersed, the women in many cases being only too happy that it hadn't come to a fight.

But no one was listening to Anstan. The body of women who surrounded her, and were protecting her, whilst being amongst the most fanatical of her supporters, were nonetheless realistic enough to be aware that things had not gone to plan.

"Our troops have returned to their quarters."

It was Quilik's friend and colleague Formack who spoke.

"We are in no position to fight!"

Anstan's rage boiled over again. Grabbing a crossbow from one of the old troopers who was providing what little protection she had, she elbowed her way to the edge of the piazza. Uncertain of what she had in mind, no one attempted to interfere with her.

Only having a rudimentary knowledge of how the crossbow had to be fired, Anstan fitted the bolt she'd also grabbed and fired it into Quilik's back.

Pierced by two or three arrows from the ever-alert forest bowmen, she collapsed and writhed in agony. No arrow proved fatal, the forest people following Tareck's injunction to wound but not kill.

Then a figure, clad in part of the uniform of a woman soldier and part the woven garments of the forest people, moved to kneel beside Anstan. Hidden by her body no one saw the blow she delivered, but Anstan lay still.

Shirler!

When it was apparent what had happened, Nasa was appalled. Sorak, Charlan and the rest of the officers and officials were taken completely by surprise and were instantly saddened. It wasn't the outcome they'd wanted.

Signalling to Tareck, Nasa followed Shirler as she returned to her group of women standing at the edge of the piazza.

"Shirler, you must come with us."

A wave of tension flowed through the forest women; weapons were grasped. Quick also to sense the change in mood, Charlan signalled the administration troops onto alert. The forest men, however, watching Jarson for a signal, remained calm and waited.

It took some time for the tension to ease. The remnants of Anstan's forces were as uncertain as the administration's.

Finally, Formack and the remaining attacking women slowly withdrew into Sector Seven and the atmosphere relaxed. Charlan approached the forest men to offer hospitality. Jarson responded, knowing that the city people would nonetheless want them to leave as soon as possible. He was only too happy to do so. The events of the day had more than anything convinced him that they should still keep a safe distance from the city.

Charlan might not have had a name for it but the feeling of anti-climax was very real for her.

43

Nasa had no thought to punish Shirler. What she'd done she should not have done, but Anstan's life expectancy was hardly long in the circumstances.

Tareck took her to the building that housed Sorak, Nasa and most of the senior administration officials but installed her in an apartment remote from the main quarters. By posting a guard on her door he signalled that she had to remain until it was decided what to do with her. In Sorak's new society she would have been interviewed by a group of officials in public and then a punishment decided. But Tareck had no expectation that this would happen.

After having joined Nasa to meet Jarson and to thank the forest people for their help before they set off back to their compounds, Sorak forbore to ask about Shirler, although she had at least now learned who she was. The conversation with Jarson was friendly and social and avoided any discussion on what was actually going on in the city. Sorak got the impression that he really didn't want to know. He didn't.

"We should set up a formal arrangement so we can keep in touch."

Jarson looked doubtful, although he was hardly surprised at the suggestion. Now that contact had been made, he supposed that Sorak and the city authorities would want to know about any approaches from the groups that had been involved in the fighting or who were in opposition to them. That was only sensible.

Nasa's parting with Jarson was particularly difficult. Neither really wanted to mention Shirler first but clearly Jarson needed to know what might be likely to happen to her. In their society, killing another person was a very serious infraction. Under the city's old regime and during the rule of the male administrations, violence and killing had been commonplace. Under Sorak and the current Senate, things had changed dramatically. But Jarson expected Shirler to be punished.

Nasa explained the process. Jarson acknowledged that it was largely how they would have treated the killing. They parted on good terms.

* * *

The episode in the piazza, the death of Anstan, something Sorak would have avoided if it had been possible, left her saddened and depressed. Within the space of one circuit of the distant star it seemed to her that all of her efforts at changing society in the city had been undermined.

Sorak knew that a major challenge to her and the administration's authority had been avoided and that her vision for the city and its future had been preserved, but it had been a close-run thing. She also knew that there would still be some diehard fanatics, like Anstan, who would continue to want a return to the past. These would have to be neutralised but tolerated, otherwise they'd have resolved nothing.

Back in their quarters, with the forest people gone, and the guard patrols stepped up but with clear orders not to be aggressive, Sorak lay in Nasa's arms and pondered her life and achievements. Such retrospection was rare for her.

And of course, compared with the days of the women-dominated city, she'd achieved a massive amount. Sorak herself probably recognised this rather less than those around her. But she'd had her streak of independence essentially from birth and had always done what her conscience prompted her to do; not something too common amongst the women of old, but more usual now.

The concept of justice, something that most of the more thoughtful of the city's current inhabitants would have recognised, if not giving it such a name, was now well-established. There was a residual feeling amongst the older and less flexible elite that they should be exempt from this concept, but Sorak would have no truck with such ideas. It was the built-in exclusivity of the pre-rebellion system that was so offensive to people like Sorak.

A range of courts, again not that that was the name given to them, had been set up and penalties determined for infractions. There had been much debate about the ultimate sanction, even for killing another citizen. But in Sorak's new world there was no death penalty.

Slowly, as men began to be accepted and then taken for granted, the people of the city, depending on what their intellectual capabilities were, became increasingly in command of their lives and their activities.

As Sorak and Nasa had observed, and the diehards had perpetually objected to, such freedoms produced mixed results, and attributes and behaviours previously unknown began to appear. The biggest area of change, and of infractions, was around property. In the pre-rebellion days no one owned anything beyond their personal clothes; everything else belonged to the Senate. This was no longer the case, and people, in ignorance of the property concept, often just took what they wanted, irrespective of who it belonged to. Regularising this and introducing the idea of individual personal property, Sorak would admit was still to some extent a work in progress. But establishing punishments of ranging severity was slowly taking hold, and Sorak was hopeful that soon the worst abuses would disappear.

The biggest problem for Sorak was getting the Senate back into being and in charge again. How she was going to do that without reintroducing the weaknesses and inadequacies of the most recent Senate, she was far from clear. Many amongst those closest to her questioned why she needed to bring it back at all. This was a thought that Sorak resisted.

"But I won't live forever. We need a Senate and administration that isn't dependent on one person."

But suspicions of the Senate emanating from the past were entrenched and hard to overcome, notwithstanding the introduction of male senators.

As Sorak pondered on how to heal the wounds generated by recent events, Nasa pondered on what to do about Shirler, and about some vague rumours reported to him concerning another fanatic trying to take Anstan's place.

Sorak's brief encounter with Jarson had created a favourable impression. He'd apologised for Shirler's action but offered no explanation for why he thought she'd acted as she had. He had no explanation. But he did know that Shirler had feelings for Nasa and held him in high regard. The thought occurred to him that she was seeking to please him by putting an end to Anstan's rebellion. It was not a thought that had occurred to Nasa.

"Jarson asked what we would do with Shirler," Sorak said when she and Nasa discussed the forest leader and the events of the previous day.

It was late at night.

Nasa was immediately aware that something was bothering Sorak. Her interest in Shirler caused him some concern. Whilst he gave no thought to his two sessions with the forest woman, he had no idea what Sorak would truly think. If nothing else, he knew that she would see him as disloyal; and disloyalty was something she hated most amongst the people of the city.

But somewhere in the depths of Sorak's mind, the political situation and the dissatisfaction that she supposed many women still felt, began to push to the surface.

"Killing Anstan hasn't brought the uprising to an end."

It was the first time Sorak had referred to the troubles as an uprising. It told Nasa a lot about her way of thinking. He pondered over whether to tell her about the rumours he'd heard. He decided he must.

"Have you ever heard of another mangeneer called Benlik?"

But he had no need to be concerned; Sorak appeared to be as knowledgeable as he was.

Benlik was another older civilian much like Anstan. A fierce fighter in her younger days, Sorak might have recognised her as one of the women, or rather young girls, who had been involved in the brawl that introduced Sorak to Lenen way back before she'd fled the city with Nasa.

"I must have come across her before we left the city. She was a friend of…" But painful memories cut off the thought.

To Sorak's way of thinking, Benlik was a much more dangerous opponent than Anstan. What she couldn't understand was why she'd deferred to Anstan. But mostly what she was beginning to worry about was what Benlik might now do following the collapse of the uprising.

* * *

Pilar, Pelar and the few remaining Defenders cautiously made their way to the old training area in Sector Five and to the office accommodation that they'd previously used. Their caution was justified. There was evidence of occupation.

"We must find somewhere else," Pilar said; "if whoever they are have stationed a guard, they won't want us around, interfering with what they're up to."

"We should know who it is. There must still be people who want to carry on after Anstan."

Of course, Pelar was right, but her sister was reluctant to get drawn into the risk of any more fighting; there were too few of them.

"Mother's heart, another mangeneer!"

The twins' attention was suddenly drawn to a small group of women who'd moved out of the training buildings and were heading towards Sector Six.

Pelar recognised the leader of the small group as much by her clothing as anything else.

"Benlik!"

The whisper came from one of the Defenders, the youngest of them, who was herself a civilian. She immediately had everybody's attention.

"Ran the weapons factory," the woman said. "She was famous as a fighter in the dream-pits in her youth. Most people are frightened of her."

All of this was news to Pilar and Pelar.

"I think if there's more trouble developing we must tell Sorak."

"But, Pelar, we need more information." This was true.

As Benlik moved first to Sector Six and then to Sector Seven, all the while gathering the odd new member, the Defenders followed, watched and waited.

44

"So, what are we going to do about Shirler?"

The question had been hanging there.

Two circuits of the distant star had passed with Sorak, helped by Nasa, heavily engaged in discussions, through the administration, with as many groups of women as she could reach. It hadn't been easy; many of the disaffected women wanted to have nothing to do with Sorak. Nonetheless, since there was no possible evidence to suggest any man, in the light of their role in Sorak's world, would want a return to the past, she concentrated only on women. Re-establishing the Senate no longer seemed to be a priority.

From these discussions two things quickly emerged. Notwithstanding the defeat of Anstan's forces, Sorak was surprised to discover how many women did yearn for the past; however, except in a very few cases of conviction, this was largely because they found the new freedoms that they'd acquired difficult to deal with. These women were unlikely to pose a problem if their fears and anxieties could be dealt with. Needless to say, Sorak fully intended that they would be.

The second thing that was revealed, which she hadn't expected, was a desire by both the ex-soldiers and the civilians to integrate, share living areas, and to coexist in a way that had been unthinkable in the old military dominated pre-rebellion society. The members of the administration with whom Sorak discussed this second issue were as bemused as she was.

Sorak was also surprised to find that Nasa understood this desire for integration better than she did. But she immediately recognised that such a society would be an ideal basis for the future and an obvious development of the gender equality world that she had achieved.

But there was still the issue of Shirler and, as more intelligence was gathered, the issue of those who still wanted a return to the past. Benlik was very much in Sorak's thoughts.

Tareck rushed into Sorak's quarters, agitated and looking for Nasa.

"She's gone!"

"But you said you had a guard on her!"

Tareck's expression instantly told Nasa that something serious had happened.

"She's dead. Her neck was broken."

Both had immediately thought the same thing – a man was involved – but then both realised that this was perhaps more complicated than an old slave killing from the past.

"We've searched. Shirler doesn't know her way around the city; on her own she can't have gone far."

But Tareck didn't sound very convinced by his own argument.

What if someone released her deliberately?

Nasa didn't want to think about this. Benlik and Anstan's old supporters were the obvious likely culprits. But they wouldn't have been rescuing Shirler for her own good.

Tareck and Nasa's estimation of what had happened was initially largely true.

* * *

Benlik herself hadn't been directly involved but the plan had been entirely hers. The group of three ex-soldiers, one a former capral, easily discovered where Shirler was being held. Aware that there was a guard, their approach had been cautious. As the distant star sank below the horizon the guard, confronted by the three ex-soldiers, was able to draw her weapon and seriously wound one of the troopers before being struck down.

Alerted by the noise, Shirler was ready when the two uninjured attackers rushed into her quarters. Not expecting her to be armed, they immediately sought to seize her. However, known by Tareck but not by Nasa, Shirler had retained the knife with which she'd killed Anstan.

Quickly shortening the odds by slashing the capral across the neck, and taking advantage of the pause that this caused her opponents, Shirler rushed out of the room and the building and into the mass of streets and derelict buildings that surrounded the more luxurious accommodation that she'd been kept in.

She didn't run very far. Well aware that she didn't know her way around in the city, she hid herself in a ruin that was only a street away from both the house where she'd been held and Sorak and Nasa's quarters. She found signs of occupation in the ruin – food and discarded clothing – but no evidence of the people to whom this belonged.

She was lucky. The group of civilians who'd taken up residence there, after the military had occupied their building in Sector Three, had recently taken an unexpected opportunity to return to their former homes. Not, of course, that Shirler knew this.

But she was lucky and she was safe.

Benlik was furious. How the three troopers had failed to deal with Shirler was beyond her understanding. She accepted that the woman would have been expected to fight back, but how she'd successfully disabled her attackers, in the circumstances, she simply couldn't conceive.

But she had more important things to deal with. Exacting revenge on Shirler could wait.

The meeting that Benlik had called in Sector Five was reported to Sorak but without any indication of the purpose of the gathering. It would certainly have been of great interest to her had she known.

The six women Benlik eventually chose to accompany her on her mission were all ex-officers, all with some form of resentment of Sorak, and all with a desire to still push forward the cause of women's rule of the city. But all were showing signs of desperation that concerned Benlik.

Nonetheless, briefed and armed, the party set out for Sector One, in search of their target.

* * *

Pilar, Pelar and five of the Defenders had spent the time since the non-battle partly in Sector Six in the old military headquarters, and partly in Sector Seven. Disappointed that things seemed to have fizzled out, they were on the point of disbanding when a couple of elderly men, former slaves in the manufacturing plant, sought them out. This was so unusual that the twins immediately gave them their attention.

It quickly transpired that the two men knew who the Defenders were, although Pilar and Pelar never found out how they'd come by this knowledge, or why they thought they'd be interested in the goings-on of Benlik. However, they were correct in their assumption.

"Benlik is heading for Sector One. With six others."

It was the only information the men had. But to them it was important. It was clear to the twins that these two were highly suspicious of the mangeneer. Having worked for her in the pre-rebellion days, they realised that she hated Sorak and all that she was trying to achieve in the city. For them, Sorak was a heroine, and they were fearful that Benlik meant her harm. In this they were absolutely correct!

"Sorakmam ought to be warned."

"We should go to Sorak's quarters," Pilar said. There was no dissent.

* * *

Shirler knew she couldn't just stay in the ruin. She had either to make her way to one of the gates and then head off to the forest, or she had to make contact with Nasa. Since she wasn't sure that she could find her way to the appropriate gate from where she was hidden, or that the gate guards would let her leave anyway, making contact with Nasa was her preferred option.

I need to see Nasa again!

Her feelings for Sorak's partner were even more jumbled up in her head than before. She'd never felt so confused yet so joyful at the thought of a man. The fact was, Shirler really didn't want to return to the forest; she wanted to be with Nasa. Love was a concept that in the pre-rebellion city had largely been eliminated by the old women's Senate, yet amongst the forest people it was the basis for all relationships. Shirler was well aware of the concept, even if Nasa might not have been.

She knew that Nasa lived with Sorak and that they had strong feelings for each other, but nonetheless Nasa had had intercourse with her, twice. That counted for everything with her.

The forest people had been aware of the pre-rebellion city, but since a women-dominated society was totally foreign to them they'd avoided any real contact. It was only when they discovered that things had changed – how, was still a mystery to Nasa – did they begin to welcome contact. Nasa and Tareck's visit, first to the wrecked spacecraft and then to the compounds, had opened up a new era. But she was still confused by Nasa's dealings with her; did he have feelings for her or not?!

But Shirler's thoughts were suddenly interrupted. Someone was approaching. She moved to one of the ventilation openings in the building where she was hiding to see who it was. A group of women, clearly not concerned about being seen or heard, paused in the narrow lane running alongside the ruined building. She had no idea who Benlik was, but her instincts told her that these women were not likely to be friendly.

The group eventually moved on as Shirler looked down on them. They were headed towards Sorak and Nasa's quarters, not that she was aware of this.

What motivated her to work her way back down through the building and out into the narrow lane, Shirler couldn't have explained. The seemingly hostile attitudes of the women had certainly registered with her. But as she did so, she was conscious of another group of women. These were proceeding much more cautiously. Dodging into another derelict building she was both curious about these new women and anxious for her safety. She wasn't sure whether she'd been seen. She hadn't.

Shirler thought she recognised the two black women obviously in charge of the group. Familiar with twins, she recalled that the two women and their accompanying troopers were in the background during the confrontation in the piazza. Her recollection suggested that these women would be friendly, but she wasn't inclined to show herself.

"I must find Nasa," she kept telling herself.

Pilar, Pelar and their party moved carefully forward. Their caution suggested that they knew that Benlik's party was in front of them but that they didn't want to make contact with them.

* * *

Charlan and the other military commanders were gathered in one of the old Senate offices in a reconstructed part of the building. They were seriously concerned about the inconclusive outcome of the confrontation with Anstan and her supporters. And their intelligence was beginning to alert them to the emergence of a new leader, Benlik, known to be far more uncompromising than Anstan.

"Our watchers have lost sight of this Benlik," Charlan's deputy said, "but we know that a small party has detached itself from her main group. However, where they are we don't know. But we must assume they are likely to be heading our way."

With limited numbers of troops and the still uncertain alliances amongst the old officers in Sector Four, Charlan was reluctant to institute a rigorous search in the outer sectors. She simply couldn't afford to disperse what few resources that she had. All agreed that their best course of action was to provide the best protection they could for Sorak and the administration officials where they were, and await events. But in view of the extensive offices and quarters scattered amongst both derelict and restored buildings, they knew this wasn't going to be easy.

"We must talk to Nasa. He needs to know about the ongoing threat."

But Nasa needed no telling.

45

Benlik's timing wasn't the best. Having carefully worked their way into the morass of buildings in Sector One, the group found themselves at the large compound used by 147, the last of the male administrators and the man who had finally come to terms with Sorak and the women seeking to establish a new society. However, Benlik herself was unaware of the significance of the place.

Creeping through one of the passageways, the group spread out around the edge of the central courtyard and underneath the veranda. They were immediately aware that the upper floor was occupied. Noise, talking and laughter, suggested that both women and men were present. This they hadn't expected.

Benlik was just about to signal their retreat when a young man came out onto the veranda and started to walk down the ramp to the ground. They froze. Just as he reached the end of the ramp he pitched forward, struck by a crossbow bolt from one Benlik's supporters. Whether he'd detected any of the group, they'd never know.

Benlik was furious. They'd only intended to use the compound to hide in until the distant star began to wane. To engage with any of Sorak's forces, administrators, anyone who could expose them, was the last thing she wanted. The women hurriedly retreated to one of the access alleyways and waited for any reaction. They didn't have to wait long.

"Reack! Reack!"

The young woman who'd followed the dead man out onto the veranda, calling to him, looked over the railings and saw his body. She screamed.

As she rushed back to find her companions, they were arming themselves and preparing for a possible encounter with whoever had arrived at the compound.

As Benlik's group quickly headed into one of the adjacent abandoned buildings, a different cry went up. They'd been detected.

Then nothing appeared to happen. But recognising that surprise would now be impossible, Benlik quickly headed deeper into Sector One. They weren't followed, but equally they were unaware that a messenger had been sent to Charlan to report what had happened. No one knew the identity of the attackers but clearly the way they were behaving said that they were hostile.

There's no way now that we can go directly to Sorak's office and quarters.

Benlik's anger was bubbling to the surface. The plan for them to head straight for Sorak once the distant star had begun to set was now too dangerous. They would have to work their way back through a whole mass of derelict and unoccupied buildings, with the risk of being challenged. But they were committed; they had no other choice. Resisting the temptation to take her anger out on the woman who'd fired on the young man, she sent her forward to reconnoitre. Maybe the enemy would take care of her! They didn't.

The scout returned to report that, having located Sorak's office, there were no signs of any activity around it or the quarters. For Benlik this was suspicious. But they had to press on. The administration offices surrounding them were also ominously quiet. Finding an unguarded entrance, Benlik's troopers crept into the corridor that ran down the middle of the lower floor, and she began to get a sense in the gloom that they were not alone. But as they checked each office and each room as they came to it, there were still no signs of any occupation.

It's a trap. We're being drawn into a trap.

But they'd arrived at the last of the offices at the end of the corridor. It was lit, unlike the other offices. If it was a trap, this was it!

"Hold!" Benlik shouted as the first of her followers entered the room.

She was too late.

The door was suddenly smashed shut. The room hadn't been empty, and now Benlik's forces had been reduced to just five.; and two of her troopers had been captured having entered.

* * *

Shirler found it hard to keep up with the twins. The need not to expose herself meant that she had to stay well back, and it wasn't always obvious which route they'd taken.

* * *

Benlik and her remaining supporters quickly escaped the building. Once again, it occurred to her that, even so, it had been too easy. Why did Sorak's forces – she assumed that it was they who had captured her two troopers – not pursue them as they hurried out into the maze of streets surrounding the administration buildings?

In fact, Benlik was convinced by now that they were being manipulated. As they rounded the side of the main administrative building they found that all but one of the exits from the junction they'd arrived at was blocked.

This could not be by chance!

With Benlik leading and the four other members of the party bunched up tightly behind her, they headed for the entrance to the building at the end of the street. They had no other choice; their route was being predetermined.

"We're clearly expected to re-enter the private quarters," Benlik told herself.

The building was well-lit, and a corridor of closed doors, something unusual in most of the city, opened into what was clearly a communal dining area. The area was empty, but the entranceways to several rooms that led off it were exposed. Benlik had been into this communal dining area before so she knew that some of these side rooms were accessible from other parts of the building. Whatever was going to happen was going to happen here.

* * *

"Hold!"

It was more a whisper than a shout.

As Shirler crept by the entrance of a low building, that unknown to her had been accommodation for prison warders, she was grasped from behind. A hand over her mouth, her arms pulled behind her, she was powerless to resist.

"Hold!" the voice said again.

She saw that she was being held, and was surrounded, by a group of four women. In the dim light she could just see the outline of the woman who'd spoken.

One of the black twins, Shirler told herself.

She wasn't sure what this presaged.

Then she was aware of hands running all over her clothes and body. She reacted violently. She was unused to being touched; such action would only have been possible in the intimacy of the bedroom in her culture. Lashing out, she jumped back against the wall and pulled her knife from its sheath.

The group froze in front of her. This wasn't the reaction they'd been expecting. For them, touching was a friendly gesture.

"It's the forest woman, Pelarmam."

As the group tightened around Shirler, Pelar moved in front of her, careful to keep out of range of her circling weapon.

Pelar was joined by her sister.

"We mean you no harm," Pelar said. "We were following Benlik and her party, but we lost them in the burnt-out buildings."

Shirler had no idea who Benlik was but what the twin said confirmed what she'd observed.

Then in one of the silences that often emerges even during the most frenetic periods of activity, they heard the sounds of a clash of weapons and then of running feet.

A young woman, panting from her exertion and bleeding from a wound to her sword arm, ran out of the entrance of another nearby building. It was the seventh member of the group who'd been reconnoitring the area around the administrative buildings and the quarters of the main officials.

As one of her colleagues bound her wound, she reported.

"They're in the main quarters, in the communal dining area. The Senate guard have the building secure but haven't confronted them yet."

The twins looked grimly pleased. Shirler was simply confused, but she correctly assumed that 'they' were this Benlik and her followers.

What none of them knew was that Nasa had ordered the guard to stay out of sight, until Benlik was in the trap.

But now that she was, Nasa was hesitant to talk to her, as the evidence told him she was very angry and unlikely to listen to reason.

What the twins' scout couldn't tell them was how many people Benlik had with her. However, she was clearly outnumbered.

Retracing the scout's steps, and by gesture, forcing Shirler along with them, the party set off to make their entrance into one of the side rooms of the communal dining area. Seeing but not being seen, they were in time to observe Benlik and her four remaining followers build themselves a barricade of tables and chairs and settle to await events.

Sorak, Nasa and Charlan, meanwhile, had also entered one of the side rooms and were equally observing Benlik's furious defensive measures.

* * *

"Hold!"

The universal challenge was whispered at the young man who had attempted to enter the communal building.

"Lenar!"

The guard tenant was surprised to see Sorak and Nasa's son. Himself a guard commander, Lenar had been given responsibility for the external security of the city after the raids of the herdsmen from the forest. It wasn't an onerous task and was regarded as a way of keeping Lenar safe whilst giving him a role in the city's management.

"You must stay out of sight."

A guardswoman was delegated to accompany Lenar to one of the side rooms on the opposite side of the dining area, and opposite where the tenant knew Charlan and the other principals were.

The tenant would hardly have thought of it in such terms, but the scene was set for the climax of the drama building in the dining area.

46

Nasa!

Benlik had been reviewing their situation. What had started out as a campaign to halt Sorak's reordering of the city, taking in the killing of the forest woman responsible for Anstan's death, had now become a desperate fight for survival. Not that, she told herself, she relished survival in Sorak's world. But her situation was critical, and it was the more practical things that were now bearing down on her. Only she and two of her followers had crossbows. One now had no bolts, and she and her colleague each only had one. She knew that she had to make them count and her problem was how, which was why Sorak's partner was uppermost in her mind.

All five of them had swords, but Benlik supposed they'd be given little opportunity to use them. Why would Sorak want to risk casualties when Benlik was within her grasp?

"Nasa," she said again, aloud this time.

Benlik was well aware that she would be given little or no opportunity to attack Sorak directly. Attacking Nasa was her next best option. But she needed him to be present for that to happen.

A flutter of movement in one of the rooms off the dining

area, opposite where they were hiding within their barricade, attracted her attention and her colleague's last crossbow bolt. A scream said the bolt had at least found a mark.

Shot in the shoulder, the Defender standing next to Pilar and Shirler staggered away out of the building to receive medical aid from the Senate guards. Again, this brief episode made Benlik angry; it was a waste of effort and weaponry, as it was unrelated to Sorak or Nasa.

More movement from a different area then attracted her attention.

* * *

"We have to end this."

Sorak and Charlan agreed with Nasa, but neither was sure how to achieve this without the loss of Benlik and her supporters' lives. That was what they wanted to avoid.

They can't have many crossbow bolts left.

Nasa assumed this to be the case. None of the women he'd been able to see had been carrying quivers for bolts, which meant they'd only had a small number each. He also knew that they had had to fight their way to Sector One and therefore would have very few, if any, bolts left. Nonetheless, confronting Benlik directly carried a risk, but it was the only way to bring things to an end. They all knew that.

* * *

"Nasa, you are welcome!"

As he stepped out into the open in the dining area, Nasa doubted that Benlik meant this greeting. Covered by an array of crossbows from the Senate guard and the twins' group, he moved towards the barricade. He could hear her but couldn't see her.

"There's nothing you can do here," Nasa said. "If you throw out your weapons and then follow yourselves, no harm will come to you."

There was total silence in response to this offer. Nasa hadn't been expecting any sort of immediate reaction.

But the final act of the drama was in play and no one expected the confrontation to last very long.

Behind Nasa, several of the Senate guard and some from the twins' remaining group moved out into the open, ready to return fire if any hostile action took place.

Behind the barricade, Benlik was gathering herself for what she saw as her final endeavour against Sorak.

The scream this time came from Sorak herself. It was followed by an anguished grunt from Lenar.

Nasa pitched forward, Benlik's bolt going straight into his heart.

With no target visible there was no return of fire.

Unconcerned about what was happening around him, Lenar rushed across the dining area to his mother, who collapsed into his arms. Silent now, she clung to her son in silent anguish and despair.

There was another frozen moment in time.

Then, in a flurry of rapid movement, Pilar, Pelar and their remaining Defenders rushed the barricade and began to pull it apart. They were met with no more crossbow fire. The Senate guard confronted Benlik's last two supporters.

Benlik herself, sword in hand, nonetheless took no part in this fighting, but with a nimbleness that belied her age she leapt from the collapsing barricade and advanced towards the sounds of Sorak's distress. Her intent was obvious.

Lenar, aware of the danger, drew his sword and eased his mother further back into the side room in front of which they'd been standing. But what he was also soon aware of was another figure moving to confront the raging Benlik. Uncertain, Lenar paused and watched, and prepared himself to intervene if the need arose.

Shirler, standing only a short distance away from Nasa when he was struck, had felt the blow almost as if it had hit her physically. Her feelings were in a jumble again but a towering rage began to emerge as the dominant one. And there was Benlik advancing towards her; or at least towards the group behind her containing Sorak. From the glazed look in Benlik's eyes, Shirler had no way of knowing whether she'd seen her.

But then she did.

Oblivious to anything but her own raging desire to kill Sorak, Benlik was suddenly brought to a halt, both Sorak's disappearance and by the curiously clad figure that had darted past her and swept up a sword discarded by one of her dead companions. Recognition dawned.

Benlik turned to face Shirler.

Benlik's two remaining supporters, knowing no mercy would be available to them from the Senate guard, had fought tenaciously. As the twins and their troopers had dismantled the barricade and created space, these last two supporters had stood back to back and fought doggedly, their swordplay superior to that of the Senate guardswomen. But they were hugely outnumbered and weren't going to survive for long. Ignoring Charlan's call to them to surrender, they were finally cut down, much to her regret.

"Mother's heart," muttered Charlan.

It was almost as if they were in one of the city's arenas. As the guard commander's exclamation went unnoticed, an impromptu circle was formed around Benlik and Shirler. Charlan knew she ought to intervene and take Benlik to the Senate prison but long-buried instincts told her to let the fight go ahead. Giving Benlik the chance to die with dignity was a thought that pushed up into her conscious brain. That Shirler might be the one to die she gave no thought to, knowing the guard would see to it that that didn't happen.

Overcome by her grief, Sorak was guided back to her quarters by the two administration officials who were the closest to her. They stayed with her, as Lenar had remained in the communal building. Not entirely clear in his agitation why he'd remained, he like Charlan readied himself to intervene if the forest woman, now stripping off her outer garments, was at any risk. Unlike Charlan, Lenar would be very happy to see Benlik killed in public.

Grasping the unfamiliar sword, longer than she was used to, Shirler waited as Benlik stood totally still, and strove to control her breathing. Seeing Anstan's killer in front of her had steadied Benlik's nerves.

Shirler's anguish at the death of Nasa probably wasn't as deep as Sorak's but her hurt was real and powerful to her. She wanted revenge, but she knew that she had to push such thoughts from her mind if she was to overcome Benlik.

Benlik's first powerful thrust was parried by Shirler. Battle was joined.

After this initial show of intent, Benlik seemed to withdraw into herself. By far the superior swordswoman, her cold calculating brain had slowly overtaken her original blind anger. As a consequence, she was growing more dangerous by the minute. The fact that Benlik was an ex-mangeneer and not an ex-soldier would have been lost on Shirler, but for those who were watching her skill as a swordswoman was obvious.

Shirler, on the other hand, was beginning to have doubts about the wisdom of what she'd undertaken. Fond as she had been of Nasa, was he worth dying for?

Enough of such thoughts. You have to kill this woman.

Unaware that neither Nasa nor Sorak would have wanted Benlik to die, she forced her mind to a level of concentration that she hadn't known she was capable of.

Her vigilance and wariness paid off.

Confident in her skill, Benlik now advanced on Shirler, alternately thrusting and slashing at the retreating figure. Shirler bided her time.

Although she didn't understand the words that Benlik threw at her, she understood their meaning, but she wasn't going to stand and fight until she was more familiar with such a long sword.

But she was never going to get that chance.

Parrying another of the mighty thrusts that seemed to be Benlik's speciality, her blade broke and Shirler was left holding not much more than the hilt of her sword.

"Mother's heart!"

The invective escaped from almost every woman watching.

But Shirler was too concerned for her survival to realise that it wasn't *her* broken sword, but Benlik's, that had attracted such attention. It was only as Benlik tossed the useless remnant of her weapon aside and it clattered across the floor that Shirler realised how the situation had changed. Both weapons had been destroyed in the previous clash.

Before she could take up any sort of defensive posture, Benlik had leapt on her and was attempting get her hands around her neck. Jabbing the useless hilt into the mangeneer's stomach, Shirler was carried backwards into the scattered remains of the barricade. Forced to a halt, Shirler grasped Benlik's wrists and attempted to prise them apart, trying to ease the pressure on her neck and prevent herself from being choked. Buckling under the weight of Benlik's body, but free of her grasp around her neck, the two of them found themselves rolling around on the floor amongst the debris of the barricade, each searching for a hold on the other's body.

Benlik was proving to be the more powerful of the two, but the women watching intently were quick to observe that Shirler was adept at using her opponent's weight and movement to her advantage.

After a period of rolling and writhing on the floor Shirler ended up on top and, smashing her forearm down onto Benlik's neck, she scrambled to her feet, leaving the mangeneer twitching and panting for breath.

Shirler walked away… but Benlik still had fight in her.

As Shirler sensed that the other woman was back on her feet she turned to see Benlik sweep up another stray sword and throw herself forward.

"She must have had the knife on her all the time!"

Charlan was appalled by what finally happened.

As Benlik attempted to throw herself onto Shirler and bear her down with her body weight again, she let out a strangled groan, collapsed, rolled, and ended up on her back with the knife all too obviously sunk into her chest.

Shirler just stood there, no one seemingly prepared to approach her, until Tareck, Nasa's friend and Sorak's bodyguard, and one of the few people Shirler knew and liked, quietly took her by the arm and led her into one of the empty side rooms.

Other than positioning two guards, Charlan took no further action until much later when the communal area had been cleared.

The outcome of the encounter was reported to Sorak, but in her distress she gave no thought as to what had motivated Shirler, or what she might now have to do about her.

Shirler shrank into herself and spoke to no one, not even Tareck. Overwhelmed finally by her grief over Nasa's death, she lay on the floor as if dead and awaited her fate. She didn't care what happened to her now.

47

The city was in shock for many days after Nasa's death. Significant numbers of people, even amongst the civilians, had no idea who Benlik was, least of all why she'd so disastrously sought to kill their leader, but they did know Nasa. The story of Sorak and Nasa was a part of the folklore of the city. Nasa was a popular figure and someone whom the men of the city, be they former slaves themselves or young men who'd known no slavery, looked up to. His easy relationship with Sorak had become a model for countless others in the new society. Nasa's loss was felt by almost everybody in the city, even by people that he'd never met.

Tired of death and killing, the growing reaction towards fanatics like Anstan and Benlik was one of anger. If Sorak had created any legacy at all it was stability, something very few of the younger citizens wanted to be threatened. And it was the younger people who were now very much leading city life.

A sense of doom, however, prevailed amongst many of the older citizens. They'd been through too much to share the optimism of the following generation.

Not only was there great sadness over Nasa's death, there was also universal sympathy for Sorak in her loss.

Keeping herself to her quarters, Sorak had very little awareness of the shared angst over her partner's death, but had she known of it she would have been both heartened and humbled.

After her battle with Benlik, Charlan had spirited Shirler away again to one of the more remote areas of Sector One, uncertain of what Sorak might want to do with her. Having learned of Shirler's feelings for Nasa, from the bodyguard Tareck, Charlan would have preferred to have sent her back home immediately once the events in the communal building had ended, but to do so seemed to her to usurp Sorak's authority. The guard commander had no idea what Sorak might be thinking.

* * *

Lenar was distraught.

Having quickly sent for Desak, he hoped that she and their child might be of some comfort to his mother. But aware of their presence, Sorak had nonetheless retreated into herself and had accepted Desak's gentle ministrations almost without seemingly to notice them. But Desak had lived with Lenar long enough to know that his mother was not one to show her emotions or inner feelings publicly. Yet she knew that Sorak was desperately hurting inside.

As the days passed, Lenar became more and more conscious of the loss of his father. Hunting expeditions in their hidden valley, long before the place became untenable, surfaced in his mind. His father's love – that mysterious word again – and his careful tutoring of him in the necessary skills for survival poured into his mind. But with his mother's distress, he knew he had to keep his feelings to himself.

Eventually, after many circuits of the distant star, nurtured within her small family, Sorak began to show an interest in what was going on in the city. And she was prepared to have contact with people again.

"Mother, here are Pastak and Risak to see you."

The two old ex-officers had decamped from their quarters in Sector Four to be close to their friend and to provide her with some extra protection.

Past history since the rebellion had taught the two of them just how fragile a leader's hold on power could be. At such a time they knew that Sorak needed reliable friends about her to add to the physical support provided by Charlan and Tareck and her family.

And then one day, as the distant star rose over the horizon, Sorak appeared in her office and demanded that the guard commander and certain of the administrative officers be sent for. She was back in business.

* * *

"The city is in turmoil."

Sorak wondered where the normally direct and straightforward guard commander had got such a word from. However, she was quick to notice that Charlan seemed unconcerned about this 'turmoil'.

It seemed that two momentous things were happening, two things that Nasa had always claimed would need to happen if the city was ever to settle down and be free from the sort of tensions that in the past had so often been generated.

"Most of the common soldiers who'd been living in Sector Eight have moved in to Sector Three. The civilians asked them to come and help rebuild one of the commercial areas, and to even work with them in the manufacturing plant."

The final integration of the military and civilian populations was underway.

"The military barracks in Sector Four are being made over to young families."

Pastak, when she reported this, still seemed surprised that such a thing could happen. But with managed breeding long since abandoned, providing a safe place for families to live and thrive had become essential if the city wasn't going to die from lack of citizens.

The concept and invention of money was Nasa's second anticipated innovation. Once the city authorities had ceased to provide for every need, the commercial areas of the city took on a new importance. But as a barter system to feed acquisition quickly proved inadequate, Nasa had foreseen this concept of money. And as this universal medium of currency developed, so too did the concepts of enterprise.

Of course, Nasa had had no knowledge of money in a physical form, only that there was a need for a medium of exchange that gave fixed values to things.

* * *

Life moved on.

Sorak was always acutely aware of just how many cycles of the distant star had passed since she'd lost Nasa. Life in the city had evolved and settled into routines and patterns that had essentially become self-perpetuating. Her son Lenar and his partner Desak now had three children, and multiple-child families were on the increase. For the first time in many cycles, as far as the Senate could calculate, the city's population was on the increase.

None of this obvious success of Sorak's desire to create a long-term and stable society, however, could overcome the pain of Nasa's loss. Her success in the city had begun to evolve long ago, and that success had been his success too. Sorak knew this.

But the city was thriving. The administration had been reorganised and was now being paid for by a levy. Nasa's concept of a fixed vehicle of trade was well established, and Sorak, drawing on long-past memories of browsing the old Senate library, acknowledged that the introduction of money had brought the city closer to the world from which its original inhabitants had come.

Specially trained administrators dealt with those citizens who committed a range of infractions; the punishments were agreed and approved by the citizenry, and then by the Senate. The benefits and necessity of this were recognised by everybody.

Gender was longer an issue. Apart from their biological functions, women and men were equal and free to pursue whatever path they chose for themselves in the city.

And as she began to grow older and increasingly infirm, Sorak felt well satisfied with what she'd achieved and what she would leave behind when she died. The world she lived in was unrecognisable from the one that she was born into, not that there were many left who would still remember.

Sorak's legacy was acknowledged by most of the people in the city. The city had a future. Yet far away, in one of the more remote forest compounds, another aging woman pondered this legacy too.

* * *

"But what," Shirler had asked herself more than once, "is the point of the city? What are the people living for? What are any of us living for?"

She had no answer, and without Nasa to ask she thought she'd never find one.